PRAISE FOR HEIDI CHIAVAROLI

The Edge of Mercy

"*The Edge of Mercy* is most definitely one for the keeper shelf. With her characteristic depth of emotion and willingness to address hard issues, Chiavaroli delivers a beautiful and gentle reminder that hope can persist even in the darkest of circumstances."

LINDSAY HARREL, author of *The Secrets of Paper and Ink*

"A book as rich as it is raw. Heidi Chiavaroli takes readers on a journey that is often painful for the realistic trail on which many have tread. But she doesn't leave us in the shadowy places—she shines light on the source of hope, forgiveness, and unconditional love."

SARAH MONZON, author of *The Isaac Project*

"With a skill akin to an expert quilter, Heidi Chiavaroli has taken the experiences of two women born centuries apart and pieced them together into a heart-wrenching story of hope, forgiveness, and the understanding that no one, no people group, is all bad or all good. *The Edge of Mercy* was an emotional journey that lasted long after I read the last word. I encourage you to take that journey too."

SANDRA ARDOIN, award-winning author of *A Love Most Worthy* and *A Reluctant Melody*

The Hidden Side

"*The Hidden Side* is a beautiful tale that captures the timeless struggles of the human heart. Exploring both contemporary and historical relationships, Chiavaroli has woven two worlds together seamlessly. With lyrical depth, she has delivered a story that is particularly relatable to parents who are struggling to guide teenagers through today's tumultuous climate."

JULIE CANTRELL, *New York Times* and *USA Today* bestselling author of *Perennials*

"Heart wrenching and real. Heidi Chiavaroli's *The Hidden Side* draws two equally compelling timelines in one novel, their stories connected by conflicts and emotions steeped in our worst modern-day nightmare and our history's painful birth. I could not stop reading this book—cannot stop thinking about the characters and the conflicts they faced. A novel not to be missed."

CATHY GOHLKE, Christy award-winning author of *Secrets She Kept*

Freedom's Ring

"Chiavaroli's writing flows easily and the pacing keeps the pages turning in this moving novel that covers tough topics such as PTSD, sexual assault, and forgiveness with realism and nuance."

PUBLISHERS WEEKLY

"First novelist Chiavaroli's historical tapestry will provide a satisfying summer read for fans of Kristy Cambron and Lisa Wingate."

LIBRARY JOURNAL

"*Freedom's Ring* is a powerful journey into past and present that will inspire, encourage, and uplift. Prepare to indulge in this masterful love story of God and country that both haunts and heals long after the last page."

JULIE LESSMAN, award-winning author of *The Daughters of Boston* series

THE EDGE OF MERCY

A NOVEL

HEIDI CHIAVAROLI

HOPE CREEK PUBLISHERS

Library of Congress Control Number: 2019901263

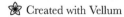 Created with Vellum

To James,
I am so proud to be your Mom.
I love you so much!

CHAPTER 1

Swansea, Massachusetts

I slipped the two rings off my finger to cradle them in my palm. Warm and bright beneath sunlight, no one would guess they taunted echoes of a failed marriage.

I stretched out my left hand and glared at my naked fingers. I couldn't imagine never wearing the rings again, couldn't imagine who I was without Matt to define me.

Sudden anger made me tremble. I'd been faithful. I'd held up my end of the wedding vows. This was not how things were supposed to be. Fumbling with the rings, I gripped them tight with my right hand, prepared to shove them back on my ring finger with force, but they slipped from my quaking fingers.

Time slowed as I watched my wedding rings tumble downward, bouncing a couple times off the side of the large rock I stood upon. I fell to my knees and a pathetic whimper escaped my mouth as I heard the first *clink* against the stone.

My blood ran like ice. I caught a glimpse of platinum, then nothing. I'd have to search on my knees for hours if I expected to find them.

I remembered what Dad taught me to do when I dropped something.

Don't lunge after it. Stop, think. Let your eyes follow what you've lost. You'll see where it's gone. Then, Sarah, you'll be able to get it back.

Strange how when I told my parents Matt was leaving me, Dad hadn't encouraged me to stop and think. He'd told me to fight for my husband. He wanted to know if I planned to live on alimony for the rest of my life.

I sighed heavily and stood to take in the scene I'd come for in the first place. The scent of pine and warm earth wafted through the air. Bright sunshine pooled around me, and the massive boulder stood solid beneath my feet. Like an ancient warrior, it offered majestic security, and I gleaned comfort from it. This rock wouldn't betray me. It wouldn't crumble beneath me as my marriage had.

Maybe that's why I came here whenever problems encroached upon my life, pressing in, squeezing tight. Eleven years ago, my neighbor, Barb, introduced me to these hiking paths, and to Abram's Rock. She told me stories of this boulder —legends, really—and though I wrote them off as fictional, I found myself returning here in times of need over the past eleven years, bonding with the sensation that another had indeed suffered in this place too.

Much older now, Barb hadn't been able to make the trip here in years. But that didn't change my attachment to this place.

I looked down to where jagged rocks and hard earth met, swaying before me until I grew dizzy—though likely more from my circumstances than the incredible height of the rock.

I hadn't seen it coming. My husband of seventeen years wanted a separation and I couldn't fathom why.

At least that's what I told myself. Sure, Matt and I had been distant of late, but I chalked it up to busyness—a mere ebb in the many up-and-down waves of any normal marriage.

Yet even Kyle had noticed, commenting just last night on

the fact that his father hadn't been home for dinner more than twice in the last month. Not one to bare his feelings, I could tell our sixteen-year-old son was bothered by his absence. I wondered how such a separation would affect him.

As I started down the gentle slope of the opposite side of the boulder, my cell phone vibrated in my pocket. Its upbeat tone rattled the peaceful quiet of the forest.

My heart ricocheted inside my chest at the thought of hearing Matt's voice on the other end of the line. Maybe he'd realized his mistake. Maybe—

I fumbled to see the screen and gulped down the bubble lodged in my throat. My sister, Essie.

"Hey."

"I thought you'd be at the hospital. Where are you?"

I groaned. Calling out of my shift two days in a row wouldn't put me on the director's good list, that was for sure.

I picked my way toward the base of the rock, to where I thought the rings had fallen. "I'm in the woods, trying to find the lost symbols of my marriage."

"I take it you won't be done in another hour or so, then?"

"Ha. Ha." My sarcasm fell flat when I told my sister what I'd done with my wedding rings.

"Your marriage can't be hopeless, Sarah."

I leaned over a hollow area between two rocks. Dead leaves cradled the middle. No rings.

"What's Matt's deal anyway? Did you two talk anymore last night?" Essie's assertive voice knocked against my eardrum.

I knew what she was thinking. Another woman. I'd already entertained the thought. It was one of the many reasons I found myself seeking the solitude of the woods.

"No, and he left before I got up this morning." I'd made sure of it.

"Well, maybe you two can work through this. Lots of couples go through slumps."

Was "taking a break," as Matt put it, a slump? I grabbed

hold of a tree branch and pulled myself up the first part of the steep slope, on top of another rock that created a small cave. "Working through a marriage requires two people. Matt doesn't want to work. He wants out."

"Come out with me and the girls tonight. Get your mind off things."

I scrambled for an excuse. "Kyle has a track meet."

"Come after."

"I planned on taking Kyle out. You know, talk things over."

Essie snorted. "The person you need to talk to is Matt."

"I—I'm not ready." This could be worse than a simple "break." There could be another woman. Matt could insist on divorce. My chest began to quake. "I have to go."

"Call if you change your mind."

I hung up the phone, shoved it in the pocket of my jeans, and resumed searching for my wedding rings with newfound exuberance. For what must have been an hour I pushed aside leaves, scraped crevices with my fingernails, stepped back to search for a glint of platinum beneath the sun's rays. Nothing. I sat at the base of the rock and let the tears come.

In the aftermath of my quaking sobs, a numbing quiet overtook my soul.

This place seemed ageless, as though the channels of time sometimes overflowed their banks. It reminded me that many other women had walked these very trails, and I felt certain some of them must have known a pain similar to mine.

———

I wasn't supposed to fall in love with Matthew James Rodrigues. Not according to my parents, anyway.

The first time Matt showed up on my doorstep, Dad took one look at his rumpled hair, his Elvis tattoo, and his idling jalopy and told him he could take a long hike off a short pier if he thought he'd get anywhere near his daughter.

Back then, Matt had been nothing more than a teenager with a lawnmower, a shovel, and a good tan. But he had something else—business smarts. He knew how to work people.

He knew how to work me.

He used to visit me at the high school lunch table while all my friends tittered not-so-conspicuously. I still didn't know why he approached me that first time to introduce himself. I wasn't anything to look at. Matt smelled like fresh wood shavings from the vocational shop. His rugged dark looks and persistence caught me off guard.

Before long, I was begging Daddy to change his mind about Matt. He didn't budge.

"Do you think I worked hard all these years to have my oldest daughter marry some trailer trash? And a Catholic at that?"

He said *Catholic* as if the devil himself had spawned the religion. As if half the boys I went to school with weren't Catholic.

"I don't want to marry him, Daddy. I just want to get to know him."

"No. End of conversation." He went away mumbling about how he should have never taken the pastorate position in New England all those years ago.

I snuck off to meet Matt that night. It was the first time I'd disobeyed my parents.

Matt had a Volkswagen with a tape deck. That first night we drove to Newport, listening to Elvis tapes. Matt wasn't like other boys I knew, listening to Pearl Jam or Billy Joel. He liked what he liked, whether it was popular or not.

He liked me.

I'd never known such attention before and I fell. Hard. Every night I snuck out my bedroom window to the end of the long drive where Matt's car waited. We went everywhere the water was, but that summer our favorite place was Newport. We shared our dreams beneath a vast sky. Matt told me about his fatherless childhood, how he avoided his trailer park home—and his mother—whenever he could. He hated being poor and vowed that someday he'd be successful.

My dreams seemed less important beside his. More than anything, I wanted him to succeed. And I wanted to be by his side when he did.

I lost my virginity in a fold of earth alongside the flat rocks of Newport one warm August night. I still remember the crash of the waves, the spray of the surf, Matt's arms around me, his heart beating heavy against mine.

The night I told my parents I was pregnant was the worst night of my seventeen years.

Mom cried. Daddy got so red in the face I thought he'd split open and burst like one of the overripe tomatoes in Mom's garden. He said God would curse me for my sin and if I didn't repent I was on the road to hell. Then he left the house—Mom, in tears, calling out after him.

I felt sure my father went to find Matt and kill him. Instead, he dragged him back to our house, and inside for the first time. I could scarcely look at him from my petrified spot on the bottom of the red-carpet steps.

"You will marry my daughter."

"Yes, sir."

"And you will provide for her if it takes every ounce of your strength. Is that understood?"

I felt Matt's gaze on me and I looked at him, telling him with my eyes I was sorry. I knew he wished it wasn't this way.

"Yes, sir."

And that was as close to a proposal as I'd ever gotten.

Matt quit school to mow lawns and landscape yards full time. Three months later we'd both turned eighteen. I graduated and Matt saved up enough money to rent us a room at the Holiday Inn on the night of our wedding. It was a simple affair, with only my parents and Essie and Lorna, Matt's mother, at the ceremony.

When I lay with him that night, Kyle already grew strong within my womb. I nestled my head in the crook of Matt's shoulder, felt a tear on his cheek.

"Are you sorry you married me, Matthew Rodrigues?" I asked, scared to death of the answer.

He grabbed my wrists and pulled me on top of him. Shook me slightly. "I never want to hear you say that again, you understand me Sarah *Rodrigues*? I love you. I will always love you." He crushed me to his chest. "You saved me, Sarah. You saved me."

I never asked what exactly it was I saved him from. Now I wonder—if I'd saved him so good back then, why was he so eager to get rid of me now?

CHAPTER 2

I stared at the pristine quartz countertop of my kitchen. Atop the perfect marbled specks of black and green sat a loaf of bread. I'd taken it from the breadbox without thinking.

I shoved the loaf back into the box with a bit more force than necessary. Matt could make his own stupid lunch. I yanked on the handle of the refrigerator, searching for comfort food.

The front door opened and I straightened so fast I slammed my head on the inside of the fridge. Stifling a yelp, I rubbed the sore spot and closed the refrigerator door too hard.

Kyle walked into the kitchen, dumped his backpack on the floor, then sat at the breakfast bar. "Hey, Mom. You okay?"

Oh, how to answer that question.

I released a frustrated sigh and shook off the hurt. "I'm fine. I thought you had a meet this afternoon. I was going to head out in a few minutes."

"Dad called, said he'd take me. He wants to ask me something."

Ask him? More like tell him his decision to leave his wife and son.

I looked at Kyle, nearly an adult. Lucky for him, he'd inherited both his father's height and looks. More and more lately, I noticed a younger version of Matt in our son. Those brown eyes, so like his father's until . . . until when? Until he'd married me? Until the combination of stress and success had rubbed the shine from them? When had my husband stopped being happy?

I blew a strand of hair from my face. "I guess I'll meet you two there."

Kyle grinned, a shadow of guilt playing on his dark features. "Dad said something about us catching up. Mine is one of the first races, so even though Coach'll kill me, I'm going to skip the rest. Dad has a meeting tonight so it's the only time we can talk."

Behind Kyle, the grandfather clock my great-aunt handed down to us called out the hour with four simple chimes. I loved that clock. Always steady, always consistent, even through the night while we slept and didn't pay it any attention.

"I thought this was a big meet."

Kyle shrugged. "Aren't you the one always telling me family's more important?"

"Okay . . . I'll see you there, then."

"Don't even bother, Mom. D-R has the top sprinter in the state. Enjoy the rest of your day off. I can hang with Dad."

Did he not want me there?

"I don't care if you come in last. I love watching you run."

He shrugged. "Whatever makes you happy."

But I had a terrible sense he really didn't want me to go. Had Matt said something to him? We should all talk together, shouldn't we, as a family?

I brushed off the feeling, tried to convince myself it was only my imagination.

A warm arm came around me and I gave my son a hug, grateful he still let me. When we parted, I tapped him on the top of his chest, and when he looked down I chucked him on the chin. "No worries, kiddo. Go out there and whip those Falcons, okay?"

He gave me a lopsided smile and ran upstairs to change. Ten minutes later he was out the door, his father's shiny Rodrigues Landscaping truck waiting in the drive.

I headed upstairs to the master bathroom, peeled off my clothes, and pulled on some jeans. Who was Matt to dictate me missing my son's race?

I checked my makeup in the rearview mirror and grabbed my purse from the passenger seat. Just before my fingers pulled the handle of the door, I thought of my husband, certainly in the bleachers, ballcap on, watching our son complete warm-ups.

Something like a soggy tennis ball settled in my stomach. I remembered the last time I'd seen him—night before last. The way he'd stood at the mantel, one hand on it, facing the window. Telling me he needed a break. He didn't want to be with me.

Bitter bile gathered in the back of my throat. I thought of Kyle's not-so-subtle suggestion that I not come to his race, and quite suddenly my hand felt too heavy to pull open the door.

I grabbed my keys back up and started the Mercedes. Half an hour later I walked into Chardonnay's, and glanced around the posh room. A squeal from a corner booth caught my attention. Essie—dark blond hair primped and large silver hoops dangling at her ears—waved from the center of the group of women.

I greeted the ladies and squeezed in next to Jen, Essie's friend from college and now my coworker at the hospital. She gave me a sideways hug, a thousand unspoken words in the action.

My sister always did have a big mouth.

"So she told you guys, huh?" I ordered a chardonnay from the waitress.

Across from me, Mariah reached out a perfectly-manicured hand. "I've been there, honey. I know it hurts like the dickens now, but when he's dishing out those alimony checks, he's the one who's gonna be groaning."

Essie slapped Mariah's arm. "I didn't say they were getting a divorce, stupid."

Mariah stared blankly between Essie and me. "I thought you said—"

"A break. I said he wanted a break."

Mariah raised her eyebrows and grimaced, as if to say, *What's the difference?*

Indeed. Besides a few signatures, what was the difference?

"My friend and her husband split apart for a time and it did wonders for their marriage," Katie said from where she sat on the other side of my sister. "Maybe good will come of this yet, Sarah."

I closed my eyes and shook my head. "Listen, I appreciate you all trying to make me feel better, but I didn't come here for sympathy. I just want to get my mind off things."

They nodded. An awkward silence filled the table as the waitress brought my wine.

"How are the boys?" I asked Jen.

She folded her napkin on her lap. "Let's just say the promise of this night out was the only thing that kept me sane today. Would you believe I left those boys alone for ten minutes outside and next thing I know they're making our shed into their own personal bathroom? Complete with a beach pail urinal." She stuck her tongue out. "I'm lucky I got to it before they decided to do more than pee in it because believe me, that was coming next."

Katie laughed. "At least your kids are old enough to be alone for a few minutes. I got in an argument with my trash man today. He refused to take my trash because it was too heavy. I told him three infants in diapers don't make light trash. He told me I should try cloth diapers."

Mariah wrinkled her nose. "You all are sure making me want to pop out a few. Rick's been hounding me. I can't imagine. I told him no ring, no babies. And truth is, I'm not even sure I want a ring that badly after all I went through with mistake number one."

Essie breathed in deeply, then out. Then again, with dramatic flair. I stifled a laugh. "What's she doing?" I mouthed to Mariah.

"It's some yoga-Buddha technique she's learning."

Essie, with much show, continued her breathing. "T'ai chi. I'm learning a calming technique. When I'm tempted to contribute to the complaints and negative thoughts of those around me, I try to center myself into a state of peace. You guys should try it. It works."

While I embraced—or rather, never contended—my parents' faith, Essie had done all she could to avoid it. Whether through self-help books, t'ai chi classes, a study on transcendentalism, or many hours on a shrink's couch, she tried everything, drinking in each new venture with wholehearted enthusiasm.

"Well I don't know about the rest of you, but I didn't come out tonight to center myself. I came to get a buzz and complain about life." Mariah tipped back her gin and tonic.

Jen flagged down the waitress and ordered nachos for the group. "I'm just happy to go back to work tomorrow and get a break from their shenanigans. We're still short on CNAs though, so chances are I'll be bleaching out bedpans anyway. Beach pails, bedpans . . . I suppose I'm destined to clean urine."

"'The only person you're destined to become is the person you decide to be.' Ralph Waldo Emerson." Essie tossed her honey-colored hair over her shoulder.

"Will someone shut her up?" Mariah rolled her eyes.

Undeterred, my sister put a hand on my arm. "Speaking of making your own destiny . . . maybe now's your chance to do something more than bleaching out bedpans yourself. You've always talked about going back to school, becoming a nurse practitioner. This is an ideal time, sis."

I'd learned long ago not to be offended by Essie's offhand comments. Still, I loved my part-time job as an RN. I didn't even mind cleaning out the occasional bedpan. Besides, now was not the time to find my wings. Now was the time to stay grounded, to fight for my marriage, fight for my family. "I'm still processing the fact that my husband's leaving me. I don't think I'm ready to hurl myself into school just yet."

"Why not? Maybe now's the perfect time. What else are you going to do when you're not at the hospital your twenty hours a week?"

"Remind me why I came tonight?" I said. Yes, I knew I had no life outside of work and my family, but it never mattered to me. Even now, I didn't need anything else. Didn't want anything else. What I needed was Matt, Kyle, and my part-time job.

Essie crossed her arms and rested them on the table. "Sorry. Didn't mean it like that. It's just . . . you've been living for Matt and Kyle all these years, even for your patients. Maybe it's time you did something for yourself."

Maybe she was right. I thought of the other night, of Matt standing at the mantel of our spacious living room, his hand rubbing the back of his neck, his soft yet piercing words.

"I need some time, Sarah. Some time away to think. We need a break."

Suddenly all I'd worked for, all I put my hope in, unraveled before my eyes. Essie was right. What did I have to show for my thirty-five years? An outgoing, handsome son, yes. But what else? A broken marriage? A boxy, three-story colonial? A part-time job I'd originally taken as a step toward my true dream?

I wanted to go back home, climb into bed, pull the covers over my head, and not come out again until God realized I did nothing to deserve this disorderly bump in my otherwise smooth life.

Mariah's face blurred before me. The room swayed. I fumbled for my purse and keys, throwing a twenty-dollar bill on the table. "I need some air."

I stumbled toward the door, my chest tight and my stomach queasy. My life was not supposed to fall apart like this.

I pushed open the heavy black doors. The cool night air washed over me in swift waves. I sat on a bench and breathed deep. In and out. In and out.

"Hey, that's some good t'ai chi."

I looked at Essie, rubbing her sleeveless arms against the chill. She slapped my leg to signal me to move over before she sat. "I'm sorry, Sarah. I didn't mean anything by it. I get it, and you're right—it's too soon to start rearranging your life. You haven't even talked things through with Matt."

I nodded. Ground my teeth.

"Are you mad at me?"

"No. I think I am going to head home, though. I shouldn't be out tonight. I should be home, trying to fix things."

Essie gave me a hug and walked me to my car. I slid into the silver Mercedes Matt bought me on my thirtieth birthday and lowered the window.

"Sometimes things need to break," Essie said. "That way they're stronger when they're put back together."

I forced a smile. "Who's that, Henry David Thoreau?"

"No, that's an Essie Special."

I gave her a wave and pulled onto Route 44.

I didn't want a broken marriage, a broken anything. After I married Matt, I'd worked hard to have my life—our lives—neat and orderly. Essie was wrong. Broken things never became stronger. They weakened, were more susceptible to damage. That's why I kept Grandma Martha's teacup on the top of my hutch where no one could see. If I ever dropped it again, it wouldn't be a single crack.

It'd be an unfixable mess.

CHAPTER 3

I turned off Netflix when I heard the truck pull in the drive. I pushed my hair out of my face, stuffed the remote in the couch, stood, sat, then finally stood again as the door opened.

Kyle entered first, his track bag and cleats slung over his shoulder.

"Hey, how was the meet?"

He shrugged. "Second place." For one heart-wrenching moment I thought he'd burst into tears as if he were seven years old again and finding out the truth about Santa. Instead, he booked it up the stairs just as Matt crossed the threshold.

My bottom lip quivered along with my stomach.

My husband threw his keys in the woven basket atop the pine entry table, purchased from a top-end furniture store. I'd wanted to refurnish a table I found on the side of the road. Matt wouldn't hear of it. "Hey."

I didn't respond.

He walked into the living room, sat in his La-Z-Boy, and splayed his fingers over the tops of his legs, as if poised for battle.

I wanted to give him one. Either that, or a two-year-old's tantrum. He had started it, after all.

"We need to talk," he said.

Yes, we did.

"I told Kyle."

"And?"

"He was upset."

"You don't say?" I didn't care that my sarcasm was ugly, I didn't care that it certainly wouldn't win him back. All I wanted to do was hurt him like he'd hurt me. Like he'd hurt our son.

"No one's saying this is for good, Sarah. Let's get through the summer. I need some time to think, to get away."

To get away from me.

"Why, Matt? Why all of a sudden do you need this?" I didn't have the guts to ask if there was another woman.

"We've been together for seventeen years, every day. Don't you ever want some time to yourself?"

No, I didn't. I wanted to be with him. My husband, my best friend.

Silence ate up the space between us. I studied his profile, the slight crook in his nose he'd incurred at the age of fifteen from one of his mother's many boyfriends.

His gaze fell to my left hand. "Made meatballs tonight?"

Making meatballs. The only time I took off my rings. I didn't want to lie to him, but I didn't want to tell him I'd lost my wedding bands either. He'd know something was up when he didn't find meatballs simmering on the stove.

He shook his head, released a long sigh, letting the question drop. "Do you ever think that Kyle's as old as we were that night your dad dragged me to your house?"

The back of my eyelids burned. I swallowed down hot emotion. "Is that it, then?" Was our entire marriage only obligation to him? "You've done your time, now you want out?"

He stood, fists clenched. "I didn't say that. But that's just like you to twist my words around, isn't it? All I want is some time away, but you have me lining up lawyers."

I grabbed on to the hope that it could be so simple. Just some time away.

I pressed my lips together. Arguing wouldn't get us anywhere. "I'm sorry." I stood, placed a hesitant hand on the tight muscles of his forearm. He'd worked hard all these years. For me, for Kyle. Maybe he did just need a break. "D-do you think we should see a counselor?" He turned toward me and I buried my face in his neck, inhaling the smoky scent of his cologne. The stubble beneath his chin brushed my forehead as I leaned in farther. "I don't want to lose you," I whispered.

"You're not losing me." But his return embrace felt halfhearted, as though he offered it out of obligation. "And I'm not ready to do the counseling thing. Let's just see where the summer takes us."

I wondered if this was his way of easing out of our marriage. I clung to him tighter, breathed him in, not caring how pathetic I looked.

"There's one more thing." He dropped his arms and I concentrated all my efforts on restraining myself from seeking them again. "I've asked Kyle if he wants to spend the summer with me in Newport. He can work for the company and—"

I reeled back as if physically struck. "What?"

"We have a couple big jobs in Newport. You know, the Waterman mansion and the new golf course going in. There'll be plenty of work and it'll give us some time together."

"It's his last summer before graduation."

It seemed Matt was trying to pull every tangible thing that held me from beneath my feet.

"He'd be at work all day anyway and out with his friends at night. I've been too busy this spring. This'll give me some time with him. We can work together, catch up, play a few rounds of golf."

I couldn't fault Matt for wanting to spend time with our son. Besides, if there was another woman, surely he wouldn't want his son so close by.

"Listen, I gotta run to the office for a few things. I'll be home later, okay?" He gave me an awkward peck on the cheek. "I do love you, Sarah."

I forced a smile onto my lips, but it fell as soon as he left. He loved me, but clearly it wasn't just our home or work or our family he needed a break from.

It was me.

––––––

The next morning Matt's suitcase sat on the bed in the guest bedroom. I called in sick again to work, for quite suddenly I did feel sick. I didn't bother with my hair or makeup but took up residence on the couch with a box of tissues and the NBC website open on my laptop to catch up on *This is Us.* Several times the messy heap of dishes in the sink called to me, but each time I attempted to load the dishwasher another wave of nausea would send me to either the bathroom or the couch.

Kyle came home after track practice and sat on the coffee table. I closed my laptop. I shouldn't do this. I shouldn't drown in pity. I should have at least checked in on Barb today—my elderly neighbor probably could have even put a smile on my face.

I missed her. I'd go over as soon as I spoke to Kyle. It had been too long.

"Hey honey. How was your day?" I said.

"I've had better."

I sniffed. "So have I." I put a hand on his knee. "You okay?"

He shrugged. "I guess. Dad just said he needs some time . . ."

"So he's been feeding you the same lines too, huh?" I laughed, but the words reeked of bitterness.

"Are you mad I'm going to stay with him for the summer?"

I dragged in a deep breath, not wanting to let a lie escape, and yet not wanting to hurt my son's bruised feelings any

further. "It's good for you to be with your father. I'll sure miss
you though. You're growing up so fast." My voice cracked,
betraying my emotion.

Kyle's mouth pulled into a straight line before he gave me a
rare peck on the cheek. In it, I felt all he wanted to say, all the
pity he felt for me. "I love you, Mom."

"I love you too, kid."

Except he wasn't really a kid anymore.

He went upstairs to his room, and though I told myself I'd
get up and check on Barb in a few minutes, time passed and I
couldn't summon the strength to move. Instead, I curled into a
tight ball.

The day Kyle was born was the happiest of my life. Funny
how just seven months earlier, sitting on my parents' red-carpet
stairs had been the absolute worst. Matt's grin couldn't have
been wider as he held our squalling newborn son in his arms.
He didn't stop kissing him, kissing me. When we finally came
back home to our small apartment with our bundle, no more
than kids ourselves, I remember passing Kyle's room where
Matt rocked him. I didn't miss my husband's whispered words.
"Thank you, God, for all of this."

Matt never spoke of God, especially not to me. Faith—
religion—was the one thing we simply couldn't find common
ground on. So we'd just stopped talking about it altogether. It
worked for us.

But standing at the threshold of Kyle's bedroom, staring at
the back of my husband's head and seeing my son's puff of dark
hair in the crook of his elbow, I too was overcome with
gratitude. Surely Matt and I could find common ground in this,
being thankful for our precious son. Conceived in a place of
secret and passion, God had nevertheless shown us favor,
brought good out of a mess.

Four years later, when Matt and I were ready to have more
children, God's favor didn't prove so tangible.

"Sarah?"

I sat up on the couch, rubbed my sleepy eyes, and swiped at a wet spot on the side of my mouth. I'd fallen asleep, and now before me stood my husband, suitcase in hand.

"I just wanted to say good-bye."

It would have been easier if he had let me sleep.

I slung my legs onto the floor. I wanted to yell at him for leaving, I wanted to clasp my arms around his legs and demand he stay.

"Are you going to tell me where you're staying—in case I need to get ahold of you?"

"You have my cell. I left the address on the counter."

I nodded and tried to quell the burning sensation working up my throat.

"I just paid the mortgage and the electric bill, so you should be good for a while. I'll be by Saturday to pick up the mail, and Kyle."

We were really having this conversation.

I lifted my arms to him, then let them drop. He put a hand on the back of my head and leaned down to kiss my forehead. I regretted not doing my hair and makeup that morning. I regretted that my wedding rings were lost in the woods. I regretted falling asleep on the couch, waking up with bad breath. His last picture of me would surely not make him hesitate to leave.

"Bye, honey," he said, as if he were just leaving for a short business trip. My stomach twisted as he scooped up his keys and left. I opened my mouth to call out to him, but no sound came forth.

Quiet filled the house, the grandfather clock eerily silent of its normal comforting ticks. Nausea climbed my insides.

Matt and Kyle…they were what was truly important. They were my all. Without them, my life threatened to be swallowed up into a black hole of failure.

CHAPTER 4

"Are you kidding me?"

I tossed the bag of Reese's Pieces I'd been nibbling onto the coffee table and craned my neck toward the door. "Nice of you to knock."

"Nice of you to return my phone calls." Essie waltzed into my living room and turned off *Downton Abbey*. "Is this what you've been too busy doing—stuffing your face and watching addictive dramas?"

I groaned. "I've been throwing up a lot, but my nausea cleared yesterday, so yes, since then that's exactly what I've been doing."

Essie looked in disgust at the used tissues crumpled in a scattered pile on the coffee table—the uncharacteristic disorder of my entire house. "Get up and shower. We're going out."

"Don't want to."

"Tough cookies. You need to get out of the house."

Before I could form a counterargument, my phone jingled where it lay on the coffee table.

I grimaced at the sight of the hospital number. I'd called out sick four days in a row. Truthfully, I didn't want to deal with the call, even if it was just one of the other nurses reaching out to show concern, but responsibility bade me answer. I could at least promise to be in tomorrow.

I slid the answer button and put the phone to my ear. "Hello?"

"Sarah, hey . . . how you doing?"

I let out a sigh. "Glad it's you, Jen. I'm okay. Listen, sorry I called out again. I'll be back tomorrow. Promise."

"Actually, I'm not calling about that. It's something else. . . . Do you know a Barbara Lyne?"

I lowered myself to the couch. "Yeah . . . sure, she's my neighbor."

"She's at the hospital, suffered two heart attacks last night."

"Oh no." I stood, already looking for my keys. I should have checked in on Barb last night. I'd intended to. How could I have been so careless?

"I usually go over there every couple of days. With everything happening—"

"It's okay, Sarah. But you might want to come down."

I moved to the foyer and slid on my flip-flops. "Of course. How's she doing?"

"Not well. I'm sorry, honey. And you're her only listed contact."

Huh. Strange. I thought Barb had a daughter—it was why I didn't check up on her more than a few times a week. She loved her independence, and in my mind her daughter was keeping an eye on her as well.

I scooped up my purse. "No proxy?"

"I know—practically unheard of for someone her age, but no. Just you."

I hung up with Jen and quickly explained to Essie the situation before heading to the hospital, popping a mint into my mouth along the way.

I drove onto the highway, my mind on overload. Matt was gone. Barb had a heart attack. I was her only contact.

Someone should find her daughter. She *had* a daughter, right? I'd been so certain . . . Mary, that was her name.

I sank into the many memories I'd shared with my neighbor —how Barb had babysat Kyle more than once when he was small, insisting Matt and I have date time. Barb was the one who had shown me the walking paths in our town, including Abram's Rock, telling me legends dating back to colonial times. I thought of the fierce love she held for the dog she'd recently lost—Howie, who never left her side. I thought of the many quilting projects scattered around her old home, of how she often comforted with a cool hand and soft words when I was upset. I pressed the gas pedal harder.

"Hang in there, Barb. I'm coming."

———

My flip-flops slapped against the linoleum of the long hospital corridor—a much different sound than the crocs I usually wore. I breathed in the scent of disinfectant, comforting after so many years.

When I entered the geriatric ward, the nurse at the desk greeted me by name. I ignored the need to explain why I was here when I had called out sick and instead headed to the room number Jen had given me over the phone.

I knocked on the partially open door, hoping that Barb's cheerful "Come in!" would greet me.

Nothing.

I pushed open the door.

My neighbor lay on the hospital bed, looking especially small and frail. Amazing how such a strong-willed woman could wither to such slight existence.

I moved closer, listening to the rattling breaths coming from her body. I lowered myself to the chair beside the bed, wondered if I should try to wake her.

Jen came in a minute later. She put a hand on my shoulder.

"Dr. Wyczyk doesn't think she'll last much longer. She called the ambulance after her first heart attack, but she had a second after she was brought in. She's too weak for surgery. I'm sorry, Sarah."

I pressed my lips together, nodded. "I meant to check on her last night. I should have."

"There's nothing you could have done, girl."

Truth or not, it was what I needed to hear, even as I struggled to believe the words. Maybe I couldn't have done anything medically, but I could have been there for my friend. She shouldn't have been alone. "No one else is listed? What about her daughter?"

Jen scooped out Barb's chart, examining it, shaking her head. "Just you."

Barb and I were close, but not *that* close. I nearly said as much, but I didn't know if Barb could hear me and I didn't want to hurt her feelings. Apparently, she thought differently.

After Jen left, I slid my hand into Barb's. It was cold, and the skin on her bones lay limp and wrinkled. I squeezed. "Hey, Barb. It's Sarah. I'd really like to talk to you."

No movement.

I spoke again, about anything and everything. I told her how Matt left, how Kyle was taking his finals this week, how I'd lost my wedding rings at her rock.

"I wish we could go for another hike . . ." I'd been rambling too long, was probably saying things I shouldn't say to someone on the brink of death, but somehow I felt that Barb, if conscious, would understand.

From beneath the covers, her toe twitched. She moved her head back and forth, as if in a restless sleep. Her eyelids fluttered.

"Hey, neighbor," I said gently.

She blinked again, her breath coming forth raspy.

"Take it slow."

"Sarah . . ."

"What are you thinking, giving me such a scare?" I arranged the blankets around her and counted it a victory when she smiled.

All too quickly it vanished.

"Barb, shouldn't we call your daughter to let her know . . . you're here?"

She gave a short, humorless laugh. "To let her know I'm dying, you mean?"

"Barb . . ."

"She wouldn't care. Told me as much last time we saw one another."

I tried to hide my surprise. True, I didn't know my neighbor that well, but I also couldn't imagine anyone harboring such resentment toward her, especially her daughter. "People say things when they're angry. I'm sure your daughter would want to know you're in the hospital." I took out my phone. "Do you know her number? Or maybe I can find it if you tell me her name and where she lives."

Barb stared at the empty wall as if she stopped hearing my words. Something foreign surrounded her and it reeked of loneliness. I found myself searching beneath the covers for her hand again.

"It's never too late . . ." My words sounded desperate even to me. I thought of the brokenness between me and Matt. Was there truth to my words? Or did there come a time when such a flimsy thing as hope was no longer viable, no longer worth investing in?

My neighbor slapped her lips together and I scooped up a cup of water and lifted it to her lips. After she'd drunk, she leaned back on the pillow, exhausted, and dragged in a deep breath. "Mary . . . she blames me for her father's death. She blames me for our family falling apart."

I shook my head. "I don't understand."

"You don't need to, honey. I should have loved better, is all. Worried more about loving than judging . . . especially my family. But I never lost hope . . . Elizabeth—you know, my ancestor? She taught me that. I'm still clinging to it now."

She wasn't making sense. "Elizabeth?"

Barb shook her head back and forth, as if uncomfortable or in pain. "The rock. Abram's. She was there that day. I wish I could have shown Mary. But she'd left by then, wanted nothing to do with me. Then you and that precious baby showed up next door. Thank you, Sarah. I'm leaving it all to you. You'll know . . . what to do with it."

I inched so close to the edge of my seat, I almost fell off the end. I grabbed for Barb's other hand. The heart rate monitor beside her beeped in quick succession, rattling my nerves. I knew another nurse would come any minute. "Do with what? Barb, what do you want me to do?"

"Tell Mary . . . Tell her I'm sorry and that I love her."

"You can tell her yourself. Do you know her number? Do you—?"

The monitor flat-lined. A rattle sounded in my neighbor's throat and I stood, squeezing her hand.

I could accept that Barb was dying, but not that she should die like this, with her daughter just a phone call away and a mountain of regrets between them.

"Barb, no. Barb."

Jen entered the room. Her gaze landed on my elderly friend and she slid past me, positioning her stethoscope in her ears and listening to Barb's chest. I gripped my neighbor's hand tighter.

Minutes passed as Jen probed and then felt for a pulse. I knew what would come next.

"She's a DNR." Jen let her fingers drop from Barb's wrist. "I'm so sorry, Sarah."

I released Barb's hand slowly, tried to gather my thoughts. "I —I wish we had just a few more minutes."

I wish I had paid more attention to her, I wish I had known about the rift between her and her daughter, wish I could have done something to help before . . . this.

Jen patted my arm. "Take a minute if you want, okay? I can call you when my shift's over."

I nodded, numb from the events of the last couple of days. "I was her only contact? What about the arrangements . . . a service . . . ?"

"I'll look into it, honey."

I forced a tight smile and a nod. My friend left the room. I sat with Barb for a long time, until I could no longer stand the emptiness of the room, the pallor of her lifeless skin. I leaned over and kissed my elderly neighbor's cool brow. "Goodbye, Barb. I'll give Mary your message. I promise."

I blew my nose and wiped my eyes before looking at my neighbor one last time. I gathered a breath and made my way down the hall, past a vaguely familiar doctor who gave me a peculiar look, past the nurses' desk, and into the elevator. I gasped for breath when I reached the first floor and stumbled down another hall.

I couldn't shake the feeling that there was more I could have done, more I could have said. I couldn't shake the guilt that I had chosen wallowing in my own problems over the well-being of an elderly woman who depended on me more than I knew. Without warning, a fresh burst of anger toward Matt erupted in my chest. If he hadn't left, I would have been paying more attention. Maybe I could have seen early signs of Barb's attack, maybe I could have prevented it.

I slid back into my car and turned the key, loneliness near swallowing me up. I needed to find Barb's daughter, give her my neighbor's message. She was sorry. She loved her.

Were the words enough to heal their broken relationship?

CHAPTER 5

I slid the key of Barb's house into the side door, but one quick turn told me it had been left unlocked. The door swung open with a creaking sound that caused a shiver to chase up the back of my neck.

Her kitchen lay spotless as always, save for a cup of tea with a bag still soaking within. The thought that this must have been the last thing my neighbor did—make herself a cup of tea—before her heart attack, caused the backs of my eyelids to burn.

I took out the bag and threw it in the trash before dumping the cold tea down the sink. The rancid scent of the wastebasket called for my attention, and I went around the bedroom and bathrooms, grabbing the trash from each room before dumping it into the larger kitchen one and taking it outside. I opened windows, allowing the sweet scent of fading lilacs from a nearby bush to sweep in and replace the smell of decay.

I paused at the sight of Barb's living room and sat on the corner of her couch—my usual spot—to stare at her well-loved rocker, a quilt in turquoise and brown triangles sitting crumpled on the edge. I put my head in my hands. "Oh, Barb."

I ran my hands over my face, the task before me clear. Deep down, I didn't want to worry about this now-abandoned property. I didn't want to worry about an estranged daughter or making things right. What I really wanted to do was go to my own home, bury myself deep beneath my covers, and hug Matt's pillow to my chest where his musky scent still clung. I wanted to grieve my marriage, grieve the fact that I hadn't been there when Barb needed me. I just wanted to be sad.

I gathered a breath and stood before going to the old rolltop desk in the corner. I opened it, noticing the thick layer of dust in the grooves, and began to search for an address book.

Barb had never asked for help from me. For anything. In fact, most of the time, she was the one offering help—whether it be taking care of Kyle or getting our mail or offering a listening ear. Why hadn't I made more of an effort to be a part of her life?

I shuffled through an untidy stack of papers, ignoring the answer that needled my conscience.

Quite simply, it was too much work.

I had my own family, my own home, my own job. In my head, I wasn't responsible for Barb. She had a daughter to help her—family.

I riffled through another pile, continuing my search.

My gaze landed on a spiral-bound address book behind one of the piles and I scooped it up. I took it to the couch and flipped it open to the first page, perusing the cursive writing for the name of Barb's daughter.

I finally found one entry under the *L's* with the listing of simply *Mary*. A single phone number lay beneath it.

I reached for my cell phone and dialed the number. A voice recording came on telling me that the number I dialed was no longer in service. I hung up, flipped the address book closed. Clearly this wasn't going to be simple. I would have to find out more about Mary. A last name would help. Certainly Barb had photos around, or cards with old addresses on them. I knew she'd never ventured into social media, but there certainly had to be something in this house that would tell me how to reach her daughter. I could search Mary Lyne online, but I could only imagine the results I would get. And besides, if Mary had gotten married and taken her husband's last name, searching for an *L* may not even help.

I wandered into Barb's bedroom. The sheets lay rumpled and without thinking, I pulled the covers up, revealing a beautiful quilt done in grays, oranges, and reds. I squinted at the familiar scene and went to the bottom of the bed to get a better view.

While I knew Barb quilted, I hadn't realized how intricate her designs. And there was no doubt she had made this quilt. Its vibrant colors pictured a large gray rock, the hint of a cave at the bottom. At the top stood a shadowed male form, feathers sticking out of long hair, a brilliant sunrise behind him. The pattern spoke of a Native American tribe, though I couldn't be certain which. Either way, I knew who Barb had intended to picture.

Abram and his rock.

Though Barb had spoken often of the legend surrounding the rock and the hiking trail, I hadn't known until today how much it had all meant to her. Even at the hospital, I wondered if she didn't only ramble in confusion. Now though, seeing the quilt she'd labored over along with its prominent place on her bed made me realize how serious Barb had been. I thought of the woman, Elizabeth, whom my neighbor had mentioned, how she wanted Mary to understand something having to do with her ancestor.

But none of that would matter if I couldn't find Mary.

I searched the pictures on Barb's bureau and nightstand, dwelling on one black-and-white photo of a young couple with a little girl in pigtails. I held it up to within inches of my face, tried to make out Barb's wrinkled profile hidden within the young woman, and thought I could see a glimpse behind her eyes.

The little girl had light hair like her mother, and while the picture was nice, it wasn't helpful in finding an estranged daughter. I put the photograph down just as my phone rang from the other room.

I saw Jen's name and answered.

"Hey."

"Hey, I'm so sorry about your neighbor."

"That's okay." I wanted to reassure her we weren't close, and yet how should that matter? And whether or not we'd been close, in some ways we were bound tighter in her death than we'd ever been. "Were you able to find out anything? I know she has a daughter named Mary."

"There's nothing in her records, or that of her primary doctor."

I pushed the screen door open and breathed in the fresh air. It felt strange to talk so blatantly about such things while I was alone in Barb's home.

"What happens then? I mean, Matt and I could take care of the arrangements, I suppose . . ." Matt and I. That was how things used to be. Now though, my husband wanted to get away from me. But surely he would help me in this. He'd want to know of Barb's passing and help if he could.

And yet Matt had left for his break. I could take care of this myself—a last tribute to Barb.

"We've contacted her primary, who will contact her lawyer. If there's a will, it may help sort some of this out."

"Right." Barb's lawyer would have Mary's contact information.

"There's nothing more you can do today, Sarah. You should take some time to do something for yourself, you know?" I heard her unspoken words, pulling me back to the reason I'd called in sick to work that morning—what seemed like eons ago. "I'll see you here tomorrow, you think?"

"Yes." I needed to go back to work, not only because the hospital depended on me, but because I needed to go on with life, to reach some sense of normalcy, to get my mind off Matt and Barb and stories and family. "Thanks, Jen. I appreciate everything."

We said good-bye and I went back into Barb's house to close up the windows. In the distance a gray cloud mounted the horizon. I turned from it and went to my neighbor's empty bedroom. I ran my hand over the quilt, feeling the carefully crafted nips and tucks of thread and fabric beneath my fingertips.

Barb wished her daughter had known about Abram and his rock. She mentioned giving it all to me, that I would know what to do with it. But I didn't. I only knew the legend. I didn't know about Elizabeth or Barb's family story. And quite honestly, I didn't think I had the emotional energy to search for it in the attic and desk and closets of this lonely home. Maybe if it had all happened a week ago . . . but now, with my world seeming to cave in around me?

I tried not to feel anger at Barb. She shouldn't have left me with this task. It wasn't fair. This was her life, her daughter, her past sins and regrets. She did little all day besides pray and quilt. She should have made more of an effort while she was alive to make amends with her family.

Thoughts of my rings lost at the bottom of Abram's Rock niggled their way into my mind. I had my own family troubles to attend. I had a job I'd been absent from, a son to say good-bye to. Jen was right.

None of this needed to happen today.

It's funny the things I noticed now that Matt was gone.

How empty the bureau looked without his jeans, socks, and t-shirt upon it, prepared for the next workday. How my single toothbrush in its holder shouted up at me that I had failed, that I was destined for a life of loneliness, how my family would never be the same again. How the absent scent of his morning coffee brewed a bitter taste in the back of my mouth, one that echoed of anger and unfairness.

I became obsessed with our simple wedding photographs, with searching my husband's young face for a clue of the trouble that would come seventeen years later. If there was a trace of this disaster, I didn't see it. I had to believe these issues hadn't built up over a long amount of time—that they'd cropped up and caught Matt by surprise just as much as they'd shaken me.

I left for work early the next day, as soon as Kyle caught the bus to school. I drove out of our finely manicured driveway and beneath the shade of a massive red maple I'd had to fight Matt to keep. Ten years ago when we'd bought the land to build the house, I'd been discontent. I'd wanted to purchase an old farmhouse a mile farther down the road, fix it up nice, maybe add an addition with a wraparound porch. Something with character.

Matt insisted we build our own home, something no one else "had a chance to screw up." We built the huge boxy house I now lived in alone. He'd wanted to cut down the old maple, said they ruined the grass below their drop line. I fought him and he conceded. Besides the decrepit barn at the back end of our property, the maple was the only thing on our three acres older than fifty years.

Instead of taking a left out of our driveway and onto the highway, I turned right toward my parents' home. I'd avoided Mom's phone calls all day yesterday and since I hadn't yet heard from Barb's lawyer, there was something I needed to ask my father.

My stomach vibrated alongside the engine of my car when I saw a Rodrigues Landscaping truck in my parents' driveway. A man with a red bandana and glistening arms ran a weed whacker around my mother's flowerbeds. A lawnmower engine sounded from the backyard and my stomach settled. Matt was in Newport, not Swansea. Of course he wouldn't neglect his Swansea clients. Only my parents weren't true clients—they'd never paid a nickel for Matt's services. When Matt married me, he'd offered to do the yard work for free, as their son-in-law. I used to visit with Mom over tea as Matt mowed their lawn and tended their flower beds and walkways. When Kyle came along, I brought him with me. Matt took him on the riding mower when he turned four. By the time Kyle was seven, Matt began sending one of his employees over to tend my parents' lawn during the week. The only time he called Mom or Dad was to check on their landscaping needs.

I scooped up my purse and walked to the back patio, where my mother worked on a counted cross stitch. My father sat, intent on a commentary laid on the glass table, his Bible open to the book of Isaiah.

Maybe I'd come at a bad time. He didn't like to be interrupted when working on his sermon.

"Knock, knock," I said.

Mom put a hand to her chest. "Oh, Sarah! I didn't hear you." She got up and gave me a longer-than-normal hug, squeezing me tight then releasing me to hold at arm's length. "How are you doing? You haven't returned my calls."

I wriggled from her grasp. "I know, Mom. Sorry. I'm okay, though, really."

I allowed my gaze to travel to my father. He stood. "Hi, honey." He gave me a light hug and I inhaled the smell of Old Spice and leather. "Glad you stopped by."

"I'll make some tea." Mom slid open the screen patio door and jiggled it closed. I sat at the table with my father.

"Any word from Matt?"

I blew out a long breath that feathered my bangs to the side. I *really* didn't want to talk about Matt. "No, Dad. He'll be by on Saturday to pick up Kyle for the summer."

He grunted.

"Were you able to talk through things, honey?" Mom spoke through the screen door.

"We talked. Listen, I know you guys care, but this is something Matt and I need to work through ourselves."

"How can you work through it if he's not around?" Dad flipped his commentary shut. It rattled the glass of the table. "It's just not right for a husband and wife to be apart. Unnatural."

I wanted to remind him that the way we began our marriage —with Dad ordering Matt to marry me—wasn't all that natural, either.

"Lots of couples separate for a time. You know, absence makes the heart grow fonder and all that?"

"What about a man and wife becoming one flesh and all that?"

I sniffed and concentrated on the bunches of white phlox embracing the walkway. The lawnmower engine died and the sound of the whistling kettle in Mom's kitchen took its place. A moment later, Mom came out with a tray of Grandma's Shelley teacups.

"When is Kyle done with school?" Mom placed a cup and saucer in front of me.

"He has the last of his exams tomorrow. I can't believe he only has one more year of high school."

"And what are his plans for the summer?" Mom smiled at me, then at my father, and I sensed the peace she wanted between us.

"He's going to work with Matt in Newport."

"Oh?"

"It'll be good for them to spend some time together. And maybe I'll go down for a weekend or two." In truth, I'd only just thought of this idea. I didn't know if Matt would be open to it.

"Seems to me you'll have some time on your hands this summer, then. Maybe you'll think about helping out with the VBS at the church this year? You've always been great with the children."

I put my teacup down and straightened. "Actually, I'm

thinking of picking up some hours at the hospital. Two nurses and a CNA are out on maternity leave." I thought to add that I was also thinking of looking into schools—to finally pursue my long-dead goal of being a nurse practitioner, but the sudden thought gave me pause. Was I tempted to say it only to shock my parents into silence? To show them that I really wasn't that worried about Matt leaving, that I was confident it would all work out in the end?

"Oh? Well that's nice." Mom pressed her back against the vine-patterned patio chair. "How is everything at the hospital?"

"It's . . . okay. Actually, that's kind of why I came. I'm not sure if you remember my neighbor, Barb?"

Dad cleared his throat and poured skim milk from the creamer into his tea. "She used to watch Kyle some, didn't she?" He squeezed the Tetley teabag with the back of his spoon and placed it on his saucer. Excess liquid dribbled from the bag and slid toward his cup.

"Yes, a while back . . . she actually died yesterday at the hospital. A heart attack." I purposely left out the part about how I had been so involved in Matt leaving I'd abandoned my neighbor in her time of need.

Mom covered my hand with her own warm one. "Honey, I'm so sorry."

To my surprise, my bottom lip began to tremble, and I couldn't rightly understand why. It must have been everything—not only my shaky marriage, Barb's death, Kyle's impending absence for the summer, but the compassion that now came from my mother, a woman I'd never felt particularly close to.

I shrugged, sniffed away my emotion. "I was the only contact she had listed on her medical forms. I'm hoping to hear from her lawyer today, but if not, Dad . . . I was wondering if you might be able to do a service for her?"

My father's mouth tightened. I knew funerals, especially ones for those he didn't know personally, were not his favorite thing. "Yes, of course."

I tried not to be surprised at his answer, at the lack of hesitation, even at the kindness in his voice. "Thank you."

We spoke for a few more minutes about Barb before Dad turned the conversation. "So does Matt think you working more is a good idea?"

"I didn't ask him, Dad. And I don't think I need his permission."

"I just wish you'd talk to him, honey."

"He doesn't want to talk, and I can't control him. When he wants to talk, he knows where to find me." I gulped my bitter tea. About two more gulps and I could be out of here.

"You're being difficult." He sighed, rubbed his temples, forever feeling the need to be the pastor with all the wisdom and answers. Funny how in that moment I almost felt bad for him. He inhaled a deep breath, his slightly rotund belly expanding with the action. "But so is he. I wish I could drag him back the same way I did that night—"

I stood, needing escape. If not, I would blame our entire marriage mess on my father, which may not be that far from the truth.

Matt and I failed, but I think what my father hated more than anything was seeing *his* failure in all of it as well.

"I have to get to work." I put my purse on my shoulder. "I'll let you know what I hear about Barb."

"Sarah . . ." Mom's voice trailed behind me, but it was halfhearted. I gave her a smile, mostly so I wouldn't feel guilt later, then kept walking toward my car, trying to dispel the animosity swirling within my chest. I grasped for control, but realized that if the last few days proved anything, it was that I had no control whatsoever.

CHAPTER 6

I took the exit to the hospital too fast, the last gulp of tea still sour in my mouth, right along with the conversation I'd had with my parents. What did they want from me?

But I knew.

They wanted me to throw myself into the work of the church, to be the perfect pastor's daughter for once. They wanted me to tempt Matt back with sweet words and kisses and hearty meals, to drag him to church with me, where at once, he'd be converted.

Even if that happened, even if things were perfect on the outside, it wouldn't change Dad's perception of me.

I pulled into the hospital parking lot, found a shady spot beneath an elm, rolled down the windows, and killed the engine. An elderly man with a faded Red Sox cap assisted a woman with a walker to a Buick three spots down from mine. He held her elbow and together they shuffled slowly toward the car, their tennis shoes in unison.

Shuffle.

Shuffle, shuffle.

I wondered if they'd been in sync their entire lives.

If Matt didn't come back home, we'd never grow old

together. Maybe we'd never been in complete harmony, but he could have at least hung around long enough to help me with my walker.

I looked at the bare finger of my left hand. I'd been stupid to take the rings off in such a vulnerable place. I'd go back to Abram's Rock and look again soon. If Matt found out I'd lost the rings, he would flip—they'd cost a fortune.

I remember sitting in our Nissan sedan outside the jewelry store on our fifth wedding anniversary. Matt looked over the console at me with a grin on his face that highlighted the dimple in his right cheek.

"What are you up to?" I asked.

"I thought it was time to get you some proper wedding rings."

"Oh, Matt." I twirled the weathered gold band on the third finger of my left hand—his mother's old wedding ring. He'd told me it had been in a Reebok shoebox beneath his mother's bed in the corner of their mobile home since the day they'd moved there, after his father left them. "I love this ring. I've had it since the day we married. I don't want to change it now."

Something in him shut down. His grin turned tight, his Adam's apple bobbed. "I thought you'd be happy."

I placed my hand on his tanned forearm. The muscles tightened beneath the plain gold band I loved so much. "I'm happy I have a husband who cares enough to surprise me like this. But I don't need you to spend a small fortune on new wedding rings. If it's all the same to you, I'd like to keep this one."

He moved his arm from my fingers. "It isn't all the same to me. We finally have some money, and I don't want you wearing the ring of my parents' failed marriage any longer than you have to."

I reached out to him and he didn't pull away. "I didn't realize it bothered you so much."

He didn't admit that it did. "Let's just go in and look."

I agreed. Once he saw how much cash he'd have to dish out, I was certain he'd change his mind. Matt wasn't cheap, but he knew how to handle money.

We came out of the store an hour later with two new rings— a one-carat diamond engagement that wrapped around a shiny ribbed platinum band. I cringed at the price and the unfamiliar weight of the metal and diamonds on my fingers, but Matt was smiling again and I had to admit, the rings were pretty.

Now, I rubbed the skin of my bare finger with my thumb. If I didn't find the rings after looking later today, I'd dig out my old one—Matt's mother's—from my jewelry box and use it as a substitute for now.

My husband would just love that.

I pushed open the door of the car just as my phone rang. It was an unfamiliar local number, and I answered, knowing it could be Barb's lawyer with news of Mary.

"Hello?"

"Hello. Is this Sarah Rodrigues?"

"This is she." I checked my watch. I'd have to talk and walk if I didn't want to be late for my shift. I shouldered my purse and waited for a blue sedan to cross the drive before I walked beneath the covered portico that led to the entrance of the hospital.

"Hello, Ms. Rodrigues. I'm Wyatt Sullivan calling on behalf of Barbara Lyne."

"Yes, hi. I was with her when she passed yesterday. It was . . . unexpected."

"My sincerest condolences."

I drew in a breath and waved to the receptionist as I passed on my way to the elevators. "Thank you. I am glad you called. See, Barb mentioned her daughter, Mary, and I was hoping you had her contact information."

Of course Mr. Sullivan had likely already contacted Barb's daughter. I didn't need to tell him how to do his job.

I entered the elevator and pushed the button to the third floor, cradling the phone against my shoulder while searching for my name badge in my purse.

"No, I'm sorry. She's not listed in any of my paperwork."

I caught the phone with my hand. "What?" The elevator jolted to a stop, and my stomach lurched. How could he not have Mary's information? I got out and stepped off to the side, behind a decorative plant. I could see Jen at the nurse's station, pointing at a computer screen, face concentrated. "How can that be?"

Mr. Sullivan cleared his throat. "Unfortunately, I don't know much of Barbara's family situation. She only came to me to have this will done four years ago."

"Is there other family we could contact, perhaps? Someone who would know where to find Barb's daughter?"

"I'm afraid not. Ms. Rodrigues, why don't you come down to my office so we can go over some things? Do you have any time this morning?"

I shook my head, knew I was now officially late for work. I wanted to tell Mr. Sullivan that none of this really had to do with me, that it was his job to find Barb's daughter. *That's* who he should be dealing with. "No, I actually just got to work and frankly, Mr. Sullivan, I have a lot going on right now. Could you at least tell me if there are any burial provisions in her estate? I'm happy to plan the memorial while we try to locate Barb's daughter."

"Ms. Rodrigues, you've misunderstood me. There is nothing in Barb's directives that indicate I should contact a daughter. In fact, the only person I am to contact is you."

I wiggled my toes within my crocs, expending my frustration. "Me?" Did Barb want me to plan her funeral all along? While I knew her faith was important to her, we'd never discussed the many decisions regarding a burial.

"Quite simply, if I must tell you over the phone, Ms. Lyne

has left you the entirety of her estate—all her worldly possessions are being transferred to your name."

I leaned against the sturdy wall, felt myself sliding down to the floor. "M—me?"

"She left a letter for you. I do think you should come down to my office as soon as possible."

My mind stumbled over his words. Barb had left me everything? A part of me felt sad that I hadn't realized how important I was to her—or rather, how little people she'd had in her life besides me. Another part felt grateful for her generosity and still another felt burdened by it.

"Are you certain?"

"As certain as I am of my last name."

I didn't need this. Not now. I needed to take care of my family, my life. I could never accept Barb's home—her worldly possessions—as my own. It was too much, it didn't belong to me. And more than likely, her daughter would come out of hiding to claim it eventually. Clearly Barb had regrets at the end of her life. Regrets she'd entrusted to me.

"I'm leaving it all to you. You'll know . . . what to do with it."

Only Mr. Sullivan hadn't been aware of our conversation.

It truly was all in my hands.

I leaned on the wall, depended on it to hold me up.

"Ms. Rodrigues?"

"Y-yes, I'm here." Barely. "My shift ends at four. Can I come by after that?"

"Absolutely." He gave me an address and directions, and then we hung up.

I slipped my phone into my purse and rolled to face the wall, laying my forehead against the cool paint. It was going to be okay. Maybe, with my marriage on the brink of destruction, this was God's way of assuring me He would provide.

I closed my eyes, dragged in a deep breath. Yet when it came down to it, I wasn't overly concerned about being provided for

—even if Matt left me for good and wanted a divorce, he wouldn't leave me with nothing. Besides, I had a good career, one where more hours were always available. And I would never be homeless—my parents would always take me in. No, provision wasn't my concern.

What I wanted, really wanted, was to be loved, cherished; I wanted to be enough. I wanted to know that Matt was mine, and I was his, no matter what.

No matter what.

"Hey . . . Sarah, right? Are you okay?"

I opened my eyes and a white doctor's coat filled my vision. I straightened and shook my head as if to thrust myself into reality. A reality where I had a husband and son at home, a neighbor next door, a shift to fill.

"I—I'm fine." Through the fuzz of my shock, I tried to place the familiar face before me, grasped for a name but came up short. "I'm sorry, I know I should know you, but—"

"Pete. Pete Keller. We were chem lab partners at Bridgewater."

My mind cleared, taking me to another time, another place. Still newly married and with an infant at home, I'd decided to take a couple classes at the local state school to get my degree. Chem lab. Huh. That'd been ages ago, but . . . "Wait . . . sulfuric acid Pete, right?"

He slid up his sleeve to reveal a nasty scar on his forearm where he'd spilled acid during an experiment. "The one and only."

I groaned. "I felt horrible about that for the entire year."

He shrugged. "It was my own fault."

"Yeah . . . but I should have been paying better attention when you were handling it."

He smiled and I could just make out the curve of a dimple beneath short, dark whiskers. "I lived to tell the tale, and as I recall, we ended up with the best grade in that class."

That's right. "Not sure how that happened, considering we were the only ones who required a hospitalization with our experiments." We laughed until it petered out to an awkward silence. My left hand suddenly felt ten times more naked, and I hid it behind my purse.

"So, everything okay? You looked pretty shaky there just now."

I rubbed my temple with my right hand, my conversation with Barb's lawyer wiggling to the forefront of my mind once again. "Yeah, just some crazy news."

"I take it not good news." When I didn't answer, he spoke again. "Well it was nice to run into you. I'm new around this place, so it's great to see a friendly face."

I searched my mind. Yes, Jen had mentioned a handsome new doctor.

"It's great to see you again too. Dr. Keller now, right?" I pointed to the nurse's desk. "I'm actually late for my shift, but I'll be seeing you."

He flashed another easy smile. "Hope your news turns out okay. And it's just Pete. Nice seeing you, Sarah."

I smiled politely and waved good-bye before scooting down the hall, tried to focus on what Barb's lawyer had just told me. But instead, I found myself watching the back of Pete's white coat, thinking how unbalanced I suddenly felt. As if one more thing might be enough to topple me over. Trouble was, I couldn't decipher whether it was the news from Barb's lawyer, the uncertain future of my marriage, or my old lab partner, that had done the unbalancing.

The envelope felt smooth and sleek beneath my fingertips. It reminded me of everything Barb wasn't, and I didn't see how this thin enclosure could properly represent her. Barb, who reminded me more of a wrinkled old manuscript—worn around the edges, full of life and character—than a smooth, crisp piece of correspondence.

But here it was, no matter how it appeared.

I unrolled the windows of the car, still in the parking lot of Mr. Sullivan's office. On the passenger seat sat a file of papers, copies of documents I'd signed for the last forty-five minutes along with a smaller envelope containing a safe deposit box key.

Barb had indeed left me with everything. Save for a generous portion she'd set aside for a museum in nearby Plymouth and for her church, everything else—her home and property that abutted ours, her rather substantial bank account and retirement savings, and the unopened letter I held in my hands—belonged to me.

Even as I grieved for my friend and tried to mentally create a memorial service that would do her justice, I felt . . . blessed.

Barb had left me with more than enough to pursue schooling full-time. In three years, I could be a certified nurse practitioner. The last hour had potentially changed my life.

I wondered what Matt would say, what he would think. I wanted to talk to him, to get his take on this entire crazy turn of events. More than anything, I wanted to plan with him—Barb's memorial, what these provisions meant for our future.

I rubbed my eyes, still baffled by the fact that Mary hadn't been mentioned once in Barb's will. Had she died? Maybe in the confusion surrounding the last moments of her life on earth, Barb had forgotten of her daughter's death?

I flipped the envelope over and slid my finger beneath the edge. I slipped out a single page in black, cursive ink, and unfolded it with care.

Dear Sarah,

I have no doubt you will be surprised to read this letter. No more surprised than my decision to bequeath to you what I have.

Dear, I don't think you realize how very much your friendship has meant to me. *I know to you I may have been an old, stubborn woman, but allowing me to help with Kyle and allowing me to share hikes with you has made all the difference in my last days.*

I am leaving you with my earthly goods because you have been a true friend, and because I know I can trust you. I suppose you may think this old woman presumptuous, but dear, I have seen a lot in my life and I can judge a person's character better than most. And I know something—you are a woman to be trusted.

And so I am entrusting you with my final request. It may appear at first that I am off my rocker, but I ask you to be patient and not write it off as you might want to do.

My daughter, Mary, has been lost to me for all too long. The circumstances of our departure are not so very important, but please know going forward that the fault is mine to bear. We parted when Mary was but twenty-one, and I have not seen her since. Lord willing, she is still alive and well.

Please don't think me pitiful, or ignorant. I hired a detective to find her back in the 90s. He did find my daughter, but when I tried to contact her, she returned my letters unopened. When I traveled to her address, I was told she had moved to an unknown location.

I respected that, or at least tried to. But I can't leave this life without one more attempt, even if it comes from beyond the grave. I pray you don't think me selfish or a coward, though perhaps I am. To be honest, part of me is frightened to reach out to Mary again, frightened of rejection. Yet I feel I can rest by placing it in your hands—presumptuous of me, I know. I see your gentle heart, Sarah. I also see your warrior heart. You remind me of my ancestor, Elizabeth, and in this, I find hope.

Just before you and Matt built your home on the land I sold, I came upon a journal of one of my ancestors during a genealogical search. While it took much persuasion on my part for them to allow me to read it, proving I was directly related to Elizabeth Baker was helpful. It was kept at Pilgrim Hall Museum, and I visited many times to read it through.

I hope you don't think me crazy, but recently I cannot release the idea that Mary should have this story of our family. It is a part of our legacy, our heritage. It made me see things differently, and I can't help but hope it will do the same for Mary. Perhaps it will bond us even beyond death.

I realize what I ask is no small task, yet I am hoping with all the computers today and the funds I am leaving you, that you will not find it so very hard. Perhaps there is a digital version available now.

Please, Sarah. Please find a way to tell my Mary of Elizabeth's story. I have told you some of it couched in legends, but I trust you will find the rest worthwhile. The records from the old investigation of Mary's whereabouts are in my safe deposit box, which Mr. Sullivan has given you the key to. Find her, please. Tell her I'm sorry. Tell her I love her.

Thank you, dear friend. You never acted as if I were a nuisance, even when I was. Take care of that sweet son of yours and that hardworking husband. And in time, I trust I will see you in glory.

Love, Barb

I pressed my head back into the seat and closed my eyes, taking in the enormity of the task before me, not a question in my mind that I would do it and do it to the best of my ability. Barb was gone. She'd never reconciled with her daughter. Was it possible it could occur beyond the grave?

I placed her letter on top of the files on the seat beside me and turned the key in the ignition. My life had turned upside-down in the last seventy-two hours. There was so much to fight for, so much to sort out.

Barb had said I had the heart of a warrior. Strange, I'd never thought of myself like that. Now, though, I might need to prove it.

I thought of the many hours it would take to fulfill Barb's request, the many hours it would take to sort through her things, to track down Elizabeth's story, to decide what to do with the house—and all without Matt.

I now had more possessions and money than I'd ever had on my own—along with a heavy loneliness that settled upon me. I wondered if Barb had felt this way often, and if so, how had I not known?

I pulled out of the parking lot. There was nothing I could change now, either in Barb's life, or in my marriage. I could only move forward, hoping that something better lay ahead, on all fronts.

CHAPTER 7

I stood at the threshold of Kyle's bedroom. Slants of morning sunlight poked through the half-pulled shades, splattering narrow ribbons of light on the pair of jeans that lay in his open suitcase.

"How's it going?"

He looked up from the top drawer of his bureau. "Almost done. Dad said he'd be here at ten."

While Matt hadn't called to talk to me once, apparently he and Kyle kept an open line of communication.

That was good. It was. I shouldn't be jealous of their relationship.

I ran a hand through my hair, conscious that ten o'clock was ten minutes away and Matt wouldn't dare be late for an appointment with a snail, never mind his son.

"Do you have enough underwear and socks? And don't forget your bathing suit."

Kyle raised his eyebrows at me, one side of his mouth tilted in a patient grin. "Got it, Mom. I remembered my toothbrush and floss too."

I came in the room and ruffled the curls at the top of his head. He was such a cute kid. Almost a man, really. "I'm gonna miss you, kiddo. But I'll see you for the service on Monday, right?"

His expression grew heavy at the mention of Barb's service. I hadn't told him about the details of the will yet. "Yeah, Mom. Of course." He allowed me a hug, but pulled away too soon. "Hey, maybe once I'm settled down there you can come for dinner or something. We can all, you know, hang out." His hopeful tone pierced my heart. He didn't pursue many deep conversations with me, but of course this split bothered him too.

"That sounds nice, honey. Really nice. We'll have to see what your dad says."

He flipped his suitcase shut and zipped up a blue duffel bag beside it. "I'll work on him for you, okay?"

I choked back a sob and squeezed out a pitiful "Okay." My son shouldn't have to convince his father that he belonged with his mother. That he belonged home.

The sound of Matt's truck pulling up the drive caused my heart to vibrate against my ribcage. I recognized the tune of "Don't Be Cruel." My gaze locked with Kyle's, and I was struck by how unnatural this was—this nervous expectation over seeing my husband of seventeen years.

A moment later the door opened. "Guys, you upstairs?"

My insides were like a damp sponge and Matt's voice was the hand that wrung it dry. I missed him. Never mind all the distractions surrounding Barb's will, getting Kyle ready to leave, the walks in the woods, and funeral planning. I missed my husband, and I wanted him home.

I twirled Matt's mother's wedding band around my finger as I followed Kyle down the stairs on legs that felt like Mom's grape nut custard.

"Hey, buddy, enjoying your freedom yet?" Matt clasped Kyle's hand with his own.

Kyle shrugged. "Yeah, all two days of summer vacation."

Matt looked over Kyle's shoulder at me. I imagined he'd come home from a Saturday morning round of golf, that he was here to stay, that it wouldn't be completely awkward for me to greet him with a kiss.

"How's it going, Sarah?"

It would be easier to be mad at him if he wasn't such a gentleman about this whole thing.

"Okay." I hid my left hand behind my back. "You?"

"Good. Good." He turned his attention to the stack of mail with his name on it on the kitchen counter. I watched the back of him for any clue how his time without me was going. He looked relaxed enough in a green polo shirt and jeans. Beneath his close-cropped haircut, the back of his neck shone dark from the sun.

He banged the stack of mail lightly on the counter to make the envelopes neater, then turned to Kyle. "Ready?"

"Sure." Kyle gave me a hug. "I'll call you tomorrow, Mom."

I resisted the urge to ask him to call me when he got there so I'd know they'd arrived safely.

"Have fun, honey. I love you."

"Love you, too."

Kyle walked out of the kitchen. A moment later the door shut behind him. He probably thought his dad and I wanted a few minutes alone.

Matt tapped the envelopes against the open palm of his left hand. "I'll take care of these this weekend."

"Thanks."

He cleared his throat. "He told me about Barb."

I shrugged, my bottom lip quivering. "Yeah."

"I'm sorry, Sarah. I know you two were close."

I blinked away tears. "Memorial's on Monday. If you can't make it, maybe I could grab Kyle, or you could let him borrow one of the trucks. I think he wants to be there."

"We'll be there."

I managed a small smile. Barb had made a request that her funeral be done at her church, for which I found myself relieved. Dad would not have to do the service, and Matt would not have to feel uncomfortable sitting beneath Dad's preaching.

I opened my mouth to tell my husband news of Barb's will, but quite suddenly it felt too personal, as if I shouldn't simply assume my husband was interested in my life anymore.

"The grandfather clock broke," I said instead. I said it because I didn't want him to leave. I said it because I wasn't thinking. "I need to find someone to fix it."

"Consider it done."

"I didn't mean—"

"It's not a problem. I know how much you like that clock. I know a great guy who'll do it for a good price."

"Okay. Thanks." I shouldn't have said anything. Certainly, I was capable of finding someone to fix the clock. I should have already done so. I missed its cheery company, its steady presence.

"Thanks for being such a good sport about this—with Kyle, I mean."

"You don't know what I said about you when you weren't here." I laughed lightly to indicate I was joking.

Matt didn't smile. "Well, call if anything urgent comes up. I've changed most of the bills to paperless, so you won't need to worry about that."

As if I ever worried about the bills.

I nodded and followed him to the side door. "Enjoy him."

"I will." He looked at me one more time, the chocolate of his eyes sincere. "Thanks, Sarah."

I waited for a hug, a good-bye kiss, something to suggest that all this would be all right in the end.

Nothing.

He walked down the steps, leaving me alone in my beautifully landscaped house with not a single bill to pay and everything I could need. Everything except my family.

"What a stupid thing to do." Essie placed her hands on her hips and stared up the fifty feet to the impossible-to-scale face of Abram's Rock.

I knelt in the dry leaves and bent my head so I was eye level with the ground. "Yeah, I know. But I didn't ask you to come here to confirm my stupidity. I need your help."

She looked down at the ground before crouching alongside me and sweeping her perfectly manicured fingernails over the leaves. "I hope you know I'm risking getting infected with Lyme disease and West Nile right now. If that doesn't show how much I love my sister, I don't know what does."

I laughed as I crawled into the small cave below the face of the rock. Spider webs brushed my face, and I pushed aside the thought of snakes burrowing in the cool crevice. I switched my phone to flashlight mode and shone it in the sheltered spot. Not a glimpse of diamond or platinum shone back at me. A mosquito buzzed in my ear and I slapped it away.

"You looked for how long the other day?"

"A couple hours." With no luck. I thought another set of eyes might do the trick. If Essie and I didn't find the rings today, I'd have to break the news to Matt sometime soon. He was going to be livid.

I crawled out of the cave and searched the tight crevice of another smaller rock. "What are you up to tonight?"

"Date."

"With who?"

"A guy I met at work. He's a chef in the kitchen—makes a stellar lobster ravioli. Plus, he's not too bad to look at."

It amazed me that Essie could manage an entire hotel while I couldn't keep a single house in order. Or a family intact.

"What time's the wake tomorrow?"

"Four. You know, I haven't told anyone this yet, but Barb left me with just about everything."

Essie straightened from where she'd crouched upon the ground. "Everything? You mean . . ."

I nodded. "House, safe deposit box, life savings. Everything."

"Whoa."

"And something else." I told her about my neighbor's unusual request.

"That's some bad karma right there, sis. How'd you get in the middle of all that?"

We stood and walked slowly around the base of the rock, our eyes on the ground. Essie poked the toe of her sneaker in the brush.

"I—I really don't know."

"So do you think she gave you all the money to ensure you'd carry out her wishes?"

"No—no, she wasn't like that. I mean, I want to do this for her. It's really not that much trouble. I guess I only wish I'd known how much I meant to her when she was here, you know?"

The words hung in the tree-laden woods, heavy. It seemed everything I'd considered precious was being swept from beneath my feet. And now that they were slipping away, I realized just how much they'd all meant to me.

I caught a glimpse of something shiny beneath a leaf. My stomach dropped and I brushed aside the leaf.

A crushed Sprite can.

"Sarah?"

"Hmmm?"

"Just be careful, okay?"

"What do you mean?"

"I mean you have a lot going on right now. Becoming third party to your dead neighbor's past regrets, trying to make things right . . . well, I think it was wrong of her to put all that on you. They weren't your mistakes. You had nothing to do with it."

"There's no way I'm walking away from—"

Essie held her hands up. "I'm not saying you should. I just

don't want to see you get hurt or feel like you're disappointing someone who's cold in their grave."

"You make it sound like doing something for others is a bad thing. I feel like all my life I've been looking out for me, for my family. And look where it's gotten us. This"—I gestured to the rock before us, the woods around us—"I'm here because of Barb. I've always felt a connection to this place. Maybe this is just the distraction I need right now."

"Okay, okay. I get it. Once again, my mouth goes before me. Sorry." Essie waited for a mosquito to land on her pants leg before squashing it. She took a leaf and wiped the guts off her palm, then looked at me. "You got this, and you got whatever else life throws at you."

I smiled. "Thank you. That's just what I needed to hear."

My sister stood. "Good, because I'm about to tell you something you won't want to hear—those rings aren't here. We've searched every inch of this place. Someone might have found them the day you dropped them. Maybe check with the police to see if they were turned in. Hopefully no one pocketed it for themselves."

I groaned. "I should have looked longer that first day. "I'll check with the police after I drop you off."

"I can come with you if we make it quick. I gotta get ready for my date."

We turned west, out of the woods.

"I'm thinking about going to church tomorrow. Want to come?" I asked.

Essie scrunched up her face. "No thanks. Besides, if my date goes well, I'll be too tired to get up for nine-thirty service."

Since I had no plans, I wouldn't have a problem waking up bright-eyed and bushytailed. Maybe I'd find some answers at church, or at least find peace. Peace about the quest I was about to embark upon. Peace about my marriage. Peace about my future. Maybe for once, God would help me.

CHAPTER 8

God didn't show up at church the next morning as I'd hoped. At least, if He had I missed Him. All I felt was Dad's intense gaze from the pulpit, set three steps higher than all the pews, as if he were about three steps farther on the road to eternal life than the rest of us. I sat in the front row with Mom, listening to Dad speak of the Good Samaritan, how we should all strive to be more like this man—a true neighbor, a true friend.

I wondered if I'd ever be good enough for God. I wondered if I'd ever do enough, or pray enough, or say enough. At the same time I couldn't help but wonder—if Jesus was supposed to save me, why did I feel like I constantly had to save myself?

My parents invited me for lunch after service, but I told them I had something I needed to do before the wake that night. To disprove myself a liar, I drove to the trailer park where Matt's mother, Lorna, lived. I stepped up to the white screen door and knocked. Red geraniums grew in a lopsided window box, wilting from lack of water.

Poor Lorna. She tried. I had called her often during Kyle's growing up years, filling her in, even taking him for visits to the trailer park. Matt never offered to come. We invited Lorna for Kyle's birthday celebrations and graduations from kindergarten and middle school. We invited her to a handful of Kyle's track meets. She showed up as often as she didn't. Matt didn't act bothered when his mother forgot a celebration or even his own birthday. In fact, he pretended she didn't exist at all. I tried to fix them too many times. After one particularly heated conversation, he let loose in a rare show of anger.

"Will you just leave it, Sarah? Some things are just too broken to fix. My mother and I are one of those things."

Did he view our marriage as one of those "too broken" things as well?

I knocked on the door again. It rattled in its frame. The scent of fried chicken from next door wafted to my nostrils.

"Comin', comin'! Hold your horses, will ya?" A shadowy figure emerged from inside the double-wide.

"Hi Lorna. It's me."

"Oh, hey, doll. I wasn't expectin' you."

Doll. I don't think Matt's mother ever called me by my given name.

She opened the door and I stepped onto a rough green mat sitting atop a fuzzy brown carpet the shade of dried pine needles. I hugged Lorna, adorned in a flower-print house robe and fluorescent pink slippers. Her stiffly sprayed hair, the color of faded tree bark, rubbed against my neck and cheek.

"I was just unwinding today before it's back to work again tomorrow. You're welcome to join me, sugar. Want a Coke? I didn't get Diet this time, figured I'd go crazy."

I laughed. "Sure, I guess I could stand a little crazy."

"That's the spirit, doll." She turned off a bull riding competition on the television and walked to the refrigerator, stuck her rather slender top almost all the way in. Her ample backside hung out the other end. "Now, where'd I put those little suckers? Ah, there they are!" She pulled out two Coca-Colas, her rouge-caked face triumphant. She set them down on one of three plastic mats on the semi-circle table. The mats held pictures of a variety of birds, each labeled underneath. Blue-jay. Cardinal. Yellow finch. Chickadee.

Lorna shuffled through one of the cabinets. "I bought some cookies case company stopped by. Now I'm glad I did." She pulled out a package of Great Value vanilla wafers. "There. Let's have a sit-down."

We sat at the small table and despite myself, I enjoyed the cozy feeling. I always did when I came to Lorna's. Matt thought I was insane, but there was something about the community feel of the trailer park, the small, simple space of each residence, that put me at ease. Or maybe it was the lack of pretense from the people who lived in them. Most times, what you saw was what you got. Living so closely, they couldn't hide much, so most didn't even bother to do the hiding.

"You sure dressed nice, doll. You come from church?"

I nodded.

"I went to mass last night. Needed my beauty sleep this morning, you know?" She took a swig of her Coke and gave me a long sideways glance. "You know, darling, you can come to Saturday night mass with me anytime. Looks like you could use a little extra sleep yourself."

I exhaled. "Yeah . . . your son's been keeping me up nights."

She slapped her hand on the table. "Well, it's good you kids haven't lost the passion, you know? Nothing like a hot bed to keep a marriage together. Not that I can claim to know much about marital things."

I almost choked on my soda. "No, Lorna." Then I began to laugh, small giggles at first until I couldn't stop. Lorna laughed with me. The laughing became near hysterical before it finally gave way to tears. It was as if a floodgate opened, fast and strong and cleansing. The release lifted a knotted burden in my chest.

Lorna patted my arm and handed me a tissue. Nothing seemed to surprise her. "There, there now, honey. You let it all out. It's good for the soul, you know."

Once I gathered myself, I wiped my eyes and sniffed. "Thanks."

"Things aren't so great in the bedroom then, I take it?"

"Things aren't great, period." I took a wafer from the package and a napkin from the wooden holder on the table. Wafer crumbs flaked onto the white paper. "Matt's staying in Newport for the summer."

"For work?"

I shrugged. "He is working down there, but the commute's only a half hour. He didn't try to hide his reasons. He wants a break, Lorna."

"You saying my boy left you?"

"Yeah. I guess that's what I'm saying."

"Sheesh, child, if I thought I could speak some sense into him I'd call him up and give him a talkin'-to right now." Her expression softened, the gloss on her lips almost pretty. "But you and I both know that would do more harm than good."

"Kyle's with him."

"Aw, darlin'."

My eyes burned. I rubbed Lorna's ring between my two fingers.

"I didn't come here for your pity. I just . . . Well, I thought you should know and I wondered if . . . I wondered if you might be able to tell me about Matt's father and . . ." I couldn't finish my thought. This was unchartered ground between us.

"You want to know why he left us, is that right?"

"Kind of."

"Oh, child." Lorna took a long swig from her can. "Cola might not be enough to get me through that story."

"Maybe this isn't the right time, or maybe I don't even need to know. It's just that Matt never—"

"He never told you? Did you ever ask him?"

"Sure I did. He just never wanted to talk about his dad or —" I stopped short of saying "you" or "childhood." I didn't want to hurt Lorna by stating the obvious. She must know how Matt felt about his past—she'd have to be brain dead not to.

Matt would be angry knowing I even brought up this line of questioning to Lorna. But Matt wasn't going to find out. Didn't I have a right to know? He should have told me everything long ago.

"I want to help me and Matt, Lorna. I want to save our marriage. If there's anything from Matt's past that you think I should know, would you tell me?"

I looked into her cocoa-colored eyes. She didn't avoid my probing gaze. "Doll, Matt's father had an affair. Only it wasn't with another woman. It was with money. He left us to chase gold. Gold! Can you believe that? A regular old forty-niner." Lorna shook her head. "He always had some hare-brained idea of getting rich. But he never left us until some guys at the bar convinced him he could strike it rich a few states over. The gold was his ultimate downfall."

Matt had hinted as much. I figured it was why he prided himself in providing for me and Kyle so well all these years.

"Anything else?"

Lorna studied me. "Maybe the fault isn't all with Matt, doll, have you ever thought of that? Going back in the past isn't going to help Matt's future. And it sure isn't going to help your marriage. You can't move forward if you keep looking backwards."

I wanted to argue. I wanted to say that you couldn't move forward if you had nothing to stand on, and a healed past was the only firm foundation. I wanted to tell Lorna that *I* wasn't the problem. I wasn't the one who left. I was willing to work at our marriage, to see a counselor, to do what it took to restore us.

But I didn't say any of those things. Instead, I finished my wafer cookies and soda in silence as we chatted about Kyle and bingo night in the trailer park and other safe topics.

All the while, I wondered if Matt knew how alike he and his mother actually were.

Matt did come to the funeral. He and Kyle sat one on each side of me, dressed in their best. The pastor of Barb's church spoke of the hope and treasure waiting for her in heaven.

Other than my parents, Matt, and Kyle, I didn't recognize any of the other attendees, but strangely, many seemed to know who I was. One middle-aged woman said she knew Barb from their church quilting club, and that she had spoke often of me.

I tried to be gracious, but when Matt and Kyle said quiet good-byes before the collation in the church hall, I felt abandoned again. I watched Matt nod in the direction of my parents and slip out the back door, Kyle lingering a few extra moments to hug his grandparents.

As I cut slices of banana cream pie for the guests who were all but strangers, I found myself dwelling on a verse that Barb's pastor had quoted. I didn't remember the entire thing, and I couldn't think of how it related to what he'd said about Barb's life, but nevertheless, I clung to it.

He'd called the keeper of Barb's soul the "God of Hope." Right now, with my husband and son driving away yet again, I clung to the seemingly impossible offering those three words stirred forth in my soul.

God, give me something. Give me hope.

CHAPTER 9

The day after Barb's funeral, I ignored the very real need to use my second personal day to clean the house, or begin organizing Barb's, and instead drove to Plymouth. I'd made an appointment to view Elizabeth Baker's journal the day before, not without some trouble. Only after I had shared Barb's letter with Jill, the curator, had she relented, telling me that such privileges were highly irregular and that I would have to watch a video on the handling of historical manuscripts before being allowed to do so.

I agreed to it all.

Now, I rolled down the windows and turned up the music, allowing Scotty McCreery's words about wanting five more minutes to swell up within my heart. Outside, the sun splashed on the roadways and forty minutes later I parked alongside Plymouth Harbor. Across the way, the replica of the Mayflower bobbed in the clear water, its naked mast pointing to the sky.

I'd come here once as a girl with my grandmother, mother, and Essie. I could still remember leaning over the rail to view Plymouth Rock at sea level, the expectation of seeing the rock great in our minds.

I remembered Essie's small voice, huffing in disbelief. *"That's Plymouth Rock?"*

True, I'd been surprised by how small it was too. I'd expected something big and grand, something like Abram's Rock. But I also remember feeling how I often felt in the woods of my hometown—like I was witnessing something incredibly special just by being in the same spot where such a significant event occurred.

I walked past the memorial now, wishing I'd taken Kyle here before, or at least explored it with Matt. So much history, right in our backyard, and yet we'd always been too busy building businesses or working or keeping up with the Joneses.

Now, beneath the cloud of recent events, exploring it alone didn't hold much appeal. I glimpsed the rock as I walked past, took a left on Chilton Street and climbed a hill toward Pilgrim Hall Museum. The large gray building stood imposing at the end of the block. I scaled the many outside steps before I reached the lobby, my laptop bag now heavy on my shoulder.

In the foyer, an older woman greeted me. I inhaled a deep breath and introduced myself.

The woman lifted her phone. "Just a moment while I call for Jill."

In a few minutes' time, a woman appeared from the staircase to my left. She held out her hand. "It's nice to meet you, Mrs. Rodrigues. We spoke on the phone. I'm Jill."

I nodded. "Please, call me Sarah. Thank you so much for making this possible."

Jill led me around to the main exhibit hall, where I glimpsed a large painting on the left that read *Signing of the Compact in the Cabin of the Mayflower.* Taking out keys, she unlocked a glass door labeled *Steinway Memorial Library.* We entered. The dark red of the paint contrasted beautifully with the many portraits along the wall. Windows allowed in splashes of sunlight. Across the room sat a grand fireplace flanked by caged bookshelves, a treasure of documents within.

"This is amazing," I said.

"As I said to you on the phone, this really is not regular practice, especially for a seventeenth-century document. But because of our history with Barbara . . . the board decided to allow you access."

"I am grateful." I wondered if Barb's generosity in her will had inspired theirs.

"We'll be using her donation to digitalize Elizabeth's journals, but we won't be able to get that together until next year sometime." She pointed to my bag. "I can give you the link to watch the video I mentioned, or I can set you up on our computer."

I took out my laptop, typing in the YouTube link. We watched the video together, in which a woman solemnly explained that every time a historical document was touched, it was at risk of damage. She went over how to wash hands properly before touching a document, what to keep away from the record, and so on.

When we were finished, Jill set up book supports, or a "cradle," that would help ease the stress on the spine of Elizabeth's journal. After we returned from washing our hands, Jill unlocked one of the cabinets and pulled out a bound book of yellowed pages. She laid it carefully in the cradle and untied the ribbon around it.

"The pages are beginning to come loose, so we have to tie it together with this unbleached cotton." She pulled the cotton with care and laid the book open. Gently, she rested chain links on either side of the first page to hold it open. I watched carefully, the gravity of the privilege I was about to partake in not lost on me. "If you notice any pages stuck together, please tell me at once."

"I will treat it with the greatest care. I promise. Thank you so much."

For the first time she gave a small smile. "I believe that you will. Please don't hesitate to come find me if you have any questions."

I sat down and stared at the journal, already open to the first page. Without touching it, I read the first two sentences, not without some struggle.

Andia wed today. 'Tis how I came by this paper.

I fought for each word of the short sentences, realizing with clarity the monumental task before me. I skimmed the rest of the page, noticing some unfamiliar words and many *f*'s in place of *s*'s.

Of course, I was curious about the story Barb had thought so important. But this would take hours upon hours. And I couldn't do it from the comfort of my home—I'd have to make the drive to Plymouth during the museum's hours.

I rested back in the chair, fought for perspective. Truly, almost anything of late seemed like a monumental task. Doing the dishes, getting ready for work, taking out the trash, searching for a clock repair guy. With the heavy press of my failed marriage upon me, I couldn't quite summon much excitement toward anything. And now, with this fresh disappointment, I battled a wave of depression.

Closing my eyes, I breathed in through my nose.

I'd never be able to live with myself if I ignored Barb's request. And I couldn't let it drag out, either. Not only would it never give me peace until completed, but Mary should know her mother died. She should know that Barb cared until the end.

Only I couldn't contact her until I'd gotten through Elizabeth's story. Until I recorded a readable copy. Mary couldn't transcribe the story long distance.

I opened my eyes and gave myself a short pep talk. It was simple, really. This needed to be done. I was the one to do it. End of story.

I opened a new file on my laptop and titled it *Journal of Elizabeth Baker*, and began.

March 20, 1675

Andia wed today. 'Tis how I came by this paper. After the vows, when all stood in line to congratulate my dearest friend and her new husband, Goodwife Elizabeth Howland gestured to me with the crook of her finger from her spot in the front pew. I was eager to escape the mass of people to see her. She presented me with this bound book of precious paper, and bid me put it in the pocket of my dress. I told her it was Andia's day for presents, not mine. She said Andia would have everything she needed provided for her by Hezekiah now, and that I was the one who may need a bit of encouragement and a place to voice my thoughts over the next few months.

I wondered what she knew that I did not.

Whether I will need a place to voice my thoughts or not, I can't deny there is something wholly satisfying about putting my musings on paper, stringing together letters into words, words into sentences. Much like the piecing of an intricate quilt, 'tis a delight to create something from nothing.

I asked Goodwife Howland if it would please her if I visited on the morrow for a cup of chocolate and some of her stories. I never tire of her tellings of her childhood in the homeland, of her frightening voyage on the Mayflower when her yet-to-be husband fell overboard and was saved by God's providence and one of the topsail halyards, of that horrid first winter, of the Indian named Squanto whom she and Goodman Howland knew well. The latter interests me most, and I long for more. Yet she never satisfies. Either she has naught to tell or she does not wish for my ears to hear it.

She bid me stay home on the morrow. I could not presume to hide my hurt. With Andia now wed, who was left to talk to if not my namesake?

Goodwife Howland leaned down to whisper in my ear as the men made ready the horses to leave Pastor Miles' meetinghouse.

"Soon thou wilt wed also, Elizabeth. Thou wilt have the responsibilities of thine own home and hearth to keep. 'Tis best thou spendst time preparing for that and not in the musings of an old woman."

My heart longed to argue, yet I kept my mouth closed.

Papa was quiet as the wagon rocked over the rough trail to the Bourne residence, but I sensed something on his mind. I pulled the lap robe closer to ward off the chill of the day.

Papa said Caleb Tanner had come to see him the day before when I was out for one of my walks. He said Mr. Tanner wishes to court me.

I told Papa Mr. Tanner was too old for me. What I didn't tell him was I thought him a bore. There is nothing surprising about him. Caleb Tanner is the most predictable man on earth. Since I was no higher than a corn stalk in the ground but a fortnight, I remember Mr. Tanner sitting in the second pew on the left in Pastor Miles's church. He has lived on a small homestead growing his vegetables and chopping his wood, never seeking to further his estate or explore new territory or befriend the feisty natives. He certainly isn't the kind of man who would be open to a wife reading and writing and keeping a journal of her thoughts.

"Elizabeth Grace, Caleb Tanner is a good and respectable man, not more than ten years your elder. He's been waiting for you to come of age."

It unnerved me that Mr. Tanner sought interest in not only a wife, but in me. I prayed he would not be in attendance at the wedding feast and my prayer was answered. I heard Mr. Lewis note in passing that Mr. Tanner had to attend a matter of import back on his homestead.

He likely had to tend his milk cow.

March 24, 1675

Mr. Tanner called on me today. He asked Papa if he and I might share a short walk. Much to my dismay, Papa did not refuse.

I stoked the fire and wiped my hands on my apron before following Mr. Tanner out the door. I didn't look at Papa, hunched over drinking his flip at the table, his cough echoing behind us.

Mr. Tanner spoke of the beauty of the day as he led me north on a familiar path away from the homestead. I mused why it was that he sought me out. We hadn't much familiarity with one another. In truth, the only memory I had of him was when I was but a lass. John Cole and Nathan Cobb took it in their minds to chase me with a big fat toad at a harvest picnic. In my panic, I hid behind Mr. Tanner, then not much more than a lad himself. He crouched down and pulled a piece of straw from my hair and asked me what was wrong. I pointed to the boys running toward me with their ugly friend. Mr. Tanner straightened and told the boys that was enough for now and to go find something more useful to do than to tease helpless little girls.

I'd run away without thanking him. It came in my mind to do so now, but he likely had no memory of the incident.

I tried to appreciate Mr. Tanner's tall, steady presence by my side. He smelled of smoke and faintly of manure. I didn't see how I could make myself love him.

He asked me if I enjoyed Andia's wedding. I told him I had, but that I'd been anxious to get home to write in my journal.

He didn't have a response to that, so I went on to tell him I often took walks in the woods in these very paths, and that I thought it would be quite exciting to meet a native or two sometime, but I never came upon them, and what were his feelings about the natives?

To my surprise, I think I saw a smile beneath his honey-colored beard. Yet his words did not indicate such. He bid me stay away from the ruffians, that none of them were a happy lot.

I told him I thought it wrong to condemn those the good Lord hath made from the same dust as he. I also told him I thought Captain Church the bravest, wisest, and most exciting man in the colony to seek them out and befriend them.

Again, Mr. Tanner had little to say on that.

I doubt he will call on me again.

March 31, 1675

Whether it be God's providence or happenstance, I can't be certain. But I must write about what happened this day. After Papa gave me my morning book lesson and I saw to the dishes and fire, I went for one of my walks. I cannot begin to understand it, particularly at this time of year, but I often feel as if the woods beckon to me. With the faint scent of pine lacing the air, I feel a peace, as if I am one with the trees and the dirt beneath my feet, one with birds the color of sky and fire, with woodland creatures the color of fresh-cut wood.

Today I sang. And 'twas not a church hymn. I sang "The Nightingale," having read the words and music from one of Papa's imported books. If he knew I acted with such boldness, he'd forbid me ever leave the safety of the chimney seat again. As it is, he is not aware I go so far. He would no doubt fear for me as Mr. Tanner made mention of on his last visit.

I so enjoyed the upbeat tune and beauty of the morning, I lost track of time. I wandered beneath a tall pine, and that was when I saw him.

He was the most beautiful creature I'd ever seen. His hair was jet black and his skin the color of the warming pan I use to rid my bedsheets of the chill at night. He wore leather leggings and breeches. I tried to tear my gaze from his shirtless torso, but I had never seen a man in such a state before, and even as my face and neck heated, I could not help but study his well-formed muscles and broad shoulders. I hid behind the base of the tree and watched as he crouched and put a pair of clamshells to his face. I realized then that he was plucking out hairs on his chin.

I do not think I breathed in the space of a minute's time. I tried to remember the greeting used in their language, but it escaped my mind. I saw a bow and arrow at his side and my heart pranced like an untamed horse. Mr. Tanner said to stay away from the natives. This one may take to his weapon when he saw me. He may shoot it and kill me. I imagined myself crawling across the forest floor with an arrow through my body.

I backed away slowly, but my foot found a twig. In one smooth motion, the native spun, bow poised in hand, his face alert.

I did not think. I ran.

He yelled out after me, but I kept running even as his words echoed through the forests.

"Nétop, nétop!"

Even as I remembered what the word meant, I did not slow my pace. The foreign expression etched itself in my mind. I will not soon forget his voice.

"Nétop."

Friend.

CHAPTER 10

My phone alarm woke me from a dream I didn't want to leave. I shut it off and fell back on my pillow, trying to recapture the vision. It wouldn't be hard. I remembered the moment—the dream—because it was real. It had happened years earlier.

Matt and I had been seeing each other under the cover of night for almost a month, but one Friday night my parents had gone to New Hampshire for a conference. Matt picked me up after he'd mowed his neighbor's lawn. For once, the sun shone bright in the sky, and I met him at the front door instead of at the end of the drive. His hair was still wet from his shower and it curled at his ears. In his car Elvis sang out "Are You Lonesome Tonight?"

He took me to the Lobster Pot in Bristol. We ate on the patio and watched the sun's rays dance on the water. I tried to order a bowl of soup as my main course, but Matt insisted I order something more substantial. I knew he'd had to mow about three lawns to afford to take me out.

After dinner, we drove to Colt State Park. We walked on the wide rocks and around the park until we found a large tree whose branches touched the ground, creating a sheltered canopy below it.

"It's a European weeping beech," Matt said as he drew me under its protective umbrella.

The tree's trunk grew so thick I couldn't begin to extend my arms around it. Its base split into a *W* where gnarled branches sprouted upward and out. Couples' initials cluttered its bark, swollen and twisted with the growth of the tree. I looked up, where the canopy of pear-shaped leaves and branches opened to faded blue sky.

"I worked here last summer and found this tree." Matt dug in his pocket and withdrew his Swiss Army Knife. "May I?"

My insides fluttered. I'd only known him a month. "How many other girls have you brought here?"

He stepped closer. He smelled of Ivory soap and woodsy cologne. He'd been a perfect gentleman so far, giving me sweet kisses then and now, but nothing more. "Only you. That's why I brought you here. I've had other girlfriends, but you're special, Sarah. I can't explain it. You make me feel like anything's possible—it's like you make me something. I brought you here because I wanted to tell you. I love you."

He lowered his lips to mine and I tasted a salty thin layer of sweat on them. I leaned into him and for the first time, he deepened our kiss. I hungered for more, felt the same ardent desire in him. But he was the one to pull back. He brushed a strand of hair behind my ear and held up the knife.

I nodded and leaned against the massive trunk to watch him climb the tree, sling a leg over a limb, and carefully carve *Matt and Sarah* below a large knot in the trunk.

There was no turning back after that.

My alarm blared again, and I dragged an arm from above my head to shut it off. Over the years, Matt and I hadn't visited the weeping beech tree nearly enough.

I closed my eyes and thought of that kiss again, of the many physical intimacies we'd shared over the last decade and a half. Not only did my soul ache for my husband, my body did as well.

Surely he'd come home soon if for no other reason than missing the warmth of my arms, as I did his.

By the time I walked out the door, coffee in hand, nerves had replaced every other desire in my body. My stomach grew tight as I thought about facing a day at work. While I was initially hesitant to transcribe Elizabeth's journal, right now the thought of the cozy library at the museum, Elizabeth's ancient words on the table before me, intimidated less than the thought of a hallway of patients dependent upon me. At work, I would have to pretend to be happy. At the museum, I didn't have to pretend anything. Tucked away in the library by myself, I could lose myself in the work of the story.

But I had responsibilities and really, I loved my job. It would be good to settle in again, to think about the patients and my coworkers instead of Barb's request or my personal problems. The journal would have to wait until the weekend.

When I reached the geriatric ward, Jen clapped her hands once upon seeing me. "Boy am I glad to see you. Doris is having a hard time in 223—Mr. Caron, a man who had a stroke two days ago. He's being a bit stubborn. Would you mind?"

I clocked in and placed my lunch in the refrigerator. "No problem."

I scurried down the hall to rescue our oldest—and sweetest —CNA, Doris. When I arrived and peered around the closed curtain of the first patient, I saw her standing with a bowl of Cheerios in her hands. On the laminate floor beside her lay a metal spoon with splatters of milk surrounding it.

"Uh oh," I breathed. I took the bowl from Doris. "I think Mrs. Taylor could use you in 301."

"Thanks, Sarah," she whispered.

While I wasn't certain I could handle this patient on my own, it often seemed as if relating to them one-on-one worked better for me. Otherwise, some of the more cantankerous sorts felt we were trying to wage war against them.

I grabbed some paper towels from their holder on the wall

and stepped toward him, putting his cereal on his tray. "Hi, Mr. Caron. I'm Sarah."

He eyed me as I stooped to clean up the milky mess on the floor before tossing the towels into the trash.

"I'd love to help you with your breakfast if you'd like."

"Fine," he mumbled after a moment.

I held up a small bottle of apple juice. "Would you like some?"

Mr. Caron nodded. "She thinks I'm deaf, you know. I can still hear fine out of one ear." One side of the older man's mouth drooped, and it took some effort to understand what he said.

"Well, I'm glad you told me." I twisted open the juice and poured it into the cup on his tray. "Should I sit?" I gestured to the empty space on the side of his bed.

"Yeah. Good of you to ask. They usually just do it."

I scooped a small spoonful of Cheerios into the spoon, and careful not to spill the milk, I raised it to his lips. He opened his mouth and chewed on his left side. Some soggy Os fell from the other side of his mouth and I wiped them up with a napkin. By the time he was done with the one spoonful, the rest of his Cheerios sat in a mushy heap in his bowl.

Sunlight streamed onto the white blanket of Mr. Caron's bed. I remembered the beautiful quilt on Barb's bed with the picture of the Indian. *Nétop.* Would Elizabeth see him again? And was he truly who I suspected him to be? Barb's legend . . . alive?

"Are you expecting any visitors today, Mr. Caron?"

A long silence. "My wife is supposed to come by later."

"That's nice." I lifted the juice to his mouth, and Mr. Caron slurped down a wobbly sip, then swallowed.

I turned back to the Cheerios when an unintelligible sound came forth from the man. I looked up, thought I might see him crying. I pondered whether to pat his arm or ignore it. Maybe I should coax him to take another bite.

From behind the curtain beside us, a man spoke to the other patient in the room. Perhaps a doctor or nurse. I hoped Mr. Caron wouldn't burst forth in a show of emotion that might interrupt any exam being done.

But instead of tears, words came out, slurred. "Hate for her to see me like this, not able to care for myself, having to be fed like a baby. Can't even take care of my bathroom needs." Shame shrouded his words and pity erupted in my belly. What could I do to help this man? I felt confident in taking care of a patients' physical needs, but emotional? I could barely take care of my own these days.

"I'm sure your wife loves you," I said, though in truth I hadn't the faintest clue if being classified as a spouse meant you were in love. I'd been sure Matt had loved me up until last week. Now . . . well, I hadn't talked to him in days.

"She does . . . sweetest thing ever walked this earth."

"Then she's not about to be bothered by you needing a little help, is she?"

"Still humiliating."

I lifted another bite to Mr. Caron's mouth, but he didn't open. "How did you and your wife meet?" I figured if I could get Mr. Caron's mind off his current circumstances, it would improve his mood and his appetite.

His mouth loosened. "I used to be a firefighter. Got burned bad one run. Eileen was a nurse at the hospital—not this one, we were in New York at the time. My leg was burnt something awful, couldn't walk for weeks, but I sure had the prettiest nurse taking care of me."

I was about to point out that since his wife fell in love with him while she nursed him, she certainly wouldn't mind doing so now, but I didn't want to interrupt his thoughts. Mr. Caron talked for some time. I couldn't always understand his slurred words between mouthfuls of cereal, but I listened until he was done.

When he finished his story and his cereal, he rested back on his pillow. "You're good," he said. "Stay like that. Don't get too busy."

I wiped the dribbled milk from his chin with a rough napkin, thankful I hadn't passed on the task to a CNA. "I'll remember that." I moved the tray to the side for food services to get later. "Get some rest. I'll be back to check on you in a bit. Maybe I'll get to meet Eileen."

The good side of his mouth lifted and I walked toward the door. The other patient's curtain rustled and Pete emerged.

My face warmed. I hoped he hadn't heard everything, and if he did, I hoped he thought I handled the situation well. More than likely, he believed me to be a sentimental nonprofessional who hadn't a clue about medical care.

"Hey, Sarah. I heard about your neighbor. So sorry about that."

"Uh, thank you." He must have heard one of the other nurses talking about my absence, though truthfully, most of the doctors that came through the ward didn't pay too much attention. They were in and out, usually happy to be back at their offices. "She was . . . old."

He made a sound of acknowledgment as we walked toward the nurses' station. "How'd your crazy news turn out?"

"My crazy news . . . oh, right from the other day." I shook my head. "Wow, if you remember what your patients tell you half as well, you must be a great doctor."

He smiled, dimples tightening his face, stethoscope hanging loosely at his neck. I realized then how handsome he was, and suddenly I wondered whether I'd been inadvertently flirting. I'd never felt quite so insecure around another man, mostly because I had always been secure in the fact that I belonged to Matt. But now . . . did I belong to Matt?

I forced the thoughts aside. Of course I did—I was his wife.

"My news was . . . crazy, but it's all good. Thanks for asking."

He stopped outside a room, his green gaze landing on me.

"Well, nice seeing you again. And not that it matters what I think, but I'd say Mr. Caron's pretty lucky to have you as his nurse." He winked, and then ducked into the room, his sneakers squeaking against the linoleum.

Pretty lucky to have you.

There were so many wrong things about our awkward conversation, and at the same time, something about the man's presence intrigued me. His compliment swirled as smooth as homemade ice cream in my belly. It had been a long time since someone acknowledged me for doing something well. While I knew I was a competent nurse, the praise didn't often come, and truth be told, I didn't need it. But at this vulnerable time in my life, when I was questioning my ability to be a good wife, a good mother, a good neighbor, a good *person* . . . well, the compliment seemed to be a sort of lifeline. Pathetic, maybe, but I didn't care. *Someone* thought I was good at something.

That would have to be enough for today.

I sipped my iced coffee, creamy and rich as it slid down my throat. As I'd done since returning to work each day, I left the hospital to go directly over to Barb's. There, I played soft music inspired by the original inhabitants of North America. It was something Barb played often, and with the light flute sounds and beating drums wafting along the breezes of the open window, I'd almost felt like my friend was with me.

I went around the rooms, taking inventory of Barb's possessions, trying to decide on the benefits of an estate sale. In the end, I was overwhelmed by the task and closed the windows, turned off the music, and crossed the wooded trail to my own home, where I settled into a seat on the patio.

Since the museum closed at four-thirty every day, I had to wait until tomorrow—Saturday—to continue with Elizabeth's story.

I leaned back and rested my head against the patio chair, savoring the pungent scent of new mulch weaving through the air in pleasant bursts. Warm sunshine caressed my arms, but the wind licked any intensity away. Above me, casting slants of shade across the cobbled patio, was the pergola Matt built. In one corner of the terrace sat a massive stone fireplace. We'd used it often to entertain guests. When we had it built, I imagined Matt and me cozy on the patio at nights—alone—but in reality we barely started the fire for ourselves. Instead, we saved it for entertainment, usually for people Matt knew through work, people I performed for, people who somehow made me feel a prisoner in my own home.

I allowed my gaze to travel over the lawn. The patio gave way to trimmed, vibrant green grass, interrupted only by several islands of richly-mulched landscaping. Soon a veritable sea of lilies and hydrangeas would color the lawn. A stone wall, too perfect to be anything but professional, boxed in the gardens, keeping the flawless landscape safe from the wild woods beyond.

The untamed forest outside the wall filled in this time of year, the faint emptiness of a trail etched through the woods. Louis and Greg, Matt's two employees who usually took care of our lawn, dumped the lawn refuse back there. All the weeds and grass and plant clippings got left beyond the stone wall, where no one could see it.

My stomach grumbled. I should go in and fix myself a sandwich. With no one to make supper for and with my additional hours at the hospital, I ate less than usual. My pants already hung looser on my already slim waist and I'd needed to tighten my bra that morning.

From within the house, the phone rang. I dragged myself off the chair and retrieved it, not looking at the caller ID but answering as I went back out to the patio.

"Hello?"

"Hey."

My breath hitched, loud enough for Matt to hear over the line.

"Hey."

"How's it going?"

"Okay." I sounded like I really meant it. Did I? Was I okay?

"How's Kyle doing?"

"He's good. Bone tired, but good. He wants to talk to you before I hang up."

"What are you guys up to tonight?" I tried to pretend a normal conversation, one where I wasn't hurt that I was left out of their plans.

"Ordering in, probably going to bed early. The sun whipped us today, but we got some good progress in on the Waterman mansion."

"Good."

"Yeah . . . good. Hey, I called the guy to fix the clock. Turns out he's not in business anymore. I'll keep looking for someone, though."

"Don't worry, I'll take care of it."

"You will?"

I dragged in a breath. "I think I'm capable of at least that."

"Sure you are. Sure. Listen, I'm putting together the employee dinner and I wanted to let you know the date."

My thoughts kicked into high gear. I hugged the phone to my shoulder. Every summer Matt held an elaborate dinner at The Red Parrot in Newport for his employees. I'd gone to every one. But now? He didn't want to live with me; why did he want me at the dinner?

"I didn't think . . . You want me there?"

"Course I do. Everyone would miss you if you didn't come."

Everyone. I wondered if that included him.

Then I knew. I knew why he wanted me there and the realization sent bitter bile up my throat.

"You don't want anyone to know, do you?"

"Know what?"

"That we're separated."

"A break, Sarah. We're still married."

"But you have to keep up appearances, isn't that right?" I knew Matt. He cared what people thought, especially people who helped him look good, people who made him successful. I was like one of the dried hydrangea flowers from last year, thrown into the back woods for no one to see. For Matt not to see. Now though, he wanted to graft me back in, fix things up to look nice when in reality there was only brittle brown death in its place.

But life didn't coexist with death. It didn't work that way. Beautiful flowers required hard work and sweat. Matt would put the necessary labor into his flowers, into his lawns, into his wealthy clients, but when it came to our marriage, he didn't want work. He just wanted a flower that looked good—whether or not disease riddled its insides.

"I would like you there. Please, Sarah."

Why did we live like strangers then?

"When is it?"

"Next week. Last Friday in June."

Friday. With my new schedule, I had committed one night every two weeks to the hospital. That was it. "I can't."

"You can't. Why not?"

"I have to work." I held my breath, knowing what would come next.

"Since when do you work Friday nights?"

"I took on more hours at the hospital."

Silence. I felt Matt's heated breath over the phone, assuring me that somehow, someway, he still cared. He cared what I did.

"How come?"

"What else do you want me to do with myself?" At the same time that I pretended I didn't have enough to accomplish with Barb's request and property, I also wanted to tell him that I liked working at the hospital more. I even thought to bait him and throw out the plan to continue my schooling just to see how he'd react.

"I like my job," I said. It was too lonely at home, too lonely at Barb's. The museum wasn't open late enough for me to visit.

I thought of how Jen made me and some of the other nurses laugh so hard we'd joked that we would need to swipe some Depends from the cart today. How Mr. Caron's wife had come to bring him home yesterday and had brought me flowers to show her appreciation for my help. How Pete had wished me a good weekend before he'd left for the day, jokingly asked if I'd had any more crazy news, then studied me with those sincere green eyes as he'd said good-bye.

"So when were you going to tell me all this?"

"All . . ."

"That you switched your shifts?"

"Oh, I don't know, Matt, maybe over dinner one night . . . wait, wait that doesn't happen anymore. Maybe before bed then, or over coffee in the morning . . . wait, that doesn't happen anymore either, does it?"

"Sarah."

I'd made my point and stopped myself from giving a fake apology.

Silence clung to the phone before he expelled a long breath. "Fine, if you can't get it off from work—"

"I can't. I just committed to it. I don't want to ask for time off already." Really, I simply didn't want to go to the party.

"I'll make it on a Saturday night, then. Last Saturday in June. That okay for your schedule?"

"That will be fine. I'll pencil you in." I put a trace of humor in my voice to let him know I wasn't holding any grudges. Over this, anyway.

"Gee thanks. Okay then, I'll put Kyle on."

"Good night."

But he was already calling for Kyle.

"Hey, Mom."

"Hi, kiddo. Working hard, huh?" I put my bare feet on the patio table.

"Am I ever. Planted about fifty hydrangea bushes today. Dad's a slave driver, man."

I laughed. "Ready to come home, then?" I shouldn't have said that. "Sorry."

I sensed Kyle walking, maybe leaving Matt's presence. "It's okay, Mom. We haven't talked much about you guys, but I will work on him for you, like I said."

"It's not your job, honey. You just worry about working and having fun with your dad, okay? I don't need any reports or pep talks. It used to be my job to take care of you, remember?"

He snorted. "Okay . . . you have fun too—not too much fun though, right? Be careful around Aunt Essie."

I laughed. "I'm working too much to have girl-time over here." I told him about cleaning out Barb's house and my new hours.

"Make sure you drink plenty of water in this heat," I said.

"I will. I'll remember to wash my armpits and bellybutton, too."

"Wise guy."

We said our good nights and hung up. I sat on the patio for a few more minutes, thinking about my conversation with my husband. Maybe I'd buy a new dress for Matt's dinner, something pretty that he'd appreciate.

I rubbed my face, grabbed my phone, and went into the kitchen. A new dress might be a waste of money. It would take more than an article of clothing to fix my marriage.

It would take a miracle.

CHAPTER 11

April 3, 1675

Andia called on me today. I had just thrust my hand into the oven to make certain the cooking fire was hot enough for the loaves I was to bake when she called to me from outside the door. I near singed my apron on the flames, so filled with glee was I to hear her voice.

I bid her come in and take some tea with me while the loaves baked. I was grateful Papa had gone to the millers for flour and to the tavern for news. We enjoyed the smell of the baking loaves and our hot drinks as I questioned Andia about married life. She said Hezekiah was kind and she much enjoyed their time together. She said she found working with him on his homestead most satisfying.

"And what of sharing his bed?" I asked.

"Elizabeth," she scolded. "You are too bold."

I told her she had a mother to prepare her for what to expect in the marriage bed, whilst I had no one but Goodwife Howland, and I could not think to question her on such a matter.

She sighed. "'Tis true, I suppose. Forgive me."

We sat in silence for the briefest of moments, as if to remember my mother's soul, borne away to heaven in the birthing room seventeen years ago the next day of my birth.

"I shan't be so indecent as to tell all, but I will say Hezekiah is a patient and gentle man, and that I have come to find——" Andia's face reddened—"comfort and even pleasure in his arms."

I did not further tempt the boundaries of our friendship by asking more.

"And what of you? Hezekiah tells me Mr. Tanner has spoken to your Papa about a courtship."

I stood to add a piece of wood to the cooking fire. *"'Tis true, though I shan't see how I could ever care for the man."*

"Whyever not?"

I couldn't voice my thoughts, even to Andia. I couldn't explain how the thought of being a farmer's wife felt like confinement. Shouldn't life have some greater purpose than spinning thread and churning cheese? I knew if I told her these things, she would declare me mad, and perhaps I am. For what young woman longs for anything more than security and the love of a caring husband?

An image of the native in the woods beside the big rock came unbidden to my mind. I could not cast him from my thoughts of late. I went to bed dreaming of him. I spoke to him when I was alone, calling him *Nétop*, since I knew no other name for him. What would Andia say if I spoke of such things? What would Mr. Tanner say? What would Papa?

Yes, I was mad.

"'Twill take some time is all. I am not certain I am ready to leave Papa alone just yet."

Andia looked at me then as if I were the sweetest girl in the settlement. I chastised myself for my deceit and vowed to try harder to enjoy Mr. Tanner's company, to be the girl I was expected to be, the woman Papa needed me to be.

"Did you hear of the news from across the river?" Andia took a dainty sip of her tea as if to draw out my suspense. *"Several of Goodman Barnes's mules broke loose and destroyed some of the savages' crops. One of their men came over to Goodman Barnes and confronted him. Goodman Barnes ran him off with his musket, thank the Lord."*

"And why should the native not be angry for having his livelihood eaten?" I asked.

Andia looked taken aback for only a moment. *"I near forgot how attached you are to the poor things. 'Twas an honest mistake on Goodman Barnes's part, I'm certain."*

"I'm certain," I all but grumbled.

It seemed to happen quite often of late. Animals would break from their holdings, ruin the natives' crops, and the natives would be forced to relocate. Men in the county would then find a way to purchase the vacant land by visiting a local sachem and offering wares they could not refuse, such as muskets and liquor.

"You should not become so attached to the heathens," Andia said. "Hezekiah spoke of trading some of his crops and wampum for a native boy, if he is able. He could use some help around the homestead."

"A slave?"

"Not a slave, truly. The boy would be better off with us, civilized and perhaps baptized."

Our conversation grew stale after that. Andia left presently.

I decided to visit Goodwife Howland soon.

April 9, 1675

Mr. Tanner called on me again this evening. He asked if I might like to take a walk in the direction of his homestead. I told him I preferred to walk toward the woods as we did last time. He assented and I left Papa alone to finish his rabbit stew and flip, his now familiar cough trailing behind us. I knew it rude not to ask Mr. Tanner if he would like some victuals, but I could think of nothing more unbearable than sitting at our small table with Papa and Mr. Tanner talking above my head, talking without saying what was truly on their minds.

We walked in silence for a time, and to my surprise I didn't find it terribly awkward. The night was beautiful, the sun refusing to rest its weary head as long of late. I made up my mind to begin anew. For Papa's sake, and perhaps even for mine. I apologized to Mr. Tanner for being disagreeable the last time he called.

"There is nothing to forgive," he said, and I noticed that this time he

smelled only of lye soap and woodchips. "I realize this is a big step for you, Elizabeth. May I call you Elizabeth?"

I nodded, though it felt odd to hear my name on his lips. Odd, but not entirely unpleasant.

"And will you call me Caleb?"

My face heated. I could not imagine calling a grown man by his Christian name, and yet that was what is expected of courting couples. "I will."

Again I thought of the native. Nétop. Why could I not push him from my mind?

"Did you hear of Goodman Barnes's encounter with the native?"

Mr. Tanner nodded. "'Tis a perverse affair."

"Was Goodman Barnes able to secure the land for himself?"

"Why would you assume he had an interest in such matters, little Elizabeth?"

I did not mind Mr. Tanner calling me Elizabeth, but the diminutive word in front of it I minded very much. "I am not little. Is that not why you chose to court me now? I am no longer a child."

I didn't miss his eyes scan my face and—almost involuntarily, it seemed—my entire frame. My heart knocked against my chest.

"You are of course right in saying you are no longer a child." He hesitated, then moved closer to me and spoke more softly. "What I see is a beautiful woman who knows her mind, foolish as it may be at times."

His nearness caught me off guard, as did his words. I did not expect such forthrightness from Mr. Tanner, and felt him goading me, putting me in my place, even.

"I see I have successfully rendered you speechless, Elizabeth. Not a small task, hmm?"

He teased me! Such jest was the last thing I expected from him. It piqued my curiosity.

"You did not answer my question, Mr. Tanner."

"Caleb."

I berated myself when I stammered out his name. "C-Caleb. Did Goodman Barnes secure the land?"

He ran his fingers through his beard, the color of honey. "Goodman Barnes visited Metacomet and settled a deal for the land."

"King Philip?"

"You know far too much for a young woman."

"Should women live in confinement with only their husbands learning news of the outside world?"

"Would it be a terrible thing to have naught to worry about but the baking and the mending and the hearth and all other such matters of import that keep a homestead running smoothly and a husband happy?"

Heat rose from the center of my belly and spread upward when he looked at me with intense eyes as he said the word husband.

"You may not wish your women so innocent if men the likes of Goodman Barnes continue to anger the natives."

Mr. Tanner was silent as we made our way back to Papa's house. When the barn came into view he said he enjoyed the walk, and he hoped I had also.

I did. Perhaps Mr. Tanner was not quite the bore I had thought him to be.

"And now, may I ask you a question, Elizabeth?"

I had not expected a proposal so soon. I may have conceded Mr. Tanner more amusing than I previously thought, but that did not mean I was ready to wed him.

I did not answer, yet he continued.

"I request—with only your good in mind—that you not wander in the woods by yourself any longer. You are an intelligent woman and you are right to realize that men such as Goodman Barnes have made the natives less than happy. We are in the frontier here, Elizabeth, far from Plimoth and Boston."

"Yet I do not see—"

"I cannot pretend to know all, but I know of the colonists' distrust of the natives. I am certain the natives feel the same of us. I do not think it safe for a young woman to be out alone. 'Twill not hurt you to reserve your walks for me?"

My heart bucked at the thought. Mr. Tanner's words were pleasant enough, but how could he already assume control over me? We were not yet betrothed!

All the pleasure I had found in Mr. Tanner that evening dissipated. "I do appreciate your concern, Mr. Tanner, but I will do as Papa and I see fit for now."

I bid him a good night and left him near the step of our front door.

April 12, 1675

I attempt to find comfort in these pages, though my ink is running low and I had not thought to collect extra walnuts to crush last autumn.

I was pouring the refuse grease from the noon meal into a tub to save for the making of soft soap when Papa asked to speak with me. I placed the used pan in the sink and we sat by the Betty lamp near the fireplace, Papa's tobacco bucket at his feet.

"Caleb Tanner told me he asked you not to go for your walks."

I tried to fix my thoughts in my head. I could not fathom that Mr. Tanner had spoken to my father about our discourse, yet it seemed he had.

"Yes. I informed him that was a matter for us to decide."

"The man cares for you, Elizabeth."

"Perhaps it is not yet his place to care so much."

"Perhaps it should be his place," Papa said. "I am getting on in years, daughter. You need your marriage settled before the Lord takes me home." He coughed then, a cough I had not yet heard come from him. It echoed in my own being, for I had heard it often from Goodwife Howland's husband many times in the months before his passing.

"Please, Papa. I am not yet ready."

"My sweet girl." Papa reached for my hand and I grasped his calloused one with both of mine. "I do not believe I am long for this world."

"How can you know such a thing that only the Lord has knowledge of?"

Papa smiled. "I suppose I do not. But I feel something different in my bones. Please, tell me you will accept Mr. Tanner's proposal when it comes. I wish to see my daughter settled and married before I leave this earth."

Warm tears spilled onto my cheeks. They trailed through the stain of dirt and dust left from cleaning the barn earlier. "I will, Papa. I will."

How could the Lord allow Papa to leave me? I pray Papa is wrong. The winter was a mite too long for him. Soon though, fair weather will descend upon us.

He will feel better soon. I am certain of it.

CHAPTER 12

I hadn't planned on going back to the museum on Sunday. I thought to visit Barb's church, clean my bathrooms, Google Mary's name, maybe take a long bath. But Elizabeth's story called to me, and I was keenly aware of the fact that if I didn't go today, I would have to wait an entire six days to get my chance again.

I found the transcribing easier now that I was familiar with Elizabeth's script. I felt for her, this long-ago ancestor of my neighbor's. I didn't want her Papa to die. I didn't want her to have to marry a man she didn't love. I wanted her happiness. And I wanted to find out more about the native I was certain was Abram, whom I had only known in legend until now.

And what was more, why did Barb feel this story so important to hand on to a daughter she hadn't seen in nearly thirty years?

I figured I could Google Mary all the other days of the week just as well as I could take a bath or shop for a dress. When I entered the Pilgrim Hall Museum, I greeted the receptionist, Callie, by name. Like the day before, she asked how my project was coming, and I assured her while it was far from complete, I was finding it worthwhile.

When I settled back into the chair behind the desk, Elizabeth's now familiar journal before me, I touched a corner of the page with my finger. Elizabeth had been a real person. She had held this journal. She had touched it. Hundreds of years ago, she'd been alive and breathing and now, like all of us were destined to be, she was but dust. What legacy had she left? How would her story unfold? How had it mattered to Barb?

I inched closer and began reading.

April 17, 1675

I have done Papa wrong. And yet I do not suppose, if given the chance again, I would do anything differently.

Yesterday Papa took to his bed. I could not sleep for his coughing. 'Tis not only the noise, but what this sickness may portend for us. I cannot bear to think of life without him. He has been the sole constant in my life. All through the night I pleaded with the Lord in earnest not to take Papa. When fingers of pink climbed the dawn sky, I rose and set about the morning chores.

Blood soaked Papa's pillow. I took to the task of cleaning him up, as well as his sheets. I made him a draft of honey and lemon tea. I helped him drink it, weak as he was, and spooned some stew into his mouth.

The house smelled of sickness. Sickness and death. I did not wish for Papa to see my tears, so I left. I ran. 'Tis not proper, running. 'Tis not proper where I ran to. I should have gone to Goodwife Howland's house to ask what to do for Papa, but I did not think.

I ran to the woods. To the very place Papa and Mr. Tanner insisted I not go. I wished to feel vibrant green pine needles between my fingers. I wished to smell their scent, to breathe in the warm spring air. There is no sickness or death or sadness in the woods. Purple and white flowers sprout on the forest floor. Birds sing a chorus. Pink buds adorn the trees. I caught a glimpse of a fawn with its mother. New life bursts forth in abundance.

And yet there was something else . . . someone else I wished to see. Nétop.

I did not sing today. My heart was too sad. I wandered in the direction I had walked last time. I saw the large rock off to my right in the distance. 'Tis easy to see without leaves not yet on the trees. I attempted quiet steps as I moved closer. I came upon the west side of the rock but did not see Nétop.

'Tis a massive rock, higher than the topsails of the grandest ship that enters our ports. Last time my attention had been on Nétop alone. Now, as I took in the view of the rock, I stood in awe of its breadth and height. A smaller boulder sat on the side of the main rock and another boulder to create a canopy. I crept closer. Below the smaller boulder on the ground was another cave. The dirt floor was swept clean and a pipe and several tin objects lay neatly to the side, along with a fire hearth and a grass-woven sleeping mat.

I backed away from the cave.

My shoe bumped something that jiggled and I looked to the ground where two clamshells lay. I beheld the area, but saw no one and so picked up one of the shells. The native had been removing his facial hair with these the first time I looked upon him. I assumed him to still occupy the area, but why? Why was he not with his own people?

I ran my thumb over the ribs of the white and grey shell and slipped it into the pocket of my dress though I could not explain why I did so other than to possess something that the native held.

I heard a sound from behind and whirled.

Before me, he stood. This time, in moccasins and breechcloths. Again, his shirtless torso stood gleaming in the sun. I averted my gaze to the ground. I did not run, though I thought to, for he caught me in the act of thievery. With the help of Papa's copy of Roger Williams's A Key into the Language of America, *I'd practiced what I would say to him while in the confines of the barn, with only the pigs and horse to hear.*

"What Cheare Nétop?" I wondered if I butchered his language.

It was a greeting of friends. I was his friend. I wanted him to know I considered him such. I forced myself to look upon his face. Smooth copper skin surrounded deep pools of brown, which studied me intently. I thought the native could hear my heart, so rapid was the beat it took up.

To my amazement, he smiled at me. His white teeth were straight and showed as pearls against his skin. "Hello, friend," he said.

I near toppled over. "You—you speak our language?"

He stepped closer and I stopped myself from backing away. He smelled of woods and pipe tobacco. "I do."

"Why then . . . that first day . . . ?"

"You surprised me. I called in the language of my tribe."

We stared at one another for a long moment, and I felt he was as fascinated by me as I was of him.

He pointed to my pocket. "You like clams?"

My face heated. It must have shown a shade darker than his own skin. I reached in my pocket and put the article back on the ground. "Forgive me. I thought to have a token of the woods." Of him.

He bent to scoop it up. His black hair fell over his shoulders and muscled, bare back. He held the shell to me. "Take for your token. I will get more." His accent was thick, but I could understand his words without a struggle.

I took the clamshell from him, careful to avoid the touch of his fingers. "Thank you, Nétop."

He smiled again. "You have found me for a reason?"

What was I to say? 'Twould not do for him to know of my irrational fascination of him. 'Twould not do for him to know Papa lay home, dying in bed, that I had not only run from the sickness, but had disobeyed Papa in coming.

"I like your rock," I said. 'Twas not a lie. 'Twas the most impressive rock I have seen.

"My home, for now." He looked at the cave in the lower part, where I had seen his things. I wanted to ask him why he made his home here, but thought my question too forthcoming. "Would you like to see the top?"

I shook my head. "Climbing rocks would hardly be proper."

"But walking alone in the woods, speaking to me . . . that is proper?"

My bottom lip trembled. He was not an ordinary native. He knew our language, even our customs. I thought of Goodwife Howland and her stories.

"You are like Squanto. You know us."

His mouth pulled downward. "I am nothing like Squanto. He brings natives and colonists together. I hide in woods." He seemed to shake himself from his thoughts. "Come. I will take you to the top." He began to walk to the north side of the boulder, where the rock rose in a gradual incline.

I followed him. I felt foolish leaning over to climb, my skirts clumped around my legs. Nétop did not seem to notice. Close to the top, a small chasm dipped and we climbed downward before climbing up once again. Nétop offered his hand to me, but I could not bring myself to touch him. 'Twould make my act of disobedience all too real.

What would Mr. Tanner say of my insolence? My willful disregard of his request? To not only walk alone in the woods, but to spend time with a shirtless native?

At the top, I was so near the tree branches I could have danced with them. I moved to the edge and looked down. Overcome with dizziness at such great height, I backed away.

"We are high," Nétop said.

My breaths quivered as I looked at the ground far below. "Yes, but I think I am ready to return down."

He smiled at me for a long moment, and I could not tear my gaze from his stare. Something unspoken passed between us in that moment, there atop the rock, yet I could not say what. I broke the connection.

"Come. We will go this way."

He took me to the other side of the rock, which overlooked the top of his cave. We curved around and went down a gradual slope until finally we reached the bottom.

"Thank you, Nétop," I said.

"Abram. My name is Abram." Again, he held his hand out to me, this time in greeting.

A native with a Christian name? Was he a Praying Indian, then?

I felt if I placed my hand in his there would be no turning back. I would be unable to go home to Papa and Mr. Tanner and pretend as if all were normal.

Time suspended for a long moment, until finally I could not leave Abram's hand lingering in the air any longer. I lifted my white hand to his dark one. His flesh was warm, and as I looked at my small hand in his larger one, I sensed this was indeed the very beginning.

"Elizabeth," I whispered.

"Elizabeth," he repeated. "Come again."

I knew that I would.

April 29, 1675

It has been too long since I have written. Papa needed the last of the ink to write a letter. He has improved some, though his coughing still keeps me awake at night. I have a mind to ride our horse to Plimoth or Taunton myself to secure him a doctor, but he will have none of it.

Mr. Tanner called on me this evening. It is the first I have seen of him since he bid me not visit the woods. I think he knew I was not happy with him. He brought me a gift of ink. I cannot stay angered at him for long after such a precious present.

We did not take a walk today. Papa was in bed and Mr. Tanner did not ask that I leave him. Instead, he helped me gather eggs in the barn and muck out Church's stall.

Mr. Tanner asked if I named the horse. I tried not to turn away from his gaze when I admitted I had.

"After Captain Church, I presume?"

I nodded and expelled a long breath, hoping to cool my flaming face.

"So he is my competition for your affections, then? A married man with children?"

To hear it spoken aloud made me feel foolish, like a silly girl. "Never have I met Mr. Church. I only admire the work he does with the natives."

"I have no competitors, then?"

What was I to say to such a bold question? I thought of Abram, of my unexplainable draw to him. I would not tell Mr. Tanner of him. He would deeply disapprove of my walking alone in the woods, of my consorting with a native.

And no matter my strange feelings for Abram, I had made a promise to Papa, for the sake of his peace during this distressing time in his life. I would marry Mr. Tanner if he asked it of me.

"There is no competition." I turned from Mr. Tanner's stare and felt his eyes watch me. I wondered if he would come closer. I wondered if he

would try to hold my hand or even kiss me. I wondered what it would be like to be kissed by a man. 'Twas not unheard of among courting couples. Andia once told me Hezekiah stole more than one kiss before the banns were read.

When I could no longer pretend to gather eggs I turned to him with my basket before me. He leaned against the pitchfork, again staring at me.

"Is this how you work on your own homestead? If so, 'tis no wonder you haven't expanded."

My tongue is the most disobedient part of my body. Mr. Tanner's mouth grew into a firm line. Why must I speak before I think? A most unworthy character trait of a courting young woman.

Mr. Tanner leaned the pitchfork against the large rock right outside of the barn and told me he would visit with Papa before he took his leave. When he was gone, I looked to the rafters of the barn, where a small field mouse perched. I wondered if he could get down, if he was frightened.

I was frightened.

'Tis why I allow my tongue to run wild. I do not wish to marry Mr. Tanner, and yet I have promised Papa, so my only device is to scare him off with my unruly mouth.

It appears to have worked.

May 6, 1675

I visited Goodwife Howland today. She gave me some ginger to soak in Papa's teas. I helped her make soap in her leach tub. I lugged the ashes and water outside for her and when we managed to make lye strong enough to hold an egg, we boiled it with her grease. I love the clean soap that comes from the filth. How do dirty ashes and vile grease create such pure beauty? I asked Goodwife Howland if she thought our lives could be like the soap. If good things could come from the bad.

She told me the good Lord promises beauty from ashes in his Word. I would like to read of such things. I will search Papa's Bible tonight.

I thought to tell Goodwife Howland of my native friend. Of all the people in the settlement, she would be the soul to understand. Yet I could not bring myself to speak of Abram. Instead, I asked her to tell me more of Squanto. She insisted she must have told me everything. I asked her might she tell me again?

She said perhaps it was time to tell me of things I had not yet heard. I begged she do so.

"When I first met Squanto I was frightened of his dark skin and unruly hair and way of dress. But after a time I ceased to see his skin or even his clothes. These things are but the trappings of what truly matters, of what the good Lord tells us is of most importance."

I placed my hand over my chest. "The Lord searches the heart," I murmured.

She nodded. "Yes. 'Twas a true blessing when I saw past these things when it came to Squanto. 'Twas a blessing to see the man himself." She gave a great sigh. "Yet the Wampanoag sachem, King Philip's father—Massasoit —did not trust Squanto's heart as I did. He did not trust Squanto alone to deal with the settlers. He sent another native to help Squanto.

"Hobomok, if this old mind can remember. I did not care for him. Squanto held nothing back from us. His motives were pure. I did not trust Hobomok. A year after John and I met Squanto, our native friend fell sick with brain fever when he returned from a meeting to repair hard feelings between the settlers and the Wampanoag. Within a few days he died."

This was not the sort of story I wished for Goodwife Howland to tell. I knew she told me for a reason. "You think Squanto was killed?"

"Only the Lord knows the cause of his death. Hark, Elizabeth, even then, when we fared well with the natives, trouble found us. There are always a few on each side, both the natives and the colonists, who refuse peace. I fear for thy generation."

Her proclamation made shivers crawl up my spine. Squanto had been caught in the middle. Was that where Abram was also? He speaks English. He lives apart from his tribe.

More than ever, I wonder his story.

CHAPTER 13

It was the same rock.

I knew as much from Barb's stories, but Elizabeth's latest entries confirmed it. Still, standing here, on top of the rock where she and Abram stood over three hundred years ago, I felt united with them somehow. Every crevice, every pebbled formation, was just as she described.

Yet, if that were true, then the legend of the rock must be true as well. My stomach curdled. I did not know if I wanted to read more of the journal if the legend proved to be genuine. It was one thing to listen to a hazy story of days long ago. It was quite another to stand here where it actually happened, to feel that I knew Abram and Elizabeth, that I had spent time communing with her private thoughts in her very own handwriting.

I stood in silence in the same place I'd dropped my wedding rings more than a week earlier, in the same place Elizabeth Baker stood all those years ago. And while I knew that Barb had asked me to give the journal to her daughter, I couldn't help but wonder if she hadn't wanted me to read it as well—if some part of her knew I would need a purpose, that perhaps I would even find an unlikely companion in a seventeenth-century girl—a girl swept away by circumstances out of her control. A girl so caught up in caring for her family that she resisted her own wants and feelings.

I began the descent down the rock, leaning back on my heels to avoid falling forward. A spider web caught my face and I wiped it away. I walked around the rock's west side and sat at the top of Abram's cave. Nothing of his existence showed in the cave now, just a small mark of graffiti, dirt and leaves, and a broken beer bottle.

Not for the first time, a whisper of the past shrouded the place. Abram and Elizabeth had stood here.

I wanted to bring Matt here.

Maybe I could tell him about the rings and he could help me look for them. Maybe I'd tell him about the journal. Maybe he'd want to read it too.

Almost as quickly as the idea came, I shot it down. Matt never wanted to walk in the woods with me. I'd asked him countless times, and each time he'd had something better to do.

But then I'd done the same thing each time he'd asked me to go golfing, or sailing, or test drive a Harley. I couldn't bear the thought of chasing a small white ball over acres of manicured grass, where trees were sparse and the sun hot. I couldn't bear the thought of sitting in a confined boat, endless murky waters and unseen rip currents beneath me, where anything under the sun could make its home. And I was none too keen about riding on an open highway, air and bare pavement all around me, ready to jump up and meet me in an excruciating crash.

I hadn't been willing to face my fears, or even my comfort level, to share in something that brought joy to my husband.

I sniffed and made my way onto the open trail leading away from the rock. Lorna's words came back to me. *Maybe the fault isn't all with him.* . . .

Well, of course there'd been things I could have done different…better. Maybe I hadn't loved my husband as perfectly as I thought. Yet, I'd never claimed to be perfect. I only claimed to be willing to wade through the ugly to fix us.

But I needed Matt to wade with me.

I unhooked the blood pressure cuff from Lila Rhineheart's pale arm and folded it neatly with the portable monitor I held in my other hand. The cuff had made marks on her wrinkled skin, leaving the loose folds slightly red. "One fifteen over seventy-five. That's great, Mrs. Rhineheart."

"Thank you, dear. Now if you'll just help me to the facilities, I'll be all set for my appointment with Dr. Keller."

"We'll get to it, then." I lowered the rail on the bed and helped the elderly woman swing her legs over the edge.

"I like your band," she said.

I held up both my hands. I only had one band on—Lorna's. "This one?"

"Yes. It's nice and simple, not overstated like all the flashy bling these young hotties wear today."

I laughed. "Oh I know all about flashy bling. Had myself some rocks on this hand up until recently. I lost them."

Mrs. Rhineheart tsked and shook her head. "Too bad. Bet a pretty thing like you has quite a looker of a husband, eh?"

I could feel the blood rushing to my face. I helped her to a standing position. "He's handsome, all right."

She curled a thin arm around my own and patted my hand. "You make it sound like that's a bad thing."

I didn't know if I wanted to divulge my personal life to this woman. She was sweet and quite likely she wouldn't remember my words next week, but I wanted to be professional. Then again, maybe Mrs. Rhineheart could give me an honest outsider's opinion. I had enough of my parents' advice, enough of Essie's, enough of Mariah's, and even enough of Jen's. What would Mrs. Rhineheart, a lady with years of wisdom behind her, have to say about my marriage?

I'd probably be able to tell her my whole life story by the time we made it to the bathroom.

"Are you married, Mrs. Rhineheart?"

"Please, dear, call me Lila. Never did like my last name as much as I liked my husband." We shuffled a few laminate blocks at a time toward the bathroom. "He died ten years ago. Heart attack. Thought my world would fall apart."

More shuffling.

"But you know, he wasn't my first husband."

I tried to hide my surprise. "No?"

Lila shook her head, wobbling the dangly earrings she insisted on wearing—the ones that stretched her earlobes almost to her shoulders. "I married my first husband young. Real young. We were two hot tickets, let me tell you. But passion fades. He held it against me that I couldn't hold a pregnancy. We decided to go our separate ways after fifteen years."

I swallowed the bubble in my throat. "Fifteen years?" This wasn't my destiny with Matt, was it? Married young, seventeen years . . . did he hold it against me that we couldn't have more children?

"Did you keep in touch?" Stupid question.

Shuffle. Shuffle, shuffle, shuffle. Halfway there.

"With no children, there was little need. He sent a card when Will died, said he saw it in the newspaper. That was it."

I wanted Lila to get in touch with her first husband. I wanted their love to rekindle. I wanted healing to take place. If for no other reason than to bolster my own hope.

She squeezed my arm. "When I met Will, he loved me without conditions. He made me happier than I'd ever been. I didn't look back after I met him. Ever." She stopped shuffling. "Things not going well with handsome hubby?"

"We're taking a break for the summer."

"Kids?"

"One great sixteen-year-old."

She bobbed her head again. "It's different when there's kids I imagine." Shuffle. "Can't stay together just for them, though."

"We're not—I mean, I don't want a separation."

"Course not, dear. But sometimes there's something better out there."

Something better than my husband? What Lila said went against everything I was ever taught. It went against the very grain of the fabric I was woven into. Divorce wasn't an option. Even if there was something "better" out there, could I chase my own wishy-washy emotions and find a happiness that endured? Was there such a thing?

We'd reached the threshold of the bathroom. A shadowed form near the hall cleared his throat. I startled, then held Lila to make sure she hadn't been frightened either.

"Don't mean to interrupt."

"Pete—Dr. Keller, I'm sorry. We didn't see you there." How much had he heard? I was grateful I could hide myself away in the bathroom with Lila for at least another eight minutes. "Mrs. Rhineheart needs to use the bathroom."

He held up a hand. "That's fine. I'll check in on Mr. Brooks and then look over her chart while I'm waiting."

We took more than eight minutes in the bathroom. And the shuffling back to the bed took at least another five, but Pete sat in the chair at the end of Lila's bed as if he had all the time in the world.

When I'd settled Lila, she clutched at my hand. "Would you mind staying, dear? This is my least favorite part."

I had more patients to tend, but I couldn't imagine denying Lila's request. I looked at Pete and he nodded.

"Of course." Feeling out of place, I stood near her bed. She didn't release my hand.

"I'm just going to listen to how it all sounds in there, Mrs. Rhineheart."

Pete positioned the stethoscope in his ears and probed

around above the thin cloth of Mrs. Rhineheart's hospital gown. After a moment, he moved his stethoscope to her back and encouraged her to take deep breaths.

Lila kept my hand clutched to her lap. When Pete was through, he helped the older woman lay down.

"Sounds good. Your numbers are much improved too. I think we can say the angioplasty was a success. Any more chest pain?"

Lila shook her head. "Does that mean I can go home?"

"I think so. But no more step aerobics for you, Mrs. Rhineheart."

"And I was going to look just like Denise Austin when I was done, too."

Pete laughed. "I strongly recommend the cardio rehab we talked of earlier. They'll help you with appropriate exercises that won't strain your heart. The stent we put in will help prevent blockages, but it's not a guarantee. It's important you take your medications." Pete put Lila's chart in the slot at the end of her bed. "I'll need to see you in another week to check how things are going."

Lila sighed. "I've always hated going to the doctors, even if it is to see a looker like you."

Pete's gaze flew to mine and then to Lila's bedsheets. He shook his head and smiled. "Thank you, Mrs. Rhineheart. You stay well, okay?"

Pete nodded to me and walked out of the room, but not before Lila asked me, "I didn't say anything wrong, did I? He is a yummy peach, isn't he?"

Somehow, I held my laughter. "Yes, I suppose he is." I tucked Lila in, told her I'd be by one more time to say good-bye before she was discharged, and walked quickly out of the room.

In the hall, I tried to hide my smile in my sleeve.

"So, I'm a yummy peach, am I?" Pete hadn't yet gone to another room. He looked like he needed to recover before seeing another patient.

I sucked in a breath to hide my laughter, unsuccessfully. "Dr. Keller, I'm so sorry. I can't help it."

He leaned against the wall and looked at me, an easy smile on his face. A lock of his dirty blonde hair fell over his forehead, and I got the strange urge to brush it away.

"It's Pete, Sarah."

My smile seemed to freeze on my face as awkward silence ping-ponged between us. Even with the vital check monitor in the crook of my arm, I still found my fingers fiddling with Lorna's ring.

"What time's your break?"

This wasn't what I thought it was, was it? Of course not. He knew I was married. But he also may have heard that Matt and I were separated. Or maybe he didn't care about any of that.

"One."

"Want to grab lunch downstairs?" His eyes locked on Lorna's ring, twirling on my finger, its luster all but gone.

"Um, yeah, that would be great." Lunch, in the hospital cafeteria, during work. There was nothing wrong with that. "I— I better go." The blood pressure cuff fell from my grip and dangled a foot above the ground. I caught it up and wrapped it neatly with the monitor.

"Okay. See you in a couple hours."

I didn't need to feel guilty. There was nothing wrong with having lunch with a coworker of the opposite sex. Matt ate meals with his clients all the time—female clients—to discuss their plans and ideas. It was professional.

I was being professional.

———

I half hoped that Pete would get tied up at one o'clock. Essie would say I was being a baby. Maybe I was. Maybe I shouldn't have piled on more hours to my schedule. Maybe then I wouldn't see Pete so much. Maybe then I'd be in Plymouth, piecing together Elizabeth's story. Or hiring a private investigator to find Mary. Or listing Barb's house.

Anything but having lunch with a guy.

But Pete waited at the nurses' station at one sharp, and we walked to the elevator together. I hoped Jen didn't see.

The doors closed behind us, shutting us in. The pulse at my throat pounded. The air hung thick and stuffy.

"Hope I'm not out of line asking," Pete said. "Gets kind of lonely eating by myself day after day."

I shrugged. "Not at all."

But my racing heart belied my words. Something didn't feel right about this. Something didn't feel quite so innocent. And while that something may very well be all on my part, it was still there—ugly, clawing for attention.

I thought about Elizabeth defying her culture's mores by going to visit Abram. *That* had taken courage. But lunch out in the open for all to see? What was wrong with me? I definitely needed to lighten up.

The elevator doors opened and I sucked in the fresh air from the outside. We took a left toward the cafeteria.

"So is your crazy news all settled down now?" he asked.

"I wouldn't say settled, but it's definitely gotten interesting. It's not so secret, though."

"I'd love to hear about it. When I first saw you that day in the hall, you looked like someone just drove over your puppy."

It was nice that he cared. That *someone* cared. And although I hated myself for it, I couldn't help but think how Matt hadn't once asked how I was handling Barb's death. He hadn't been there to see how hurt I'd been, how shaken up I was that Barb had left me with everything, even her dying wish. Was it surprising that I would want to open up to someone who asked?

We entered the cafeteria, where smells of chicken and grease met us. We grabbed trays and started down the food line. I picked up a salad, a plastic-covered fruit bowl, and a water. Pete chose the chicken pot pie and potato salad. When I reached for cash in the pocket of my scrubs, he shooed my money away. After paying, he led me to a spot by the window. Outside, a robin hopped along the green grass of the courtyard.

"My neighbor—the one that died," I started.

He nodded, didn't move to pick up his fork.

I uncovered my salad and poured Caesar dressing over the top. "She was old. But the news is she left me with everything. Along with an odd request. It involves transcribing a super-old journal that's at a museum in Plymouth. It's all just . . . yeah, crazy."

Pete swallowed a bite of his chicken. "Whoa."

I shook my head. "Right? Aren't you glad you asked?"

"No—I mean, yeah, I am. It's not every day you hear of a commission given beyond the grave."

I laughed. "Guess not."

"So how far along are you with the transcribing?"

"I'd say about a quarter, but it's slow going." I waved a hand through the air. "Enough about that. Tell me about you. What made you want to be a doctor?"

"My grandmother battled cancer all of my growing-up years before it finally took her my senior year of high school. To her, the nurses and doctors who took care of her were heroes. I guess I wanted to be one too."

My heart softened at the transparent answer. "The patients love you. I'm sure your grandmother would have been proud."

He smiled and the sight of it did something funny to my insides. "Thanks—that means a lot."

I fought for a firm place, something to ground us. I should bring up Matt, or Kyle, maybe. "You have any kids?"

He shook his head. "I keep telling myself it's all in God's timing, but I'm sure not getting any younger." He wiped his mouth with one of the rough hospital napkins I often used on the patients. "I was engaged once, six years ago. She broke it off two months before the wedding. Said my patients always came before her. It's not easy, you know? I'm on call a lot, I work long days and a lot of weekends. I care about my patients. I didn't think that was a bad thing."

"It's not. Of course it's not."

"I just always thought there would be room for both. A family and my patients. Maybe not." He grinned at me. "You going to lay me on a couch and start charging soon?"

"I wouldn't make anybody pay for my advice," I whispered.

Red warning flags went off in my head as soon as I spoke the sentence. I shouldn't open up to this man. Maybe I was the one who needed to see a shrink. First, I spoke with a sick old woman recovering from a heart attack, now an attractive doctor. Not the wisest decisions.

Pete must have read my mind. "Don't worry, I'm not going to pry, even if I want to. But I will be honest with you. I did hear some of what you said to Mrs. Rhineheart. If you ever do need someone to talk to, I'm here, okay? And I won't even charge you."

"Thanks." I appreciated his transparency, but something about his words put me on edge, as if I shouldn't simply take them at face value.

Still, in the last month, Matt showed neither interest nor care. It was nice to feel a little of both.

We cleared our trays and walked back to the elevators while Pete asked about Kyle. Before the doors opened to the third floor, he faced me. I studied the strong lines of his chiseled face. Really, how was he not married yet?

"That was nice. Maybe we can do it again sometime?" he asked.

"Yeah, sure. Thanks, Pete. It was nice."

And it was. Though I had to admit, it didn't feel terribly professional.

CHAPTER 14

May 10, 1675

I went to see him today.

I know I should not have, but the chores were done and Papa slept soundly in his bed. He told me yesterday 'twould not be long before Mr. Tanner asks for my hand. I took that to mean he has asked Papa's permission, and Papa has granted it. I expect to be wed after the harvest.

Yet I am not wed today. And today I thought to do as I like. I ran in the woods. I ran fast. I ran with my skirts hitched high above my knees and my feet leaping over rocks and knobby roots. If Mr. Tanner had seen me, he would have scolded. Andia would have swooned.

I did not care. The wind hit my face. Pine branches swatted my arms. I breathed in freedom.

When I came upon Abram's rock, I slowed even as my breaths raced. Abram sat in front of the large cave beside a fire. He twirled a squirrel on a spit. When he saw me, he stood.

"You have come."

I was not so hesitant to draw near him this time. "Yes, I have come."

He gestured to a flat rock near his own seat. "Sit and eat?"

I nodded and took the seat. When he bowed his head to pray in his own language, I did the same, though I wondered if he prayed to some god unknown to me. He broke off a piece of the squirrel and extended it to me with bare hands. I thanked him. He offered me a tin of water and a gritty substance he called Nokehick, a bland yet filling parched meal.

When we were through, he asked if I might like to walk with him. He took his bow and a crude quiver of arrows, slung them over his chest, and led me away from the towering rock.

He asked of my family. I told him of Papa and the illness that invades his breaths.

He said he knew of the illness, but not of a cure. "No husband?" he asked.

I avoided his gaze and shook my head. I did not speak to him of Mr. Tanner.

We walked toward the sun, though it hid itself in the trees, now thick with green leaves of different variety. I felt safe with Abram. Free. As if he did not care to judge me, as if he would not know how to do so had he wanted to.

I asked after his tribe. He said he left his tribe nine moons ago.

"Why?"

We walked in silence for such a time that I thought he would not answer. "You may not come back if I tell you."

I wondered if it had to do with the English. I wondered if he had committed a grievous offense against us.

"Should you care to tell me, I care to listen."

Abram walked on, his moccasins soft on the ground. His arm brushed mine now and again, and I did not shy away from his copper skin.

"It was a matter of honor. I shamed my tribe, the Pocasset. I ran from them instead of facing death."

I could see it hard for him to tell of such things. I could tell by his hesitant words that this weighed heavily on his conscience. I reached out and touched the smooth skin of his forearm, where taut muscles rippled underneath. My breath caught at my boldness and he looked down at my hand, so very light against his arm.

"What have you done to deserve death?" He did not answer and I felt the need to assure him. "You shall not frighten me away," I said.

"It is not what I have done. It is what my brother did. I am to bear punishment for his crimes. I ran."

"You did nothing, then? And yet you were to be put to death?"

Abram nodded vigorously. He seemed relieved that I did not intend to chastise him for such an act. "My brother—he took a woman who was not his. He stole her in the night and murdered her husband. Weetamoo—our sachem—sent her soldiers after him, but he was not found. It is our custom for a brother to take punishment."

He paused, seeming to measure his next words. "I was afraid. I ran. I stayed in the woods and found the English. I work for them, hunt for them. I learn the language and in some ways I am protected. I learn of your God. I come to love your God. I was happy with the English. But not for long. They grew to distrust me, think me a spy for my tribe. And again I am sent away. I sought out Metacomet—grand sachem of the Wampanoag—you call him Philip. I ask him for peace and pardon. But his brother was Weetamoo's husband and I think this is why he does not give me pardon. But he does give me my life. Again I am sent away. I come to this place. This is my home now."

Abram stopped and faced me. He reached up to brush a tear from my face. I hadn't realized I had shed it. "Chickautáw, do not be sad for me."

"'Tis a sad story," I told him.

"Yes, Chickautáw, but I would not meet you if not for this story."

I could not presume to think he meant that all of his troubles were worth meeting me, but that is how it sounded. "What does that name mean?"

"Chickautáw? Little Fire. I see fire in you, and yet innocence also." Abram patted his heart. "I name your spirit."

I was reminded how Mr. Tanner had once called me "little Elizabeth" and I had scolded him. The name Abram gave me I found endearing. He took my hand then, and cupped it against his bare chest. He never surprised me with his lack of physical modesty. I stepped closer and rested my hand in both of his. His brown eyes searched my own and my legs threatened to give from beneath me.

I should not have such feelings for a native. I know 'tis wrong.

"Do not wait so many sunsets to come again," Abram said.

I told him I would not.

May 17, 1675

Andia has gotten her native slave boy. She called on me today, the young lad in tow. I worked on a new quilt on the garden bench. I should have been preparing dinner or weeding the garden, yet last night it came upon me to make a quilt for Abram. It will be the colors of the harvest—greens and reds and yellows and browns. If I can find the time and secure the materials I will applique his rock on it, and put a figure beside it—my Nétop, Abram. I hope to finish it by the harvest, so he will have something to keep him warm at night. By that time, Mr. Tanner and I may be warming one another.

I saw Andia coming from a distance. I saw her gift from Hezekiah. I knew I could not pretend to be happy for her. The boy hid behind her skirts and she pulled him out from their folds. "Come now, Samuel. 'Tis time you meet Elizabeth."

I knelt beside him. His hair looked freshly shorn and his brown eyes vacant and suspicious. I looked into them without shame, tried to see beyond their hollowness to the life he held before Hezekiah had purchased him from his people. Had he a mother or father? Had he been torn from their arms or given over freely? What did he think about our ways? Did he cry himself to sleep at night missing his old life, forced to adopt Andia's manner of dress and speech and work and worship?

I blinked away tears. They could not come forth, at least just now. They would only serve to frighten the child. "Askuttaaquompsín?" I greeted him, though I am certain I butchered the word.

The lad's eyes widened and he answered in a short word I did not recognize.

"Tocketussawéitch?" I asked him his name.

"Piùck," he said.

I tried to think of a word to ask him if he'd like something to eat, but Andia pulled the lad back behind her skirts and told me that was quite enough. She said he needed to learn our language and that he wouldn't do so if I spoke in his tongue. More quietly, she asked how I should come by knowledge of the Wampanoag language anyhow. I told her I'd been reading Roger Williams's book. I did not tell her that on my last visit to see Abram he taught me some words.

She asked how Papa fared and I told her some days were better than others. Today he rested in bed. She sat with me on the garden bench and gestured for Piùck to go off a ways. "Would you like him to weed your garden?" Andia asked.

I told her I preferred to weed my own garden.

She said he could haul wood into the house for me, that she had trained him to do so without so much noise and that he would not disturb Papa.

"I do not desire a slave to do my own honest work."

She seemed to look down her nose at me then. "There is much to do on a homestead. I brought him here to help you, with your Papa abed."

"'Tis not in my conscience to allow a native slave to do my work."

"And yet 'tis in your conscience to gallivant around in the woods with one?"

I near swooned off the garden bench. "How . . . ?" was all I could manage.

"I overheard Hezekiah speaking with Mr. Tanner, who is in a dither over what to do about you. I know not whether he followed you or happened in the woods for another purpose, but Mr. Tanner saw you in the woods with —with the savage."

I would have defended Abram had I the ability to think aright. Mr. Tanner knew. He knew of my friendship with Abram. He knew I disregarded his request to stay away from the wood. I wondered if he would tell Papa. I wondered if I would ever be able to enjoy Abram's presence again without worrying that Mr. Tanner watched us.

Andia took my hand. "Elizabeth, please. Think. You must give up this nonsense. Whatever 'tis, it can be settled by focusing your mind on your future and a sound marriage. Mr. Tanner is a good man. Why must you resist him?"

I did not wish to confide in Andia, for fear she may repeat my confidence to Hezekiah. Mr. Tanner is a good man and I am certain I would find a good husband in him. But I know there is more to feel with a man.

I know because I feel it when I am with Abram.

May 25, 1675

Mr. Tanner came with a doctor today. He waited outside with me as the doctor examined Papa. I thanked him for going through the trouble. He said 'tis no trouble. We stood in silence, and when the doctor emerged from our cottage looking solemn and wiping his sweatied brow with a white handkerchief, I involuntarily leaned into Mr. Tanner for support.

"'Tis the consumption," he said. "I have seen cases with rapid—even miraculous recoveries. But your father's lungs do not sound well, Miss Baker. I am sorry." He handed me a packet of herbs to mix in his tea, saying it would ease the pain. I thanked him and, near tears, asked if some eggs would do as payment. Mr. Tanner placed his hand on my arm and for the first time I found myself wishing for those strong arms around me.

"Have no worry," he said. "I must see the doctor out of the settlement. Will you be well alone?"

I nodded. After they left, I checked on Papa, who seemed to have fallen into a deep, peaceful sleep. The doctor must have given him something. I ran a hand over his warm brow and sat by his side for a long time. I spoke my heart to him for the first time in years. I told him I feared life without him. I told him I met a native named Abram who gave me the name Little Fire. I told Papa I feared I loved Abram. I told him that my feelings for the native would not change the fact that I would keep my promise and marry Mr. Tanner if he asked for my hand. I told him that Mr. Tanner was a good man, that he had sent for a doctor and even made payment to him. I told him that Mr. Tanner knew I stole to the woods to meet a native and still he persisted in courting me.

After I spoke all this, I felt God calling my soul. I had never known such an insistence, and yet I knew it in that moment. 'Twas like a stirring of the wind that swept through the windows and into my heart, yet the leaves outside the window scarce moved. I prayed, then. And I felt assurance, peace, as if all would be well. And yet I am uncertain how that could be. I will continue to seek the Lord in prayer.

CHAPTER 15

I scrutinized my face in the mirror, opting for a thin sheen of gloss over my lips instead of the pale mauve lipstick I sometimes wore. I puckered my lips, pressed them together, shook my hair, and stepped back to examine myself in the full-length mirror behind the door of the master bathroom.

The new black dress I'd bought had a slight slit up the side and hugged my slim curves. I looked good in it. I looked . . . sexy. I looked . . . overdressed? Desperate? Like I was trying too hard?

I shimmied out of it and tossed it on my bed with the tags still on, crumpled in a heap. I shouldn't have stayed at the museum so long. I should have given myself more time to get ready for Matt's party. But I'd been unable to leave Elizabeth's story, unable to leave her in her plight. And when I'd finally torn myself away, it was as if a part of me was left with my colonial friend in those pages, my mind still wrapped within her words on the drive home, only returning to reality after the hot shower I'd taken.

I rummaged through my closet for a more sensible dress. I settled on one of pale yellow with a scoop neck and fitted waist.

I looked nice, more like the wife of the owner of a successful landscaping business and less like a hooker on the street corner.

I heard Matt's truck in the driveway and peered out the window. He ducked into the garage and a moment later backed out my Mercedes. I watched him exit the car and walk to the side door. He wore khakis and a gray dress shirt with a pale-blue tie that really would have matched the black dress better than the yellow. He looked toward our bedroom window. My heart threatened to leap from my chest and out the second-floor window to fall at his feet. I lifted my hand, but he mustn't have seen me because he continued toward the house.

I glanced in the mirror one last time, scooped up my purse, and jogged lightly down the stairs.

Once again, Matt stood at the kitchen counter shuffling through bills. I could pay them, but it had always been his job, something he'd liked to do.

"Hi." I took a bottle of water from the fridge.

He glanced up. "Hey, you look nice."

A far cry from the wolf-whistles I used to get when I dressed up to go out with him, but I'd take it. "You too." He'd spiked his cropped hair with gel. The spicy scent of his cologne—the same he'd worn since high school—combined with that of his aftershave to bring back a million memories I couldn't think of now lest I smudge my mascara. I pushed them down. "Ready?"

"Yup. I'll grab a water too." He moved near me to get to the fridge and I stood frozen, aware of his nearness, the knot of his tie at eye level.

I remembered the last time we'd had sex, just two days before he stood at our mantel and announced his desire for a separation. I certainly hadn't been able to tell his want to be apart from me that particular night. He'd been gentle and giving as always, intent and relentless.

His breaths fanned my forehead and he looked down at me. I felt the attraction between us, tugging us closer, drawing us with invisible force. Every fiber of my being ached for his nearness. I knew he wanted to kiss me, though I couldn't be certain of his reasons—because he missed me or because we hadn't been together in a month and he, like I, hurt physically from the separation. Or maybe a combination of both.

The bedroom was one place we never argued, one thing we had in common. Our passion for each other never dwindled for long. Sure, there were occasional dry spells or arguments that got in the way, but we'd usually find common ground in the physical act of love.

If he kissed me, we'd end up in the bedroom, late for the dinner. Matt was never late. I waited, anticipating the light pressure of his lips on mine, his arms around me in possessive gentleness.

He dipped his head. It took every ounce of willpower not to bury my face in his hard chest and seek the solace of his strong, familiar arms.

We weren't meant to be apart. Couldn't he feel it as much as I could?

"We're going to be late." His minty breath floated to mine. I moved aside. It appeared spearmint was the only taste I'd get of my husband tonight.

He led me out of the house and opened the passenger door. I slid in. The leather cooled my legs, the interior chilled from the car sitting in the garage all day.

In five minutes we sped along the highway.

"How's Kyle?"

"Good, but I think he's realizing he doesn't want to follow in my footsteps."

"You okay with that?"

Matt shrugged. "The last thing I wanted at his age was for someone to tell me what to do with the next fifty years of my life. I'm giving him space to think."

I grabbed my left hand with my right one to keep it from reaching out and touching him. "You're a good father, Matt." He seemed uncomfortable with the comment, so I plowed on.

"His birthday's next week. You two want to come back home and we can celebrate? I mean, for the day of course." Or forever. Forever would be nice.

"Got another crew starting the golf course around then. It's going to be tough to get away. Maybe we can cook on the grill and you can bring a cake down to our place?"

Our place? This conversation had about ten thousand things wrong with it, but the fact that "our place" didn't include "my place" stuck harder than the rest. I didn't voice my thoughts. "Sure, whatever works for you guys."

"You can talk to Kyle about it tonight. He's meeting us there."

"Good." At least I'd have someone to talk to at the dinner, assuming my teenager wanted to hang with his mom.

Matt veered onto Route 24 and I studied the billowing clouds on the horizon. Looked like rain. From the speakers, Johnny Cash sang out, "I Walk the Line."

"How's the extra hours going?"

I considered it a plus that he remembered. "Good. Busy, but good."

I wanted him to ask me more, indicate he cared somehow. He was silent.

"I'm thinking about going back to school." I regretted the words once they were out, knew they were a cry for attention, a cry for him to show a sign that he cared about something in my life.

A tick started in his clean-shaven jaw. "What? Why?"

My stomach trembled. "I've always wanted to become an NP . . ."

"You're serious."

I'd shared this dream with him before, I knew I had. More than likely, he hadn't been listening, or hadn't taken me seriously. I couldn't help but think of Pete in that moment, hanging on my every word about Barb and Elizabeth's journal. Anger swirled in my belly, though I couldn't be sure if it was at

Matt or at myself for thinking of another man when I finally did have time with my husband.

"Yes, though at this point it's only a thought. Nothing's definite—"

"I'm just wondering why you think now is a good time to do this? And how do you think we're going to pay for it?"

My defenses rose. I didn't need his permission. And if he'd been around, he would have known of Barb and all she'd left me and my desire to do something meaningful with it. "I have my own means."

He raised his eyebrows, gave a derisive snort. "Do you now? Well I sure as Sam would like to know how you came upon your own *means.*"

The Mercedes sped up as we drove over the Sakonnet River Bridge. Puffs of white sails dotted the bay, gliding free over the sparkling waters.

"Barb left me with some money." I whispered the words, trying not to add gasoline to an already growing fire.

"Oh." The fight seemed to leave him. "That was . . . nice. Well, go for it then, I guess."

He sounded as if he didn't care. Or as if he'd just given me his permission, as though I needed it.

"I wasn't going to apply without talking to you." My voice lost its fight, too. I didn't want to argue with him, especially tonight.

"It's okay, Sarah. Forget it."

Right. Like that would happen.

We drove through Portsmouth and Middletown, and I questioned him about his jobs and golf. Safe topics. We drove by Easton's Beach in Newport. The lifeguard stands stood empty, the crowd thinned. I would have loved for us to pull over, disregard the dinner, and walk on the beach or the Cliff Walk together. Forget our differences, forget our arguments, forget everyone and everything but us.

Matt kept driving.

"You and Kyle are around here, right?" I asked.

Matt pointed to a quaint summer cottage off Memorial Boulevard. "Right there."

Flowerboxes hung on the windows and a small porch with two rockers cozied up to the left part of the first floor.

"Walking distance to the beach. Nice." And he worried how much school would cost.

"Yeah. Maybe we can go on Kyle's birthday."

He was trying. I had to give him credit for that.

We drove past Bellevue Avenue and down the hill until we turned onto America's Cup Avenue for parking. Matt grabbed the parking ticket and found a spot close to the entrance. The billowing clouds I'd seen earlier weren't in sight near the water. The sun made its way toward the horizon. Beautiful...romantic even.

"Where's your ring?"

My blood ran cold. I'd completely forgotten that Lorna's plain ring adorned my finger, not the sparkling rocks Matt loved so much.

"I—I switched to this one for the hospital. I didn't want to dirty the others." The lie tasted like ashes in my mouth. How were Matt and I to work toward healing when I couldn't even muster the truth? I promised myself I'd tell him later. Now wasn't the right time, before his employee dinner. He'd be too upset. The lie was for his own good, really.

His mouth pulled into a tight line. "I wish you would have worn the others for tonight."

"Sorry." I was sorry I couldn't give him what he wanted. Shiny wife, shiny rings. Instead I felt more than a little lackluster, much like Lorna's ring.

I didn't wait for him to open the door for me. We walked toward Thames Street. When we neared The Red Parrot, he grabbed my hand. I savored the feel of his fingers in mine.

Even if it was only for show.

CHAPTER 16

Matt and I walked up the two flights of stairs to the uppermost floor, which he'd reserved for his employees. A mix of men and women milled about. I allowed Matt to weave me in and out of wooden columns, wait staff, tinkling glasses, and high-heeled shoes, grateful for his guidance in this sea of faces I saw only once a year.

He stopped and talked to several couples and a handful of men. He slapped them on the back, encouraged them to grab another drink at the bar on the floor below, bantered back and forth about the clients or the lawns that wouldn't stay moist, the flowers that wanted to droop in this hell-inspired heat. I waited by his side, my hand now sweaty in his, for my cue. The line that meant I was expected to step up and play my part.

"You know my wife Sarah, don't you?"

Or the occasional awkward hug from one of Matt's longtime employees. "Sarah! You look wonderful. How are you?"

I had all the right answers, of course. Subtle answers. Answers that brushed past the fact that my marriage was in trouble. I complimented the dresses of the women, smiled and listened to the men, ignored the suffocating smells of too-strong colognes and perfumes mixed into one overwhelming scent.

I didn't despise these people. They were good people. Hard workers. They helped Matt's business succeed. He appreciated them, and so did I.

But I despised the performance. Just once, I wanted to fling it off and be the real Sarah, whoever that was.

Then I saw one face in the corner I wouldn't have to perform for. He sat with two other young men his age, a smile on his face, his gaze glued to his parents' joined hands, hope written on every corner of his expression.

I released Matt's hand and walked over to Kyle. He rose, shuffled around occupied seats, and gave me a hug. "Hey, Mom."

"Hey, yourself. I sure missed you," I whispered into his ear.

"I miss you, too." He pulled from my embrace. "This is Doug and Blaine, guys I work with."

The two young men stood and I shook their hands. They went back to a conversation, and I sat with Kyle on the other side, facing the crowd of people in front of the large fireplace at the other end of the room.

"I thought you might not come," Kyle said. Gel slicked his hair. He sported a tan that must have made the girls on the beach go wild. This was not a time in his life I wanted to miss, and yet that was exactly what was happening.

"Your dad wanted me to. I couldn't say no to him." I turned my full attention on my son. "You look good. I think the hard work agrees with you."

He shrugged. "Thanks. Only I got the meanest farmer's tan this side of Idaho."

I laughed. "You having any fun outside of work?"

"Dad's taken me golfing a few times. I walk down to the beach at night, hang out with some kids. You know, mess around."

Were any almost-seventeen-year-old boys more vague with their mothers?

I looked to where I had left Matt talking to a couple other

guys. He wasn't there anymore. I spotted him with one of his foremen in front of the fireplace. He stood with his hand held up, behind a woman's back. I couldn't tell if he actually touched her, or if it was one of those invisible touches he sometimes did when introducing people.

All I knew was that the woman was wearing the black dress I bought yesterday. And while I may have looked desperate and overdressed in the shimmering piece of cloth, she looked sophisticated and confident. And from the shape of her legs, she was either a runner or closer to Kyle's age than Matt's. Maybe both. She turned slightly and leaned into the side of the staircase railing, one high-heeled shoe dangling off her tilted leg.

She was gorgeous and young—mid-twenties probably—dark-blonde hair framing a heart-shaped face. She reminded me of Elizabeth and Jessica Wakefield from the Sweet Valley High book series I read as a teenager.

I wracked my brain for who she could be. Matt had a secretary and a landscape architect, but she was neither.

I tilted my head in Matt's direction, tried to keep my voice casual. "Who's your dad with?"

Kyle leaned to the side to get a better view. "Oh." His face reddened. Did my son have a crush on this woman? "She's Cassie Waterman. You know, the Waterman mansion we're working on? That's their daughter."

I fidgeted with my purse, still in my lap. "I didn't think your father invited clients to these dinners."

"He usually doesn't. But he hit it off with the Watermans. They're nice, Mom. Not snotty like you might think."

I wanted to ask more, but Matt blew a shrill whistle. "If we can all find our seats, I think the wait staff is ready for us."

Couples filled in the many tables scattered through the large room. Outside, the sun cast red streaks on Newport Harbor.

Matt ushered the Waterman girl over, her dress swinging and clinging to her generous curves. An older couple walked on Matt's other side. The woman wore a string of pearls and an elegant baby blue dress that fell just below her knees. The man stood tall and lean with streaks of gray in his hair. They must have been in their early fifties, but they pulled off a youthful wisdom and elegance I found intimidating.

"That's the Watermans," Kyle whispered from my side.

When they arrived at our table, I stood.

"Elise and Troy, I want you to meet my wife, Sarah."

I held out my hand and tried to remember to give a warm smile and firm grip, conscious of my sweaty palm. "Pleasure to meet you."

"And this is their daughter, Cassie."

I slipped my hand into Cassie's cool one. Her blue eyes found mine. They sparkled beneath the chandeliers. It wasn't hard to see why my son had a crush on her.

"So nice to finally meet you. We've heard so much about you."

Really? Had Matt spoken well of me despite the strain in our marriage?

"Please, sit." Matt sat at my side. Cassie found his other.

In moments the wait staff poured water, set out bread, and served us baby Caesar salads. I placed my napkin in my lap and picked up my fork. Elise Waterman waited for my first bite to enter my mouth before she spoke, her attention directed at me.

"Your husband is an absolute genius when it comes to landscape design, Sarah. But of course you must already know that. The pool is Troy's favorite, but the path to our waterfront is mine. I absolutely can't get enough of hydrangeas and boxwoods."

She assumed I was familiar with their plans. Probably thought my husband talked to me on a regular basis. Go figure.

I finished my bite hastily before replying. "It sounds lovely."

"You'll have to come and see it for yourself, sometime." Cassie lifted a champagne glass to her lips. "Maybe we can all play a round of golf. You two can come over for a swim."

I didn't appreciate Matt's obvious chuckle. "Sarah doesn't

golf. I don't think she knows the difference between a driver and a seven-iron, do you honey?"

Light laughter floated across the table. Cassie's tinkled like delicate wind chimes. A thin line of sweat trickled down the center of my chest, and I wiped my mouth with the cloth napkin. I tried to think of a witty response, but it was all I could do to stay in my seat and not run out of the restaurant like a baby, unable to bear being the butt of a joke.

"Well, maybe a ride on the yacht then?" Cassie said.

Strike two. I rushed to answer before Matt could comment on my fear of open water. "That sounds nice."

Matt gulped his water. He never drank alcohol, even at social events. He once told me it was because he wound up on the wrong side of too many whiskeys growing up with Lorna's boyfriends.

"Mom, Cassie's a doctor." Kyle stepped in, likely out of pity. "You guys would probably have a lot to talk about."

"I'm not quite a doctor yet." Cassie spoke to me. "I'm still in residency. Do you work in the medical field, Sarah?"

"I'm a nurse," I said. The profession I'd been proud of until now somehow seemed less than adequate in this company. And yet when I'd expressed interest in becoming more, Matt hadn't been exactly encouraging.

He must have been thinking the same thing. "Sarah's thinking about going back to school to become a nurse practitioner."

Elise's eyes lit up. "Is that so? Well, that's a fine endeavor, isn't it, Troy?"

Troy put down his Coors. "Never a shortage of good NPs out there."

"Thanks. I—it's a little intimidating at this stage in my life, but I think I'd like to go for it."

"Oh, you should." Cassie broke open her roll. "You're still so young. You should do it now, before it's too late."

If I was still young, I wonder what age qualified as "too late."

I thanked Cassie for her encouragement. She really did seem sweet. I could almost like her if she didn't sit so close to my husband, if her arm didn't brush his every time she padded her bread with butter, if my son didn't stare at her from across the table as if the sun and moon hung on every word that came forth from her pouty, perfect mouth.

"Well, a good nurse is a great asset. If you ever need a change of scenery I'm always looking for a competent nurse on my team," Troy said.

"Are you a doctor also?"

Troy nodded. "Plastic surgeon."

I wondered if Troy had done any work on his wife. I tried to think of an appropriate comment, but nothing other than, "Wow, that must be interesting," crossed my lips.

The servers called us up to the buffet line where we picked choices of swordfish and sole, coconut chicken and steak, linguini with clams, and shrimp and scallop scampi. Matt had certainly spared no expense this year. He must want to impress his clients.

The meal dragged on. Matt spoke with Doug and Blaine, asked them how their jobs were going, joked about their farmers' tans, and so on. As the dinner wound down, Matt stood at the fireplace and gave his usual short speech of appreciation to his employees. He captured the room's attention with ease. He was in his element, soaking up the admiration, returning it with praise and gratitude that inspired his employees to keep up their hard work. The bonus checks he gave out afterward didn't hurt either.

After the speech, the Watermans excused themselves from the table and went to find Matt. I sat with Kyle and his friends, grateful the night neared an end.

The crowd thinned, and I headed for the restroom. I rounded the corner, but not before I noticed a couple in a dimly lit nook off to the side of the room. A nook that led to the kitchen perhaps. I recognized Cassie's black dress. She leaned her head, shoulder, and half of her body against the wall. Again, one leg kicked up so that her high-heeled shoe dangled off her small foot.

My blood ran cold, and then gushing hot as I realized my husband stood on the other side of her. He also leaned against the wall. He didn't see me, for he looked down at the hot little thing in front of him. A small smile pulled at his face. He didn't seem to be able to tear his appreciative gaze from her. It hurt doubly to realize that the last time he'd looked at me like that, we'd probably been teenagers.

I wondered what she said to him. I tried to make excuses for him. Maybe Cassie planned a surprise for her parents in the landscape design. There could be a million reasons they needed to speak privately. They just looked so . . . intimate.

My legs weakened, and I grasped the smooth wood of the rail that led downstairs. I watched Cassie place a casual hand on Matt's forearm. In turn, he cupped her elbow with his hand. Black spots appeared in front of my eyes. I couldn't tear my gaze from his palm against her bare skin. All at once I saw other images of them in my mind's eye. Laughing, playing golf, riding on the yacht, swimming . . . kissing . . . ?

The break Matt wanted. Did Cassie have anything to do with it? My worst fears confronted me on the crowded third floor of the restaurant.

My husband was having an affair. The question that plagued me most was, how far had it gone?

I couldn't stay in the stuffy restaurant another minute. I couldn't find the strength to walk back to our table and say good-bye to Kyle. I rushed down the stairs and pushed open the doors to The Red Parrot to breathe in the salty sea air. I took off my shoes and walked barefoot on the pavement in the direction of the parking lot. Without my heels, I felt short and stalky, clunky and old in an unfashionable yellow dress.

Cassie was a shiny new diamond rock, just the kind Matt liked. I was the plain old used ring he so often avoided. I should have seen it coming.

I ignored small pebbles piercing the bottoms of my feet. There could be a logical explanation for all of this. There could be, there could. She was just a flirty girl. Matt was controlled, honorable. I'm sure Cassie wasn't the first sassy thing he had to fight off.

Though it didn't look like there'd been a lot of fight in him in the restaurant.

I slipped on my shoes at the parking lot, covered in broken clamshells. I walked to the dock and sat. The sun had long since said its good night, and a sliver of moon shone on the water's small ripples. I sat, watching their undulating movements, draining my thoughts to nothing.

I didn't mind the water so much when my feet were planted on solid ground. It's when I couldn't trust what I stood upon that the problems began.

"That was rude."

I drew in a breath at Matt's voice.

"You didn't even say good-bye to Kyle."

"Sorry," I mumbled. "I didn't feel well."

He extended his hand to help me up. I didn't take it, but got up myself and walked toward the Mercedes.

"What? What's the matter?"

As if he didn't know. Unless there was nothing to know.

"I'm just tired. Can we go?"

He didn't open the passenger door for me. We slid in and he started the car. Elvis sang "Suspicious Minds" on the radio.

We drove up Memorial Boulevard and past his rental cottage. The lights shone behind slanted shades. Kyle must be home already.

Elvis's voice faded and Mick Jagger's took his place, singing of painting doors black and girls in summer clothes.

I needed to ask, or at least feel Matt out. I couldn't go on like this for much longer. I waited until we were on the highway, the lights from Newport far behind us and the interior of the car enveloped in safe darkness.

"So Cassie seems nice." I said it like I didn't really mean it. Ugly jealousy dripped—oozed, rather—off every word.

"Stop it, Sarah." I hated the way he spoke to me like I was a petulant child. Maybe I acted like one. But it was his fault for not filling me in on where this whole "break" thing was going. Everything I could have done for our marriage added up to a perfect equation of happiness. Why wasn't the right side showing the result, then?

"And why should I?" My ire increased, as if my spoken words were the motor of a jet on a runway, and as I said them, they built momentum, more and more, until I wanted to burst off the ground. "Didn't this break come right around the time you started the Waterman job? I'm not stupid, Matt. The girl's hanging all over you. She golfs, yachts, has parents who are made of money and dripping all over you almost as much as she is, not to mention she's drop-dead gorgeous. Everything that means success to you waiting for you to leave your homely little wife. Am I right?"

Matt pushed the accelerator, hard. We flew past cars and exits. I looked at the speedometer. Eighty-five, ninety, ninety-five. Matt never drove this fast, especially on a small byway like this. I knew I'd struck a nerve with my words, which made me feel all the worse. Right then, though, I didn't care. In the heat of my anger I thought he could go one-twenty and kill us both. At least then I wouldn't have to deal with him or Cassie or any of this mess.

But then I thought of Kyle, reading a newspaper report of his parents' deaths. "Slow down," I said.

Matt ignored me. Anger built in my gut. "You know your son has a crush on her."

He drove faster. The hedges and solid white line of the breakdown lane blurred on the side of me. Nausea swirled in the pit of my belly.

"Let me out. I'm not driving with you when you're like this."

He slammed on the brakes. The Mercedes skidded to a stop on the shoulder. I grabbed my purse, spat a curse at him for the first time in our marriage, slammed the door, and began walking north on the highway.

At least the cars would be able to see me in my yellow dress. It had been a good choice after all.

Matt peeled back onto the highway, and I stumbled forward, fury fueling my steps. He left me. He actually left me. And yet, I felt if I spent another second in the car with him, I'd go insane from jealousy and anger. Even now, I tested the boundaries of sanity.

Maybe we wouldn't make it after all. Maybe we weren't meant to be. Maybe Lila Rhineheart was right—it was time to move on.

Five minutes later I'd simmered enough to allow fear to replace some of my anger. I didn't know how I'd get home, if I'd even make it to the next exit without getting hit by a drunk driver or a frantic deer. I pulled my phone from my purse and brought up my Uber app.

Behind me a car slowed. Its headlights shone over my legs and my long shadow fell on the pavement.

"You cooled off now?"

I gritted my teeth as the Mercedes pulled alongside me, the passenger's side window open. I flung the phone back in my purse.

"Are you?" I asked.

"Get in, Sarah."

"Are you going to tell me what's really going on?"

I thought I wanted to know. Maybe I didn't.

"We'll talk."

I obeyed, but slammed the door. My breaths heaved, and I didn't buckle but lay my head back against the headrest and looked out the dark window. A warm tear meandered down my cheek as Matt pulled out of the breakdown lane, this time at a normal pace.

"Yes, she's attractive."

Anyone with eyes could see the obvious, yet it still hurt coming from my husband's lips.

"I enjoy Troy and Elise, and yeah, even the life they lead. But nothing has happened between Cassie and me."

I exhaled. I hoped he told the truth, I wanted to believe he did.

"She likes you," I whispered. "How can I compete with her? Especially now, when . . ."

He took the third exit off the highway. "You're my wife, Sarah."

"I don't feel like I'm your wife. I feel like I'm some unwanted dependent you've gotten yourself strapped with." I hated playing the "poor me" card, but if we were to be honest, I wanted to share my feelings.

We rode in silence the five minutes to the house. He pressed the garage door opener on the sun visor when we pulled up the long driveway. The door rolled open. When the Mercedes was tucked inside for the night, he pressed the button again. The doors shut, the rolling sound enveloping the garage.

Another slow tear slid down my face. Matt got out of the car. I stayed seated, not having the energy to face him again. He'd hop in his truck and leave now. I wouldn't see him again until Kyle's birthday.

The interior lights of the Mercedes flickered on when he opened my door. His hand appeared by my side, and it took me a second to realize he offered it to me. My insides quaked along with my body. I placed my trembling hand in his own calloused, solid one. He pulled me from the car, closed its door, and led me to the house.

A fuzzy sensation swept over my brain. I couldn't comprehend his sudden tenderness. I followed him up the two stairs to the kitchen, and he closed the door behind us. Without hesitation, he turned to me and placed his hand alongside my cheek. I leaned into it and inhaled the scent of his deodorant and the mint on his breath, fainter than it had been earlier in the night.

He lowered his head. His mouth hovered over my own before, finally, he brushed my lips with his. I leaned in slightly, returned the act. Our mouths met in a soft clash of desire. An involuntary sob shook my body, and Matt ended the kiss to pull me firmly against his solid chest. My tears flowed harder, and I clutched him, relishing the feel of his hands traveling up and down my arms. The last remnant of my sobs quieted beneath his soft kisses against my ear, and then my jaw, and then finally my lips.

I drank him in, not thinking about what this meant for our relationship, not thinking about Cassie or the party or even the break we were supposed to be having. All I knew was this was how it was supposed to be. Me. Him. Us.

My mind numbed save for his possessive hands and arms and presence so near, the familiar scent of his aftershave threatening to drown me in pleasure. His body responded to me quickly and he swept me up in his arms with little effort and brought me up the stairs.

CHAPTER 17

The Keurig hissed and sputtered as it drained the last of my coffee into a mug Kyle had given me in the fourth grade that read *#1 MOM*. I'd need two cups today, at least half a cup before I could begin to sort through what happened the night before.

The house phone rang, and I tied my silky black robe tighter around my waist and padded with my slippers to the portable on the counter. Matt's cell phone read on the caller ID.

I picked it up. "Hey."

"Morning."

"You were out of here fast this morning," I said. "I could have made breakfast."

"Yeah, sorry about that. I had to check on a few things, and I didn't want Kyle worrying when he woke up. You were out cold."

Probably because it was the best sleep I had in a month.

"Listen, Sarah, I'm sorry about last night. I shouldn't have let things get so far. I shouldn't have come in."

I couldn't deny the naive hope I'd held that last night had fixed us, that last night had fixed whatever bothered Matt.

"Don't be sorry." My voice cracked. "I don't regret it. I've missed you, Matt. I miss you now."

A long sigh vibrated over the line. "I just . . . We can't be doing that. We've always had trouble controlling ourselves—"

"Hey, it's how the best thing in both our lives happened, right?"

He laughed softly. "Yeah."

"Is what happened so bad? Why don't you come home? We can work through whatever this is together, like a husband and wife should." I sounded calm, rational. Reasonable. But my heart beat against my chest with the vigor of a jackhammer.

"I don't think the problem is us. I think it's me. I need to be away, Sarah. I have the rental house through September. I'm sorry."

I didn't want to push too hard. I wanted to support him, even in this. But the end of September? Three months away?

I swallowed down my deflated hope. "Okay. But I want to help."

"Keeping our distance and not letting what happened last night happen again—I think that's the only way you can help right now."

My breaths quivered, and I moved my mouth from the phone so Matt wouldn't hear them.

"I . . . Last night was great," he said.

"Yeah, it was. Say hi to Kyle for me, will you? Tell him I'm sorry about not saying good-bye last night."

"Will do."

"I love you, Matt."

"Love you, too."

The line went dead.

I rubbed my face with my hands, ate my oatmeal, drank my two cups of coffee, and planned my day.

First item: call another clock repairman. Second up: return the black dress. Third: bury myself in Elizabeth's story and try to find what Barb was so passionate about passing on to her daughter, and maybe to me.

And after the museum closed, if I had enough energy, I was having the sudden urge to hit a few golf balls.

May 26, 1675
Morning

Papa still sleeps from the doctor's medicines. Mr. Tanner came back late yesterday evening and found me again in prayer by Papa's bed. I scarce heard him knock. When I did not answer, he entered. I stood, brushed away my tears, and busied myself over the hearth. The least I could do was prepare him supper for his troubles.

I did not meet his gaze as I scurried around to stoke the fire and warm a dish of pea soup. He did not interrupt me but stared in that strange way of his that made me jumpy as a toad. I thrust the red-hot loggerhead into a mixture of cider and beer to make him a drink of flip. I gave it to him and turned to check on the soup, but he placed the flip on the table and grasped my arm.

"Elizabeth, stop."

I obeyed, my skin tingling where his fingers gripped me.

"You need not work yourself so. This is a difficult time for you. I came here to see if you needed comfort, not to garner a meal."

I sniffed. He loosened his grip. "I am well."

"I only wish to help. 'Twould be easier if you opened your mind and heart to me a wee bit."

I swallowed. I may very well be this man's wife by the harvest. I should confide in him. And yet if I did I would have to tell the whole of the truth. I was not yet ready to voice my heart out loud, at least to him.

"Mr. Tanner—"

He dropped his hand from my arm. "Caleb, Elizabeth. Have I not at least earned that much in your sight? In your heart?"

I closed my eyes. Part of me wished to reach up and touch his bearded face, to assure him of his goodness, of his right to a much finer woman than I. But I did not allow my hand to lift. "Caleb, I do care for you."

'Twas not a lie. My feelings for Mr. Tanner were complicated. He did not make my heart flutter as Abram did, but I took comfort in his nearness, in the security he offered me. I wondered if I was drawn more to his protection than to him. For if Papa should pass, Mr. Tanner would be my only hope of a sound future.

I am a wretched creature.

"Why then will you not let me in?" he asked.

I stared into the pools of hazel that were his eyes and willed him to understand without my voicing the hurtful words out loud. He saw me in the woods with Abram. What had he seen? Could he see the bond that held us? Could he see how I looked at Abram? Did he wish I would gaze upon him in the same manner?

I felt he did know, and yet wished me to voice the words.

I could not.

I turned from him and spooned a hearty serving of pea soup into a bowl, proving I could perform at least one of the duties of a wife without the giving of my heart.

May 26, 1675
Evening

I no longer feel guilt when I steal away to see Abram. I know if a time comes that Mr. Tanner and I become betrothed, I will need to end our friendship, lest I betray my marriage vows, but that time is not now, and with Papa's lifeblood draining from him day by day, I prefer to live in the present, not the future.

My friend was not at the rock when I arrived, so I sat and waited for him. From the pocket of my dress I pulled out the clamshell he gifted me. I drew pictures in the dirt with the blunt end so as not to break the delicate edges. If he did not come presently, I would trace a message for him.

When at last he came and saw me, I could not help but thrill at the look of pleasant surprise upon his face. 'Tis worth the waiting to see his severely cut, strong features light up at the sight of me. "Chickautáw," he said as he dropped his bow and placed both hands on either side of my arms. "I hope you did not wait long."

I did not tell him I would have waited hours more.

"Did you have no fortune in your hunt?" I gestured to his bow and then to his empty hands.

"I did not hunt today. I was meeting an English friend." Abram led me to his fire pit, where he stirred the still-glowing coals alive with a stick.

"I thought I was your only English friend," I said. *I* wondered if his other friend was also a woman. I wondered if she felt for him what I did.

"You are more than a friend, Chickautáw. You are part of my spirit." He said this so simply, I wondered if he knew the deep thoughts of my heart, if perhaps he even shared them with me.

He offered me some Nokehick, and I took it to be polite. High above us, a hawk circled overhead, its piercing cries splitting the air.

"I keep friendships with some English and some from Pocasset tribe, though Weetamoo does not know. Some of my tribe is not friendly to the English. I wish to warn them of threats."

I wondered if his friend was Benjamin Church himself.

"Would that not betray your people?"

Abram grew thoughtful at my comment. He stared up into the swaying trees, up to the top of the majestic rock, which was his shelter. *"I belong to two peoples, neither who want me. I side with no side. I wish for peace. If I learn that the English plan to harm my tribe, I would warn them also."*

I admired his desire for peace between two peoples who had both hurt him in some way. I told him he was a good man. He laughed. *"No one good but God, yes?"*

"How is it that you hold to the faith of those who spurn you?" I did not wish to incite anger at the English, at God even, but I had to know.

He studied me a moment and my heart thrummed beneath my corset.

"This faith—your faith, my faith—did it not belong to others long ago? The—the people the Lord brought out of Egypt?"

"The Hebrews."

"Yes. The Hebrews. Did it not belong to them first? Even to Adam at the very beginning? Is it perhaps not the faith of the English, but rather a

faith for all mankind and the English are part of that large body? What if my people are another part?"

I closed my eyes, swallowed, and nodded, feeling suddenly very small beside him.

He held up his hand to me and walked to his cave. A moment later he came back out with a small black book. A Holy Bible.

"Do you read?"

I nodded.

"Will Chickautáw teach Abram?" I tried to hide a smile at how it was that I possessed the Indian name and he the Christian one.

"'Tis much work. 'Twould take some time."

He nodded with enthusiasm. "Are you willing?"

"Yes. Yes, of course." 'Twould give me cause to come and see him often.

I left with a promise to return the next day to deliver his first lesson, if Papa did not have urgent need of me.

June 2, 1675

The early summer heat oppresses. The thick air does little to help Papa's cough, though he had a good day yesterday and was able to sit up and eat by himself. He apologized for the trouble and inquired if Mr. Tanner had yet asked for my hand.

I told Papa Mr. Tanner might be having doubts about asking. That piece of news sent him into another coughing fit and I falsely assured him that I only jested, that I was certain a proposal would come any time now.

The days are long. I sleep little. My thoughts run wild as soon as I lay my head on the pillow. I often light the Betty lamp and strain my eyes sewing by the meager light. Abram's quilt is almost pieced. 'Tis a simple pattern with bits of my old aprons scattered throughout.

I've gone to him near every day on the pretense of teaching him to read. He is a fine student and I fear 'twill not take him long to master the English letters.

Today Abram told me of a trial taking place in Plimoth Colony concerning the death of a Praying Indian named John Sassamon. Abram said Sassamon was much like him, living in both the world of the white and the world of the copper skins. He traveled easily between both worlds. Very early this year, Sassamon visited the Governor Josiah Winslow to warn him that the Wampanoag planned to wage war. A few days later his body was found beneath ice in a pond not far from his home.

I shivered when Abram told me this story. "And do the authorities blame someone for his death?"

Abram gave me a sad smile and nodded.

"Who?"

"Who does Chickautáw think?"

"The natives."

Abram nodded. "They convict three Wampanoag with little proof."

"What will become of them?"

"They will hang."

I reached out and touched the back of his hand. He turned it over so as to hold mine. My stomach tumbled and my heart sent up a pitter-patter loud enough to reach the heavens. "I fear for you."

"Do not, Chickautáw."

"You and Sassamon have much in common. 'Tis dangerous to be in both worlds."

"Then you are in danger as well."

Am I? Am I in both worlds? I feel 'tis true. I am a part of both, yet belong to neither, just as Abram does.

"What shall we do?"

I wanted him to ask if I would run away with him. As soon as the thought came to mind, I scolded myself. For what of Papa? I would never leave him for the sickness to eat away at the inside of his body, for him to die alone. And what of Mr. Tanner? I cannot say I love him as a wife should love a husband, but I know 'twould be wrong to leave him.

"I must stay here. There is good I can do," he said.

I lowered my gaze to the dirt where I had just given Abram his lesson. He lifted my chin so I would have to look at him. "We must trust God to take care of us."

"Do you truly believe there is One who sees all and cares for me?" I had *thought the question before but never felt free to voice it. Here, with Abram, it felt safe to ask.*

"I know many gods before. Vengeful gods. I never felt love from them or wholeness. I never felt good enough. I have many imperfect brothers. I too am one. But Jesus . . . he is my true older brother. He the only one who met my heart where I am."

The way he said it was so beautiful that it made me long for Jesus to meet my own heart. What would it be like to give myself fully to God? To have the intimacy with Him that Abram hinted at?

"Did you choose the name Abram?" I asked.

He nodded. "My earthly father died before I knew him. I chose this name to remind me of the father of my faith."

I looked up at Abram's rock. "I think I should like you to take me to the top again."

He did not hesitate. This time, when we reached the top, I did not pay heed to my jumping stomach. I spread my arms to the side and up. "Do you think if I were to ask Jesus to meet my heart here, He would?" I asked Abram.

He didn't answer and when I looked back at him, he stared at me. "Abram?" I repeated myself.

He shook his head as if to rid himself of a vision. "I am sorry, Chickautáw. Yes, if you ask, I believe Jesus will meet your heart."

Yet I couldn't say if I wanted Jesus enough at that moment. What I wanted stood just steps behind me.

"If I ask you to meet my heart, will you, Abram?" I said the words into the wind, into the tall tree branches in front of me.

I sensed him step forward, toward the edge of the rock, slowly. He ran his hands down the side of my arms until they met mine. His body pressed against my back. I shivered despite the thick June heat.

His breath played across the back of my neck, and in that moment I knew he felt for me what I felt for him. "Jesus's heart is better than mine, Chickautáw."

I twisted so that we faced one another. "It is yours I want."

Silence cloaked the woods. I wondered if my forward confession bothered him. He stilled, and I thought he would say something. Instead, he lowered his mouth to my waiting lips.

He tasted of smoke and tobacco and woods and freedom. My heart thrilled at what he shared with me. The length of his body pressed along mine and I hungered for him in a way that frightened me. He pulled back all too soon.

"You should go."

"Yes," I whispered. With my insides still burning, I descended the rock quickly. When I looked up he still stood at the top of the boulder, proud and straight, his silky black hair blowing in the wind. I knew that if things were to continue like this, I would have to tell him. I would have to tell him that I planned to wed another.

An involuntary sob shook my frame and I turned away from both Abram, and his rock.

June 9, 1675

News has come to the settlement of the execution of three Wampanoag Indians for the murder of John Sassamon. Andia called on me today and told me of it. My heart was not sad to see her go after a short visit.

I did not take leave to see Abram this day. Papa fell quite ill again and had great need of me. 'Tis degrading for him, I know. I must help him with all manner of things, and in his delirium he once prayed for the Lord to have mercy on him and sweep him up to heaven now so he would not have to be shamed before his daughter.

I tried to reassure him that he is not a nuisance, that I love him and 'tis my pleasure and honor to care for him. He did not respond.

Mr. Tanner has been strangely absent of late.

CHAPTER 18

I positioned my feet parallel to the golf ball perched on the tee and aligned my driver behind it. I brought back the club and swung with all my might at the little white ball.

My club met nothing but air.

I adjusted my baseball hat and looked around to see if anyone else on the driving range noticed my blunder. No, everyone else seemed busy hitting perfect balls onto the range.

Again, I positioned my feet, took aim, and swung. This time I hit the ball, but it went far to the right. I wondered if anyone ever hit another golfer on the driving range. I supposed I could be the first.

I went through half my bucket and managed three decent hits. I'd watched Matt play golf a couple times. He didn't even look like he tried when he swung. Complete perfection, total control in one powerful swing that had the ball flying three hundred yards.

He'd bought me the set of golf clubs for Christmas the first year after we built the house.

I remember opening it, praying it wasn't what I thought it might be.

To my horror, it was. A brand-new Callaway golf set in a light-purple bag. I tried to hide my dismay.

"Thought it was time to get you out on the course. Kyle's starting to play. It's something we can do as a family."

"You think you're up to teaching me?"

He winked at me. "Oh, I'm up to it."

He'd been so excited. But as the winter snows melted and the spring muds disappeared, I made excuses. I let him bring me golfing once. He'd wanted to go to the driving range to start me off, but I said if I was going to make a fool of myself I'd prefer to do it out on the golf course on a quiet day, where I could see what I was up against.

He took off a morning of work, and after we put Kyle on the school bus, we drove to Swansea Country Club's par three course.

He was patient, I'll give him that.

I tried for about the first three hits. Then I put little into it, sending my ball off the fairway, into the trees or water hazards, anywhere but on the green. I grew cranky and frustrated. He grumbled at my unteachable spirit.

"If you want to sell the clubs, you can," I said when we walked to the car.

"You kidding? You're going to quit after one session?"

"I'm hopeless, Matt."

"We're keeping them. If you ever want to put a little effort into it and learn, let me know."

They'd sat in the attic for the last nine years. Until now.

Perhaps my motivation for taking them out was wrong. And yet was anything more worthy motivation than winning back my husband?

I thought of Caleb, his persistent care and presence for a woman whose heart was more than a little wishy-washy. I didn't see how Elizabeth and Caleb's story could end happily. For that matter, I didn't see how Elizabeth and Abram's could, either.

"Sarah?"

I jerked my head up from where I'd been taking aim. Behind me, golf clubs slung at his back and a thin line of sweat on his forehead, stood a familiar man. Only instead of his usual white coat, he wore a polo shirt that showed off his muscular torso.

"Pete—hey." I tried to hide my surprise.

"I didn't know you golfed."

"Um—yeah, I don't. This is an experiment of sorts. It's not going well."

Pete set his golf clubs down. "Want a lesson?"

"Uh, no, I don't think so. I'm pretty hopeless. I came out here because I thought hitting some balls would feel good. Turns out I should have just bought a punching bag."

"Dinner didn't go so well last night?"

That's right, he knew about Matt's employee dinner. Before he left work on Friday, he'd asked me if I had plans for the weekend. I told him about Matt's dinner. I hadn't expected him to remember.

"It was fine." Instead of the dinner, I remembered the feeling of being in Matt's arms again. I looked down at my half-empty bucket of balls to hide my thoughts. "So you come here a lot?"

"Every Sunday night. Either here or the course. You live close by?"

"A few miles up the road." I tapped the head of my driver on the green turf near the tee.

"Hey, I don't mind giving you a few pointers if you want. You serious about learning?"

Good question. I imagined calling Matt up and telling him I'd like a golf lesson. More than likely, he'd see through my ruse. He'd say now wasn't a good time. He was busy with things in Newport, busy with Kyle. Why hadn't I decided this five years ago?

But if I came to him already knowing a few things . . . well, it couldn't hurt. Maybe it would be a way for us to spend more time together, talk even. I pictured Matt, Kyle, and me walking through the golf course, laughing, talking. The last few years we'd spent so little time together as a family. Kyle was busy with school and track and friends. Matt was busy with work. I should have let him teach me all those years ago. I could have tried harder, for his sake. Was a little self-sacrifice too much to ask of me?

"I don't mean to put you on the spot," Pete said. "Just thought I'd offer. I know a thing or two, anyway."

I shook my head, blinked. "No, I'm sorry, Pete. I mean, yes, I think I could use a few pointers . . . or a few hundred, whatever you're willing to offer."

He broke into a grin. I noticed the dimple on his left cheek. "Great." He moved to the empty tee-off space beside me and grabbed his driver. "Remember to keep your feet parallel to the ball. Don't worry about whacking it so hard. Maybe pause before you come back down with your swing."

He demonstrated, hitting the ball smoothly into the air to a flag a hundred yards away.

"You make it look easy." I placed a ball on the tee and dragged in a long breath.

"Relax. If you're not having fun, you're not playing golf right."

I snorted. "Then I can honestly say I've never played golf right."

"Keep your arms straight. Bring your club back just a bit. There, that's it. Now pause, focus on the ball, and come down smooth."

I followed his instructions and this time I connected with the ball and hit it about seventy-five yards out. I gave a little jump of excitement. "That felt good."

"It looked good. That's just how you want to do it." He scooped up another ball from my bucket and placed it on the tee. "Okay, this time, grip the club a little tighter."

I concentrated on the ball. When I swung, I felt as if the driver were an extension of my arms. The head met the ball and it flew straight onto the range, close to the 150-yard mark. "I can't believe I just hit that!"

Pete gave me a high five. "I think you're a natural."

He watched me finish off the bucket, encouraging more than instructing. I didn't hit all great balls, but the majority of them soared straight and, more often than not, long.

I slid my driver back into my bag. "Thanks, Pete. I actually had fun."

"You must be playing it right, then."

We slung our bags onto our backs and I returned the empty bucket to the clerk. Pete walked me to my car and hefted my clubs into the trunk. "Can I interest you in an ice cream cone? My treat."

I wanted to say yes. I liked spending time with this man. But I didn't want him to think I was interested in him *that* way. "I—I can't. Not today, anyway."

He smiled, but not well enough to hide his disappointment. "I understand. I probably shouldn't have asked—"

"No, Pete. It's not that. It's just . . . well, you know my marriage is kind of shaky now. I don't want to add more problems to it. . . . I don't know; does that make sense?"

I could have kicked myself. I shouldn't assume Pete was interested in me. He was just a nice guy, probably would have offered golf pointers and ice cream to any other woman in distress on the range. He knew I was married. Of course he wasn't asking me *out, out.*

"Say no more, Sarah. I don't want you to think I'm some kind of scumbag trying to swoop in and ruin your marriage—"

"No, no of course not." Matt and I didn't need any help ruining our marriage.

"But, well, just so you know, I'm pretty good at listening. You have a marriage that you need to fix; I get that. But I don't think it's wrong that we're friends, is it?"

Yes, yes it was. Maybe there was nothing wrong with it on the surface, but just below that, it felt all wrong. Would I want some woman—say, Cassie Waterman—being Matt's *friend* while we went through this mess?

"I think maybe for now we should keep our distance." I said the words just above a whisper. I didn't want to upset him, really I didn't. "I'm sorry."

A flash of disappointment crossed his face, but a small smile quickly pulled at the side of his mouth, making him all the more endearing. "You don't have to apologize. I'm the one who should be sorry." He readjusted his golf clubs on his shoulder. "You know what? Do me a favor and forget this conversation ever happened, okay?"

"Leave it on the range?" I asked.

He laughed. "Leave it on the range. You did great today."

"You were a great teacher. Thanks."

"See you around then?"

I nodded. "Bye."

He turned to walk to his car. After a few steps he turned and pointed at me. "Next lesson's chipping!"

I smiled and opened the door of the Mercedes.

I would need a long bath when I got home. Or maybe a hike in the woods. Something—anything—to calm the swirl of disquiet that my time with Pete had created within me.

CHAPTER 19

Presents were meant to be beautiful. The outside wrappings of silver and ribbon, held together with nothing but discreet pieces of Scotch tape, were meant to indicate the loveliness inside. As I parked the Mercedes on the side of the road near Matt's rental house and balanced the cake platter on top of Kyle's birthday present, I wondered if our family would ever be beautifully wrapped again. If how we looked on the outside would match what lay beneath.

I hoped this night would be the beginning of reconciliation. I prayed something would click when the three of us were together alone again, under one roof.

The salty scent of the sea swept up the hill of Memorial Boulevard as I climbed the front steps of the rental where my husband and son now lived. Streaks of evening sunlight shone on the wood floor behind the screened door and I paused, undecided whether to lift my hand to knock. The briny air teased my hair into frizz. I tapped on the door twice.

Kyle appeared behind the fine lattices of the screen. I couldn't help staring. Every time I saw him—especially now that I didn't see him daily—he grew more and more like his father. He wore a blue polo shirt and khaki shorts, and I returned his hug with a no-armed one when he opened the door, full as my hands were.

"Happy seventeenth, kiddo," I said.

"Thanks, Mom. Glad you could come down tonight." He took the packages from me.

"As if I would miss your birthday." I stopped myself from telling him the story of his birth, as I had every year up until now. How I'd called his father right before my mother and I left for the hospital, how Matt had been a nervous wreck and came so quickly from a job that he'd left on the earphones he wore while weed whacking and hadn't noticed until he was in the delivery room and one of the nurses pointed it out. How he held my hand the entire time, how we welcomed our first and only son into the world in a blinding burst of pain and perseverance and love.

"Dad's grilling in the back." He placed the cake and present on a black-and-white specked counter centered in a spacious kitchen that opened up to a simple living room decorated in blue, white, and tan beach decor. A fireplace stood at the far wall. Beside it sat a guitar on a stand.

I pointed to it. "You taking up guitar?"

Kyle shook his head. "Dad's. Said he always wanted to play."

Hmm, he never mentioned it before.

A small dining room gave way to French doors leading to an outside patio. I spotted Matt at the grill, his hair damp from a shower and his feet bare beneath Wranglers.

I tried to tamp down the intense ache of longing in my chest. This day was about Kyle, not about me and Matt and all we could have done—should have done—to avoid getting to this point.

"Nice place," I said as Kyle led me through the French doors.

"Yeah, it's pretty cool."

Matt turned and smiled. "Right on time. Burgers are almost done."

He didn't come over and kiss me, and I didn't feel invited to greet him in such a way. Being here in this place, in his life that didn't include me, made our separation all the more real. This is where my husband had chosen. This paradise by the sea, this cozy cottage, instead of a place at home with me, his wife.

All at once I hated the house. It was everything—and everywhere—I wasn't.

This place—so neat, so perfect on the outside, just like my husband. Wrapped up with silver and ribbon. But I had no clue what was underneath the wrapping. What was Matt thinking? Why did he not open up to me? I mean . . . guitar? Now? He could have learned to play at any other time. I wouldn't have discouraged it. Why did he choose this time and this place— even a new hobby—over me?

I forced myself to gulp down the frantic thoughts, to focus on the reason I was here. I turned to Kyle. "Your Dad didn't work you too hard on your birthday, did he?"

Matt flipped a burger. "Hey, it's not a national holiday or anything, is it?" But he winked at our son. I knew he considered the day of Kyle's birth more important than any national holiday.

Kyle rubbed the back of his neck. "He worked me hard, all right. The golf course was torture." He shared a grin with Matt.

I caught it. "You guys played hooky, didn't you?"

"It's only hooky if you're sneaking around. The guys working on the golf course saw us clear as day."

I put my hand over my eyes. "You didn't."

"We did," they said in unison.

"What's the point of owning your own company if you can't take an afternoon off on your son's birthday to try out his new clubs?" Matt split apart a hamburger bun and placed it on the top rack of the grill.

"I'm glad you had fun." It was on the tip of my tongue to

ask if they'd gone alone. But really, I didn't want to know. I'm sure it would have made Kyle's day if Cassie Waterman had joined them, but it would have hurt too much to know if she had.

"Yeah, the new clubs worked great, too. I beat Dad—first time ever."

Matt patted his chest hard, twice. "Still hurts, right here."

Kyle smiled at Matt and I saw their relationship for what it was—beautiful. Maybe this time for them together was the best thing for Kyle. He was almost a man, ready to set off on his own in another year. What better man to have by his side than his father?

"Here we are." Matt brought two plates to the table, one with buns, the other with burgers. In the melted cheese of one burger was an S for Sarah, indicating the patty most well-done.

We ate, and to my surprise, it didn't feel terribly awkward. They spoke about their work. Kyle asked me about school. I told them that I sent in my application and was considering taking a summer class in August.

"Diving right in, huh?" Matt asked.

I shrugged. Was my urge to go back to school so indifferent from his dream to play guitar?

"I've wanted to do it forever. No point putting it off any longer." I wondered if he was concerned about my not being around as much when he came back home.

If he came back home.

I helped Matt clean up, careful to avoid touching him on the way in and out of the French doors as we cleared plates, dirty napkins, and condiments.

When the table lay clean, I brought out my present to Kyle. In the past, I'd always signed his cards, "Love, Dad and Mom." This year was different, but I kept the words the same. We were still both his parents. Somehow though, I knew that Matt's present of golf clubs hadn't been signed the same way.

Kyle ripped off the silver paper. His face could still light up like a little boy's, and I savored every second of it as he unwrapped the iPad. "This is awesome. A keyboard and everything. Thanks, Mom."

Matt let out a long, low whistle.

I accepted Kyle's hug and clutched him a second longer when he made a move to release me.

"We spared no expense on you this year, kid." Matt's words were said lightly, but I was thinking the same thing. New golf clubs. An iPad. I wondered if we weren't both trying to make up for something. Suddenly, I felt ashamed.

"You can also thank Barb for my present," I added.

Though the journal transcribing could only go as fast as the hours the museum was open, I'd kept myself busy organizing Barb's house and setting her affairs straight. While I didn't yet have the heart to put the house up for sale, secretly I didn't want to make the decision on my own anyway. At the end of September, hopefully Matt and I could evaluate Barb's estate together.

At the same time, I felt more capable than I had in a long time. With the extra income coming in from the hospital as well as what Barb had left me and my plans to go to school, I felt accomplished. More confident, even. I hoped somehow these facts helped Matt see me in a different light. We'd been together a long time. We'd fallen into routine. We'd stopped seeing each other clearly. Our expectations were engraved in our minds and during the normal day-in, day-out routine, we likely saw what we expected to see—maybe Matt and I observed each other in more of a sepia tone instead of color.

"Well thanks for this, Mom. *I* appreciate the expense." He opened the box and dug out the starter instructions.

Matt went in to get the cake and came back out with a cutting knife, three forks, three paper plates, a box of matches, and a box of candles. I helped him stick the candles in the frosting. Kyle tore himself away from his iPad to appreciate our off-key rendition of "Happy Birthday." As soon as we were done singing, he picked up the iPad.

Matt insisted on cutting the cake. The doorbell rang.

He held up his fingers, slicked with frosting and chocolate cake crumbs. "Would you mind, Sarah? Probably Blaine picking up the keys to one of the trucks. They're on the counter if you'd give them to him."

"Sure." I slid through the house and rounded the corner, swiping the truck keys off the counter.

My heart did a limbo beneath my stomach.

It wasn't Blaine. Or any man. The woman on the other side of the screen wore a tiny pair of running shorts, a sports bra beneath a hot-pink tank top that somehow held her generous chest in, and her phone on her arm. She held one of the earbuds and tapped her foot on the pavement. Her blonde ponytail shook on her shoulder with her tapping.

"Cassie, right?" I didn't open the door. Did she come here often?

"Oh, hey . . . Sarah. I didn't know you were visiting."

Visiting? The word hit my chest like a hard little bullet. I would have pummeled the woman off Matt's porch steps and ordered her to stay away from both my husband and my son if Matt hadn't come up behind me at that moment. The only thing that steadied me were his hands on the sides of my arms.

"Hey," he said. "What's up?" He opened the door and let her in. Kyle entered from the back patio.

"Sorry, I didn't realize you were busy. I was going to see if you guys wanted to take a run on the cliff, but some other time, okay?"

"Yeah. Sure. That sounds good." This from my husband.

Cassie flashed Kyle a smile.

"We're about to have cake if you want to stay," Kyle said.

Cassie's gaze brushed over me, making me feel like an unwelcome intruder. My skin crawled.

"No, I don't want to interrupt. Sorry. See you guys later."

She pushed through the screen door and jogged off, her ponytail bouncing behind her.

Kyle gazed after her for a moment, shrugged, and went back to the porch and his iPad. I stood, invisible hands clasping my ankles and cementing me to the wooden floor. Tears pricked my eyelids.

"*What* is going on, Matt?" I spoke through clenched teeth, my words slow and controlled when inside I felt ready to burst.

"Not now, Sarah."

"'Sure. That sounds good'?" I didn't try to keep my voice from a small shriek. "You're going to walk on one of the most romantic places in the Northeast with that woman?"

"Run."

"Since when do you run?" Or walk, for that matter. Not once, in all our years of marriage, in all the times I'd asked him to take a hike in the woods with me, did he oblige. Now, he was *running?* With *her?*

Matt rubbed a spot on his brow as if to say, *Here we go again.* "You don't get it, do you?"

I shook my head. "No. Please enlighten me." I did not deserve this torture. I'd been a good wife. Watered our marriage with love and attention. Fed it with care. What more could I have done?

"It's all about connections, Sarah. You should know that. I didn't make it this far just because I cut lawns better than your average Joe. It's work. The Watermans know people, people with money. People who will hire me and keep Rodrigues Landscaping going. If my client wants to take me out on their yacht, I let them. If they want a round of golf, I give it to them. And if they want to go for a run with me, well that's not out of the question either."

"What if they want to sleep with you?"

Matt clenched a fist by his side. Then, with concentrated effort, he walked toward the kitchen.

He wasn't going to get away that easy.

"I asked you a question, Matt. What if they want to sleep with you?"

"Keep your voice down." He jerked his head toward the patio, where Kyle's nose was buried in his iPad, earbuds perched in his ears.

I shut the French door. "Answer me!"

"You think I don't have morals? You think I'd do anything to get to the top?"

"Oh, is it that much of a sacrifice for you to sleep with a beautiful young woman?"

"Why do you goad me? Why?"

"I just want to know the truth. Tell me!"

He slammed his fist on the kitchen counter. "Fine, you want to know the truth? I'll give it to you. I've had the chance. There, you happy? I've had the chance more than once to sleep with a woman besides you. But I never took it. Never. That's where I drew the line."

I let his words sink in. I knew they were the truth. Why, then, didn't they make me feel better?

"And was Cassie Waterman one of the women who —who—?"

"No."

I released a long breath. Just because she hadn't blatantly offered herself to my handsome, charismatic husband yet, didn't mean she wouldn't.

"It's not all about sex, Sarah."

"Isn't it? That's pretty much all it's been about for us."

He ran a hand over the back of his neck. "Maybe that's one of our problems."

Maybe it was.

We went outside, and I forced a piece of cake down for Kyle's sake. I left soon after. Matt didn't ask if I wanted to walk on the beach, even though I willed him to with all my might.

I drove away from my husband and son in my shiny silver Mercedes, feeling—knowing—that the beautiful wrappings of our family were unraveling quicker than I could have imagined. They were crumpled on the floor, stomped on.

The trouble was, I couldn't tell whose feet had done the stomping.

Mine, or Matt's.

CHAPTER 20

I thumbed through a series of musty letters I'd found in Barb's closet. They smelled as if Barb had been caught in the rain with them and then gone home and tucked them on the shelf without allowing them to dry.

While packing up dishes and glasses and silverware from the kitchen had proven an easy enough first task, moving into Barb's bedroom had required a new level of fortitude. Nothing more personal than a tea cup was found in the kitchen—here, mysteries abounded, including letters to and from a husband I'd never known. Mary's father, maybe?

Far from the first time, I wished I'd been more invested in Barb's life. I wished I'd asked more questions.

I remembered an introductory class I'd taken in nursing. One of the students had asked the instructor what she thought was the hardest part of nursing.

"Saying good-bye," she'd said without hesitation. "At the hospital the patients are never there for long. We sometimes get attached to one another. Saying good-bye is hard."

I thought of Lila Rhinehart and Albert Caron, who had gone home. I thought of Barb and I thought of Elizabeth, whose story I was halfway through.

I thought of Matt. And my heart twisted.

Good-byes were definitely the hardest part.

June 11, 1675

It has happened.

Mr. Tanner called upon me today. He looked tired and I wondered if he had gone to see the execution of the three Wampanoag Indians as some of the men in the town intended to do. I could not bear the thought of seeing a person hang. 'Tis a barbaric thing to do, even when a culprit did have guilt written on the parchment of his soul, which I am not at all of the mind the three natives did.

Mr. Tanner bid me sit in the garden with him. He asked after Papa, and I reported that I feared his end drew near.

"You serve him faithfully. You are a good daughter."

I ran my finger over Abram's clamshell, safe in my pocket.

Mr. Tanner continued. "You have many admirable qualities. I have watched you through the years and have come to care for you deeply. It is my hope that with time, you may come to care for me as well. Please, Elizabeth, do me the honor of becoming my wife."

His eloquence caught me off guard. I had expected the proposal, but not the gracious acknowledgment of his knowing that I did not love him as he did I. Still, if he knew of me and Abram, why did he persist for my hand?

"I am aware of your knowledge, Mr. Tanner."

He stared at me a moment, seeming to piece together my words. Then his eyes closed, but not before I noticed a look of defeat within them. Pity erupted in my belly, but now was the time for honesty—before banns were read, before vows were spoken. "Caleb, Elizabeth. Please call me Caleb."

I pinched the clamshell tight between my thumb and forefinger. "Caleb, you are aware of my deliberate act of going against your will, of walking in the woods. Of not only doing so, but of taking up friendship with a native man."

"Yes." The words croaked from his mouth, muffled by his unwillingness to admit them.

"Why then do you pursue me? Why do you seek the hand of a woman who disregards your request?" I hated myself for my harshness, but I would not have this cloud of deceit hanging above our heads should we wed.

"Because I love you." He pulled my hand from the pocket of my dress and clasped it to his chest. The gesture reminded me all too much of Abram's gesture and I wrested my fingers away.

"Would you love me still if you knew I not only disregarded your request, but that I have done so on multiple occasions, that I have spent much time with this native, that . . . I have even allowed him to kiss me?" My face flamed as I voiced aloud the physical intimacy Abram and I shared, the societal boundary I had crossed.

Mr. Tanner dropped my hand, stood, and paced the ground before me with vigorous steps. I knew I chanced everything. He could not only spurn my hand, but spread my secret among the settlement. I would be ostracized, cast out, ridiculed. Papa would have no one. But I was through with secrets and lies. If Mr. Tanner was to enter a marriage with me, I would have him know all.

With sudden decision, he dropped in front of me on one knee. "Yes, Elizabeth, I would still love you. I have loved you for years, since the first time you ran behind my legs, frightened of a toad. That love has grown and changed as we have, and I am ready to cherish you now and forevermore if you will accept my hand. I pray we will find love in the days we share."

I had a thought to shake some sense into Caleb Tanner. "You would wed me even though I love another?"

"Do you, little Elizabeth? Do you love your native? Or do you love adventure and freedom and life and surprises?"

I grappled for an answer. He took what I thought to be true and turned it on its head. Were these the things I loved, and not the actual man? Abram called me part of his spirit. Was he part of mine, or only a figurehead of excitement?

"I fear a time of uncertainty is coming. For you with your Papa sick. For us and for the natives as both sides harbor resentment. You want to be in both worlds, but you cannot. Ultimately, you must choose. I am offering you

a choice now. Accept my hand and we can have the banns read this coming Sabbath. Let us settle this now, while your Papa is still here to see it."

That's right. Papa. I had promised. I thought of Abram, standing tall and strong at the top of his rock. I would have to tell him. His heart would hurt as mine now did. I wondered if I made the right decision.

"I accept your proposal." Though a queerer proposal I had never imagined.

His gaze softened and he clasped my hands in his much larger ones. "You have made me happy," he said. "And will you now promise me with your whole heart not to go near the woods again?"

"I—'tis only proper to say good-bye." I could not imagine leaving Abram to wonder of my whereabouts forever.

"I will escort you, then."

"Shall a man not trust his wife-to-be?"

"Shall a man not look after the safety of his wife-to-be?"

"'Tis safe. I have gone countless times."

He must have wondered why his heart chose to love me. I certainly did. "Go then, now, while I can still be here to see of your safe return. I will watch after your father."

I hastened away to the forest, the strange truth of this pit I had fallen into not lost on me. I cared deeply for Abram but must deny my heart. Caleb wants my heart and yet he still allowed me to say good-bye to the man who'd captured it instead of him. I knew it must hurt him to see me running off with eager steps to see one of the natives he took such a disliking to.

Perhaps that, more than anything else, was the truest love ever shown me.

June 12, 1675

I am not sure if my hand or my heart grew tired yesterday. Either way, I had not the fortitude to finish all that happened after I accepted Caleb's proposal. I did indeed make haste to see Abram. He sat on top of his cave, the Holy Bible opened on his lap. I stood at the edge of the clearing and watched him, etching his picture on the tablet of my mind. I thought of the quilt I had not yet finished for him. Would I ever be able to gift it to him?

He saw me—or perhaps sensed me—and looked up from his reading. He smiled and held the Bible in the air. "I am reading good, Chickautáw."

Chickautáw. I would miss hearing his Indian name for me. He leapt from the rock with the grace of a deer and clasped my hand in his. "I will show you," he said.

I shook my head. "We have not the time." I wiped my wet eyes.

"Chickautáw, what is wrong?"

"I am sorry, Abram. I am so, so sorry." Perhaps I had betrayed Caleb, but I had also betrayed Abram. I had known our future would meet with an ending as hard as the rock under which he lived, and yet I had carried on with him. "I have come to bid you good-bye."

He cocked his head to the side as my horse, Church, sometimes did when I made a high-pitched whistle with my tongue against the roof of my mouth.

"I am to wed soon," I said.

Abram's bottom lip quivered. "And you care for this man?"

"Yes—no, I don't know! I do not care for him as I care for you, yet there can be no future for us."

He stared at me a moment, battling with himself it seemed. Finally, he nodded stoically. "It is too dangerous for you."

"And for you, though 'tis not solely that. I promised my father. He is much troubled over my uncertain future."

I felt as if Abram's thoughts were as vast and wide as the never-ending sea. Yet he did not voice them. I wondered if he thought me a coward, if I married for protection instead of love.

Perhaps I did. Perhaps I was.

"This man—he will take care of you well?"

"Yes." Of this I had no doubt.

"I will miss you, Little Fire." He drew me to himself and I sank into his embrace. He did not kiss me, though. He held out his Holy Bible to me. "Take."

I pushed it back at him. "No. You need this more than I. You have no books."

He patted the black leather cover. "This is most important. I know it in my spirit."

'Tis strange to accept such a gift from a native. Often it is the white man who imparts a gift of the Holy Bible.

"I am making you a gift," I said. "I will get it to you before the harvest. I know a native boy. I will send him. He may find comfort in meeting you."

He kissed me on the forehead and I clutched his arms, reluctant to let go. Even now, Lord have mercy on me, I wished him to beg me to stay, to offer to run away with me. I shan't ever know if I would have left with him, for he did not ask.

"Remember me with joy, Chickautáw. I will remember you the same. No . . ." He struggled for the word.

"Regrets?"

He smiled. "Yes. No regrets."

I turned to leave, my heart bucking at the space growing between us.

I pocketed the Bible next to his clamshell and ran all the way back home. When I arrived, Caleb sat in the garden. I nodded to him, mumbled something about checking on Papa, and disappeared inside. When I came out to milk the cow a bit later, he was gone.

CHAPTER 21

July swept past like a long train, each car a fleeting blur of my day. I paused only for the necessities—eating, showering, brushing my teeth and checking the mail. Work became automatic. I packed away Barb's house, setting aside things for the estate sale I planned to run in the fall. I went to the museum on Saturdays, wanting to finish the task given me by Barb and at the same time fearing its end. I hired an investigator to track Mary down after a simple Google and social media search hadn't turned up anything definite. I'd given him the old files Barb had kept on her daughter and still, I dug my feet in deeper, signing up for a class in August and pausing just long enough to call Essie when learning I was accepted for fall classes to begin my new career path.

A clock repairman finally returned my call. I left his message on my voice mail to remind myself to call him back when I got a minute, but that minute never came.

Matt didn't call. I missed him the two times he'd stopped by for the mail. I hated that our lives were settling into this routine. I hated that I grew accustomed to the everyday business of my life and the goals I'd set for myself. I hated that I was sometimes even okay about not seeing my husband for days on end.

One day Pete caught me coming off the elevators.

"Hey, stranger."

I tried not to look guilty. Yes, I'd been busy, but I'd also avoided Pete when I could. If I heard his voice in the room next door, I'd finish my duties quickly so I could be out by the time he came in. If I saw him walking toward me down the long hall, I'd duck into a patient's room to see if they needed anything.

"Hi, Pete."

His stethoscope hung uneven on his neck and I had an urge to lift a hand and tug it straight.

He stuffed his hands in his pockets. "You look dead on your feet."

"You sure know how to flatter a girl."

He laughed. "You still look beautiful. Just tired."

I tried to suppress the heat that climbed my neck. Instead, a burning sensation started behind my eyes. "I am tired."

"Well, slow down, kid." The four words were the most caring ones anyone had offered me in the past month and to my chagrin, a tear spilled onto my cheek. I hardly talked to my husband and son. I avoided my parents. Essie didn't sympathize —my go-get-'em sister only cheered me on from the sidelines.

Work, organizing Barb's house, planning my schooling— these were good things, weren't they? Why then did everything feel so wrong?

Pete pressed the elevator button and ushered me inside. I allowed him to, vaguely aware that he must have been going up to the ward for a reason. I should insist he return to his duties. He had real patients upstairs. He didn't need to take care of a single blubbering woman.

But I didn't want him to leave.

"I'm sorry," I whispered as more tears crept from the corner of my eyes. "I just need some more sleep."

He looked at me with a doctor's knowing stare. "You've run yourself ragged. And you mentioned summer classes? Maybe you should wait until the fall to start."

"I can't. I've already signed up and . . ."

The elevator doors opened and Pete led me outside to a bench set off in the garden entryway. The sun drifted lazily over the horizon. I loved summer nights, but I'd missed their beauty of late, too involved in my own problems, too busy getting Barb's house together.

"You have to live too. Dropping a course isn't going to throw you off that much. You'll probably be able to concentrate better in the fall. And maybe concentrate on living."

Right. Living. "I like the distraction."

"What do you need distraction from?"

"Oh, you know, just the living part of life." My words came out bitter. For all I knew, my husband dropped off the face of the earth. How were Matt and I to get past whatever this was if we had both become okay with a life apart from each other?

"You can talk to me, you know." Pete's voice softened. He didn't move closer on the bench. I sensed that if he had, I wouldn't have shied away. "I promise I'll keep all my ulterior motives in check."

"Those being . . . ?"

He ran a hand over his face. "I don't know, Sarah, maybe I've been kidding myself, saying I only want to be a good friend. But I'm almost ashamed to follow that line of thought."

If he was able to admit it, why shouldn't I? Why should I resist this man? He was ready to listen. He was kind, and I couldn't ignore the fact that I was attracted to him. My husband didn't want anything to do with me, was probably too busy on the Waterman yacht or taking runs on the Cliff Walk to think about his wife miles away.

It seemed I stood at the edge of a high boulder, ready to jump. Normally, I would set limits, rein myself in, guard my heart and my emotions. But I was too tired and too lonely to censor.

I jumped.

"It might be nice to talk about things."

"I'm listening."

"Now? Don't you have to go back upstairs?"

He grinned and the gesture highlighted the small dimple on his left cheek. "I was going to pick up some papers. I can grab them tomorrow." He stood and offered me his hand. "Want to get out of here?"

I lifted my fingers to his and allowed him to help me off the bench. My insides trembled at his touch. He felt steady and capable beside my tired and quivering frame, and I allowed him to lead me to his car.

He drove me out of the city and down a long stretch of byway until the road revealed glorious open space and wide sparkling ocean and sand. I smiled as some of the tension drained from my spirit.

"I haven't been to the beach yet this year." Matt should have taken me on Kyle's birthday. It would have taken us five minutes to walk there. But he couldn't even spare that for someone who wouldn't further his interests, further his business propositions.

Pete shed his white coat and rolled up his sleeves. I left my purse in the car and we strolled side by side into the setting sun. The waves didn't crash today. They trickled in. Soft and slow, like a caress upon the sand.

We walked. I told Pete everything. Matt's desire to take a break. The lack of communication. Lack of a desire to work at our marriage. I spoke of Kyle, how I missed him but didn't want to bother him and the time he had with his father. I told him of the disastrous employee dinner, of Cassie Waterman and the jab Matt had made about my golfing abilities. I told him about Elizabeth's journal, how it showed that troubles in love were as old as humanity, how I wasn't sure there was hope to be found, either in my case, or in Elizabeth's. I told him about school and the desire to prove myself, the desire to provide for myself if things with Matt continued to go downhill.

I hadn't allowed myself to ponder such a prospect until now. What if Matt asked for a divorce? Here, beside Pete on the beach, the sting didn't hurt as much as it should have. Was this Matt's intent all along? To break away from me gradually? To ease out of our marriage? A husband was supposed to tell his wife his deepest thoughts. A husband was supposed to work at a marriage, to expect bumps and bruises along the way. A husband was supposed to hold your hand through them.

Pete listened with intense interest and patience. When I finished, he didn't offer advice or apologies. My heart felt lighter. For the first time, I felt like maybe I *could* survive without Matt if I really needed to. I'd tried everything, hadn't I? The ball was in his court, and he hadn't even bothered to pick it up.

Part of me wanted to dive into this feeling—this feeling of not needing my husband. He'd put me through the wringer, that's for sure. Maybe my parents were right—maybe Matt and I had been a mistake from the get-go. And maybe my parents were wrong—maybe a pregnancy wasn't a good-enough reason for a marriage. Maybe I should have looked harder for a solution, braved the road of single motherhood, been less afraid and more courageous.

The last orange and pink rays of the sun disappeared from the horizon and Pete drove me back to the hospital. In the parking lot, I sat in his car, fumbling with my keys.

"Thanks, Pete. I needed that."

"I guess it's wrong to say I had fun listening to all your problems, but I did. I enjoy being with you, Sarah."

I swallowed the hot mass in my throat. This was too much, too fast. I was not the kind of woman who slipped into an affair so easily.

I opened the door to his Toyota. "I'll see you around?"

"You bet."

He waited until I started my car before driving away. I put my face in my hands.

What was I getting myself into?

June 21, 1675

Papa is dead.

Only he did not lose his lifeblood from the sickness that had invaded his body. He lost it at the hand of King Philip's men.

Life has turned into a nightmare this very day, as it has for our entire settlement. I am crammed into a corner in Andia's father's garrison, along with thirteen other families from our settlement. None sleep. The men, including Caleb, patrol by the windows and doors and whisper why it is that Mr. Cole, the leader of our local militia, is missing. After today, I do not feel safe despite their hovering protection.

Living in fear is a new and strange thing for me. One does not realize how terrible and all-encompassing fear can be until one must live it every minute.

I rode with Caleb to meeting yesterday. Papa insisted. I tucked Abram's Bible in my pocket, kissed my father's fevered brow, and bid him good-bye as if he would still be here when I returned.

Caleb spoke little on the way home. I smelled smoke in the air and saw it rising high above the trees as we neared Papa's homestead. My thoughts scrambled like a beaten egg as Caleb urged his mare to go faster. I had not left the cooking fire too hot, I was certain of it. Yet as we rounded the bend, my worst fears were realized. Flames licked the wood of the kitchen window and curls of smoke funneled to the clouds.

I did not wait for Caleb to stop. I leapt from his wagon, my wretched skirts in a tangle. I pushed through the door of our home. The fresh air brought a burst of heat and smoke to my face and I buried my nose and mouth in the sleeve of my dress. I pushed forward to Papa's bed. Flames had not yet overtaken it. Caleb's hands shoved me toward the door and he lifted Papa with an ease I could not manage. My chest squeezed, but I could not bear to leave two things. I lunged for the cabinet by the hearth—'tis near the door. I scooped up this bundle of papers together with the ink Caleb had gifted to me. I fumbled Abram's crude quilt out of the cabinet also, and brought it to my face. For just a moment, I breathed in the precious bit of air hidden inside the fabric instead of the clogged smoke of the house.

Caleb shouted and grasped for me as sparks and bits of wood rained upon us. He caught the quilt and pulled. I grasped it, and into the open air we fell. Caleb carried Papa away from the smoking building. He looked at me on the ground beside him, ink covering my dress, Abram's quilt still near my mouth.

Time seemed to still. I needed to check on Papa. Caleb would want to get the animals from the barn. Yet all I could see was the look of sadness on his face as he took in the picture I had appliqued on the quilt—an Indian with a massive rock behind him.

Abram and his rock.

He seemed to tear himself away from the pull of the quilt. He ordered me to stay where I was, then ran for the barn. Chickens scattered.

I shook Papa. He did not respond. His skin no longer felt heated. Black ash marred his face. I shook him again, frantic. I put my ear to his chest but heard nothing.

He was gone.

Neighbors came then. Men hauling buckets of water from the well to put out the flames. When the house was naught but a pile of ash, they left to check on the rest of the settlement.

'Tis no accident of the hearth, I heard them say. Three other homes were looted during meeting. Foodstuffs taken. Cattle shot. One other home besides Papa's was set ablaze.

'Twas the natives. They had attacked.

They killed Papa.

Caleb carried Papa's body carefully to his wagon, as tenderly as carrying a babe, as if jostling him would disturb his peace in heaven. I remember thinking about his big, strong hands, that 'twas strange they could be so gentle.

He told me I best leave the pieced quilt behind, that others in the settlement would not take kindly to seeing it. While he readied the wagon, I hastened to the barn, where one of Mama's trunks remained in the loft. I climbed the ladder, lifted the heavy cover, and placed Abram's unfinished quilt within its solid protection. I sat on the rock beside the barn and waited for Caleb to call to me. I did not look at the back of his wagon. 'Tis more than I could bear, seeing Papa's lifeless body shaken about in such a manner.

Papa died on a Sunday. 'Tis the day of the Resurrection. 'Tis a day of *miracles. 'Tis a day of rest and quiet. But death does not seem to know the days of the week.*

And neither, it seems, do the natives.

June 22, 1675
Late

Goodwife Howland snores lightly beside me. The stone walls of the garrison close around us. I know not which man is posted sentry outside the door, but I cannot sleep.

All was quiet today, and Caleb bore danger for the sake of digging a grave for Papa. We held a simple service inside the garrison. Caleb buried Papa a short ways off, near the river.

He finished his shift a bit ago. I sat against the cool garrison wall, awake. He slid down next to me. I did not resist when he put his arm around me. I buried my head in the crook of his arm and finally shed tears for Papa, tears of fear for what lay ahead.

"Will help not come?" I whispered into Caleb's shirt. It smelled of old soap and sweat, but I did not mind.

"Soon," he said, though I could tell he and the other men were worried.

I feel I know something the rest of them do not. I feel the weight of responsibility on my shoulders.

I know Abram, even if it seems as if our time together was so very long ago. Fear and sadness have a way of slowing down the days, of making all else seem unreal. The sole hope I have to grasp at this time was the garrison and the families in it. They were real to me. Caleb was real to me.

Yet Abram told me he had acquaintances—maybe even Captain Church. He may be able to secure us help quicker than Governor Winslow at Marshfield, for would not it take days to organize an army?

Part of me knew it madness to think a lone native in the woods would have better friends than our own men, but all our men were too busy here, protecting the women and children in the garrison. How else would anyone outside the settlement of Swanzey know we are in danger?

What if Abram could help?

Caleb fell asleep quick, and now I am up wrestling with my thoughts on paper.

I will wait another day. Perhaps help will come tomorrow.

June 24, 1675

A few militiamen arrived yesterday, nothing close to an army. They are scattered and unorganized, and spend their time making rounds to the homesteads while the men of our families continue to guard the garrison.

News came of more homes ransacked. Worse yet, Goodman Alby was shot by an arrow while taking his shift at the door yesterday morn. I heard the whiz of the arrow. I heard it hit flesh. He did not make a sound, other than his body hitting the dirt floor. Goodwife Howland says he will survive, that the arrow passed through his shoulder. The same is not true of one of the stout dogs belonging to Mr. Cobb. The poor creature sensed the natives in the forest and attacked. We heard a gunshot and a yelp. The beast has not returned.

Soon after, John Salisbury took opportunity to shoot one of Philip's marauding men. Our men's spirits lifted after that. 'Tis wrong to delight in death, but to my shame, I could not help feel an increase in my own soul as well.

Our high spirits did not last, for this very morning, John Salisbury and six others stole away to Goodman Alby's house. 'Tis close, but a quarter of a mile away. Their intent was to gather corn, for our foodstuffs run short. That was hours ago, and they have not yet returned.

Caleb is restless. I know he wants to see to the missing men. I also know he does not wish to leave the garrison without a proper amount of men to guard it.

And still, help does not come.

Darkness descends. I can no longer stand still.

I know what I must do.

CHAPTER 22

After reading an email from the Private Investigator I'd hired stating he'd found Mary and was putting pieces of information together for me, I sat on the back patio, sudden loneliness eating my insides.

I should be happy Mary was found. My obligation to Barb would soon end. And yet I couldn't deny that I'd been so wrapped up in Elizabeth's story that I hadn't given Mary as much thought as I should. Would the journal mean as much to her as it did to Barb? As it was becoming to mean to me?

This was why I didn't like to slow down. Slowing down meant feeling and thinking. Keeping busy meant distraction. Accomplishment.

On a whim, I picked up my phone and called Kyle's cell.

He answered on the third ring. "Hey, Mom."

"Hi, kiddo. I've missed you."

"Yeah . . . sorry I haven't called. Things have been real busy."

"Still working hard, huh?"

"Yeah." His tone stoked the embers of my heart. Something was wrong.

"Everything going okay?"

"Yeah, sure. Just getting anxious to get back to school and stuff."

And stuff.

"Talk to me, Kyle. Are things not going well with your job? With Dad?"

"No—no, they're fine." Pause. "Dad tell you he got a new motorcycle?"

The nerves behind my eyes tightened. "No. I haven't talked to your dad in a while." Too long. It had been too long. "He take you out for rides?"

"Naw, he offered, but you know, feels kind of weird . . . two guys on a bike."

"Uh huh." Somehow I felt the motorcycle was connected to what bothered Kyle. If only he'd come right out and tell me. "Bet your dad's spending a lot of time with his new toy, huh?" Maybe Kyle was hurt Matt wasn't around so much?

"Yeah. Hey, I gotta go. Greg and Blaine are picking me up in a few. I'm glad you called. Love ya."

"I love you, too."

The line went dead.

I waited ten minutes and called Matt's cell phone. I'd given him his space, but we still needed to talk, if for no other reason than the son we shared.

It rang five times, then went to his voice mail. I listened to his voice but didn't leave a message. He'd see that I called and call me back soon.

My heart stuttered as a motorcycle neared the drive. Despite the warm August night, I shivered on the patio and went to light the hearth. It had taken me a few times, but I figured if Elizabeth Baker could cook and live over an open flame, I could light one on my patio hearth. The motorcycle continued up the street and

my breathing returned to normal. I turned my attention to the
address in the email on my phone.

Mary Dawson
82 Castro Way
Sacramento, CA

A phone number was listed below it, as well as a paragraph
of information that stated Mary had been married twice and
now lived with one daughter and was a teacher's assistant in a
high school not far from her home.

I sighed. I'd need to contact Mary, but first I needed to finish
Elizabeth's journal this weekend.

I closed my eyes, my thoughts pulling.

Three days, two phone calls, and one voice mail later, Matt
still hadn't returned my calls. He'd have to talk to me sooner
or later. I half expected him to drive up on a whim with his
new motorcycle and announce that he was either ready to
come home or to leave me for good. It wasn't like him to be so
silent.

I heard a car engine in the front and held my breath.

"Sarah? You there?"

Essie. I released my breath. "In the back!"

She greeted me with a hug. "You know your eyes can fall out
from reading too much?"

I rubbed my eyes. "It's just an email. I haven't even started
school yet."

Essie sat down heavily in a patio chair and leaned back,
spreading her capri-clad legs in unladylike fashion. "You
excited?"

I closed my laptop. "I wish I were more excited than I am. I
think once the summer's over, once the estate sale is behind me
and I've made peace with whatever's going to happen with
Barb's daughter—and maybe my marriage—maybe I'll be
ready then."

"Jen told me you're the most competent nurse the hospital has. You're going to be a great NP."

"Thanks." I wanted to shout to the world, *See, I am good at something!* Maybe I'd failed as a daughter, maybe I'd failed as a wife, but I would not fail in this.

"So, Randy and I were in Newport last night."

I tried to think who Randy was, but my mind skidded on *Newport.*

"You saw Matt."

Essie pressed her lips together in uncharacteristic seriousness. "At first I didn't recognize him. He was on a motorcycle—a nice Harley. He pulled into the house you told me he and Kyle are renting, and when he took off his helmet, there was no denying it was him."

I breathed in deep through my nose. "What else," I ground out.

"I felt like you should know."

Black spots appeared before my eyes. I wanted to run upstairs to my bedroom and bury my head beneath the pillows. But I couldn't. I had to know. "Tell me." I didn't recognize my own voice.

"There was a girl on the back of the bike. I couldn't see much, but enough to see it wasn't . . . you."

Even now I tried to make excuses for Matt. Maybe he'd seen someone who needed a ride. Maybe he'd been helping someone. But only one face came to mind.

"D-did she have blonde hair?"

Essie nodded. "I didn't see much more than that. I mean, it could have been innocent—I don't know, I didn't see them making out or anything, but it just didn't look . . . innocent."

I didn't need to ask for details. I could picture Cassie's toned legs straddling my husband's hips. Her arms around him, her chest pressed against him as the engine rumbled beneath them.

I screwed my eyes shut and stifled a scream. Instead, I rose on unsteady legs and went into the house. I scooped up my purse and fumbled for the keys on the woven basket atop the entry table. This had to stop. I needed to confront my husband. If he wanted a separation, fine. If he wanted a divorce even, fine. But enough sneaking around with that—that hussy.

"Sarah, wait."

I ignored my sister's voice.

"Sarah." She blocked my way to the garage. "You can't go out now; you're not thinking."

"I'm thinking more clearly than I have in months. This needs to stop. I'm his wife!"

"Just come back and sit on the patio for a few minutes with me, will you?" Essie guided me to the back, where I'd left the fire burning.

I curled up in the fetal position on one of the chaise lounge chairs and smacked the arm with my hand. "I hate him." Riding that tramp around on his bike, and right beneath his son's nose, no less. No wonder Kyle was anxious to come home. His father was spending more time with the girl Kyle had a crush on than he was with him. Than he was with his mother.

"I couldn't not tell you," Essie whispered.

"You did the right thing. I just—I don't know what to do anymore."

"Try not to see it as black-and-white, you know?"

I raised my eyebrows, mustering all the sarcasm I could in a single expression. "No, I don't know."

"I mean, you told me yourself you've been spending a lot of time with Pete—"

"Don't go there, Essie. That's not the same at all."

"How do you know it's not the same? Would Matt be happy about you taking golf lessons from this guy, taking walks on the beach with him, talking to him about your husband? All I'm saying is give Matt a chance to explain himself before you go barging down there."

"I've given him almost two months to explain himself. He won't return my calls. What am I supposed to do? Wait around until all of Newport County knows what I don't?" I inhaled a quivering breath. "And Pete and I are colleagues. Nothing more."

I was thankful Essie didn't call me out on the lie.

"Matt started it," I mumbled into the pillow top of the chaise. I knew it sounded petulant, but it was true. I was the one who wanted to work things out, he just skulked away like the weasel he was.

Essie sat on the corner of the chaise. When the tears finally fell, she rubbed my back.

I hitched in shaky breaths through my sobs. "This isn't how I pictured things, how I pictured us."

"You need to talk to him." She rubbed small, concentric circles on my back. I closed my eyes as a last trembling sniffle overtook me. "Probably not tonight, and maybe not even tomorrow. But soon."

"I will." The smoke from the fire kept the mosquitoes away and my sister stayed with me until the red glowing coals of the embers finally died out.

CHAPTER 23

There's something satisfying about getting one's hands and knees dirty. I'd never realized it before, but I enjoyed weeding. For once, I ignored Barb's home and embraced the warm Thursday evening. Instead of waiting for Rodrigues Landscaping to pick my weeds on Saturday while I was at the museum, I donned a never-before-used pair of gardening gloves and pulled out the wide green blades of uninvited crabgrass beginning to crowd the climbing hydrangea.

I admired the clean area I worked on and moved to the left, where a bunch of orange marigolds grew with vigor. I didn't remember telling Matt I liked the color orange or marigolds, but somehow the flowers had appeared on the walkway leading up to the front porch, bright and sunny for all to see.

Cautious at first, I pulled one up by its roots.

And I thought pulling weeds was satisfying.

With each marigold uprooted, I celebrated my desire and capability to handle my own life, my own house, my own lawn. Maybe this weekend I'd go to the garden shop down the street and purchase something *I* wanted in the front of my house. Maybe a perennial instead—a purple lilac or asters or lilies— something that came back year after year despite the harsh winters and frigid cold. Something hardy and enduring. Something that persevered.

A truck engine rumbled up the drive, and I wondered what Louis and Greg would say when they saw me tearing out the marigolds. I turned to wave.

My hand fell. What would Matt say to me tearing out his marigolds?

He pulled up to the garage. Kyle hopped out of the passenger's seat with his duffel bag and raised a hand to me. "Hey, Mom." He disappeared into the house.

Matt lowered his phone from his ear and got out of the car. He walked toward me. I stood, brushing my hands on my shorts.

I would be civil. No, he hadn't returned my calls, but I would not lose my cool, even if part of me still wanted to jump down his throat with accusations.

I was about to manage a polite greeting, but he beat me to it. "What are you doing?" He looked at the marigolds, their bright, sunny heads on the edge of the lawn beneath smatters of dirt, their roots exposed to the harsh sun.

"Hi," I said, ignoring his question.

He flashed me an annoyed look. "*Hi.* What are you doing?"

"Just thought I'd plant a perennial here instead. You know, maybe lilies. What do you think?"

"I think you should let Louis and Greg do it."

I ignored the temptation to take the bait he held out. Did he think only someone who arrived in a Rodrigues Landscaping truck could accomplish such a feat? And why did he care so much anyhow? He hadn't seen the place—our home—in weeks. I clamped my mouth shut. We would end up arguing, but not about what either of us was really upset about.

"I didn't think you were bringing Kyle back until next week."

"He wanted to come home."

"Did he say why?"

"Maybe you should ask him. He's your son, too." Matt's tone was hard. I hardly recognized it.

"I know he's my son." I attempted control but felt myself losing it. "But I've barely seen him all summer." I dropped back on my knees and continued pulling up the marigolds. "I'll talk to him."

"Can you—can you just wait until I leave to do that?"

I shrugged. "Sure." I peeled off my gardening gloves. "We should talk."

"Yeah, we should."

"You want to go somewhere?" I asked.

Kyle stuck his head out the garage. "Mom, can I borrow the car? I want to meet up with some of the guys at Pizza Hut."

"Yeah, sure, honey. You'll be back later, right? I want to catch up."

"Sure thing. Thanks." I took note of how he ignored Matt's gaze, how he didn't say good-bye to his father, who likely wouldn't be here when he returned.

I stood. Kyle backed the Mercedes into the sidearm of the driveway and then drove out.

"You think that's a good idea?" Matt asked.

"What?"

"Letting him take the Mercedes."

"Did you plan on lending him your truck? Or maybe your Harley? Maybe you could let him borrow the cute little blonde attachment you've been riding around with on the back."

I didn't regret the words. Things needed to be out in the open, evaluated. It may hurt—likely me more than him—but it was time for us to have a real talk, to make decisions about our future.

Matt's jaw tightened. "I didn't think he'd tell you."

My knees weakened. Deep down I expected denial, maybe a plausible excuse. Not this, though.

"*He* told me about the bike, not about her." I couldn't manage to make Cassie's name cross my lips. Even in my mind it stirred up a blanket of nausea. If I spoke it, I'd probably be sick all over Matt's rosebushes.

"How'd you find out, then?"

A moot point. I ignored the question.

Matt lowered himself onto the porch steps. He clasped his hands over outspread legs. I tapped out nervous energy with my foot.

"Did you—are you—?" I couldn't finish. I hoped he wouldn't force me to.

Are you having an affair?

"I haven't slept with her." He sniffed, hard. "I'm sorry, Sarah."

My breaths hitched in tiny, short bursts. Black spots danced before my eyes. In some ways I wanted him to admit he'd been unfaithful. Admit he'd made a mistake. He was looking for restitution. Reconciliation. Instead, his answer was too calculated. It implied the horrible knowing that he was involved with another woman, not only physically but emotionally. And unless I read too much into his five-word-sentence, he did indeed plan to sleep with her. To be unfaithful. To move on and forget about me.

"I want to do this quietly, Sarah. I want you and Kyle to stay here, forever if you want. I'll take care of everything. But I'm not coming home. I think we need to start the process."

Not coming home . . .

Start the process . . .

I lowered myself to the ground, put a hand out to steady my unbalanced core. My fingers brushed the fuzzy head of a marigold.

Maybe I'd known it would come to this all along. That first day, on top of Abram's Rock when I had dropped my wedding rings, maybe I'd known this was where we were headed.

Or maybe I hadn't tried hard enough to fix us. Maybe I gave my husband too much space. Maybe things would have been different if I hadn't dropped the rings, if I had clung to my marriage with greater tenacity, with more intent.

"I don't want you to think this is just because of Cassie. There are about a million other reasons I think we need a divorce."

"Enlighten me, then, 'cause right now I'm in the dark." But was I? I was half of this marriage. I'd sensed things spiraling out of control for some time now.

"We got married so young, Sarah." He swore softly. "We were kids. We didn't have an opportunity to grow, to change into the people we were going to be before we were pressured into a decision to be with one another forever. But being married didn't stop us from changing. Only we didn't change together."

I pressed the palms of my hands to my eyes to keep the tears at bay. Did I believe the same? Did I believe that being young skewed my vision?

No, maybe growing older is what had skewed it. I'd grown hardened. I'd taken my husband for granted. My vision had gone fuzzy where once I'd seen clear.

"What do we have in common besides Kyle? What did we ever do together that didn't have to do with Kyle? Go out to dinner? Spend time in the bedroom?"

I didn't want him to speak of our physical act of love. It hurt too much. Like a hard, kinky ball of rubber bands wound tight around each other, one after another, after another. Hurt upon hurt upon hurt. I didn't think it would ever stop.

Images of Matt and Cassie in one another's arms, doing the things Matt liked to do. Younger. Prettier. Smarter. She'd probably be able to give Matt the other children he'd always wanted. And he was still young enough. He could be with her for another sixty years, making the seventeen we'd been married seem like a dip in the water compared to the long, deep swim marriage was meant to be.

"Please go," I whispered into my bent knees. I'd been so ready with my anger, ready to point out all the horrible things he'd done. But with his admission, I lost my fight. I just wanted to be alone.

His footsteps fell on the walkway. He went into the house, probably to grab the bills. His steps echoed loudly back on the pavement. The truck engine rumbled to life and then down the drive. Part of me wanted to run after him, throw myself at his feet, and beg him to love me as he once did.

But he'd made up his mind, probably long before today.

He no longer wanted me for his wife.

He would no longer be my husband.

I lay down, a pillow of dirt and marigold roots tangling in my hair. I allowed tears to fall and mix with the dirt at my head, a pile of slippery mud and wilting orange marigolds. They'd been thriving and surviving just an hour earlier, but now, like so much else, they were on their way to death.

The idea of divorce consumed my thoughts, Matt's words that he no longer wanted to be my husband festering and feasting on my insides, poisoning me. Even apart from papers or lawyers, his words had spread, oozing toxic thoughts and emotions into every aspect of life. They shoved into corners and crevices of my soul, stoking chords of hate and bitterness and resentment from my heart where love once resided.

I let it have its way.

I blamed Matt. Cursed him. Hated him. I tortured myself with images of him and Cassie.

Apparently, Kyle wasn't too far behind me.

He brooded the first two days he was home. I asked if he wanted to talk, but he always said no, busying himself by going out with friends or taking long runs or preparing for the upcoming school year.

I couldn't bring myself to go to the museum on Saturday. I didn't want to leave Kyle in the house alone, though by the end of the day I regretted my decision. I sat on my bed with the door open, twirling Lorna's ring on my finger. I took it off, thinking I would put it away for good. Forever. But as I sat with it, I knew it would go back on my hand that night.

I sensed Kyle's shadow at the door, and when I looked up, his eyes were red and blotchy.

It had been years since he stood at my threshold with tears in his eyes, looking for comfort.

"Oh, honey." I opened my arms and he gave me a sad smile. He didn't accept my hug but sat on the edge of my bed. The faint scent of fresh soap wafted into the room.

"I'm sorry, Kyle. I'm sorry it turned out this way."

"It's not your fault."

No, I really didn't think it was either, but there must have been something more I could have done or said over the years.

"Your dad and I . . . well, we've both made a lot of mistakes." That was the closest I'd come to admitting failure.

"I'm sorry I let you down. I told you I'd talk to him, and I tried. I did. But—"

"Stop it, Kyle. There's nothing you could have done. This is your father's decision, okay? He's a big boy."

I wanted to hurl some of my hateful thoughts about Matt into the air. I wanted to make sure Kyle saw my side, to make him as angry at his father as I was.

But anger wouldn't heal my marriage.

We were beyond that.

"I know you liked her," I said.

Kyle's face turned the shade of a second-place ribbon.

"I'm sure if your dad got that, he wouldn't have . . . I mean, I know it isn't right anyway, but with you there, it just makes it doubly wrong. I'm sorry."

"Crushes come and go. Marriages are supposed to stay." He fisted my bedspread in his hands. "I hate her, Mom. The worst of it is, Dad's so blind." He shrugged. "Guess I was too, for a while."

"A beautiful face can do that to a man."

"It wasn't just her face for me, although yeah, that wasn't too bad to look at. She was so alive. Exciting. Like anything's possible, you know?"

A wedge of hurt lodged in my chest at hearing about Cassie's good qualities, about what had attracted my son to her, about what likely attracted my husband to her as well. I pushed out a small sound that hinted of understanding, even though I understood none of it.

"But as she came around more, I saw another side of her, too. She started expecting me to get her drinks, get her bags. She'd ask me to go out with my friends so she could be alone with—" He stopped short, seeming to realize the effect his words had on me. "Sorry. My point is she's spoiled. Used to getting her way. She's the one who encouraged Dad to get the bike."

"I'm sure he didn't need much encouragement. He's always wanted one."

"Yeah, well, I don't think Dad sees her for what she is yet, but he will. Soon."

"And then what, kiddo? We forget she ever happened? Forget that someone just like her might come along again?" I placed Lorna's ring on my nightstand. "As much as I hate to admit it, Cassie isn't the only reason your dad wants a divorce. A healthy marriage can withstand a Cassie. It was already floundering when she came along; she just gave him the push he needed—or was looking for."

He hugged me then, and I tried to hold my tears back. "I love you, kiddo. We'll get through this. We will."

If only I believed my own words.

CHAPTER 24

June 27, 1675

The work of the devil is upon us. I fear that I never knew such evil could exist before this day, the most doleful that ever mine eyes have seen. I scarce know how to write of such things, but there is no other way for me to sort the events of the day than to do so.

There is nothing more for me to lose.

'Tis all gone, and I have blood upon my hands.

I am uncertain why I persist in writing. I feel my mind slipping, and I know that the only prospect to keep it sharp is to write. I often pretend I am back on Papa's homestead, writing in our garden. Then the strong scent of tobacco will overwhelm me, or the chanting of a native, and all pretense flees.

I waited until darkness swept the settlement the night I planned to see Abram. I tucked Abram's Bible and my journal in the pocket of my dress for fear another would stumble upon it in my absence. Caleb finished his shift, but lay down to sleep close to the garrison door. If we were attacked at night, he did not wish to have to step over a host of sleeping bodies to give aid.

The night was quiet, but I waited long. Mayhap too long. Sobs echoed off the stone walls. Many have been made widows and orphans in these days. The men who went to secure the corn never returned.

The garrison held a high window. A half moon shone through it and when at last it seemed all slept save for Goodman Cobb, the lone guard, I stood on a box of musket powder and silently hoisted myself through the window. I landed on a sharp splattering of pebbles and cut my hands. When I was certain I had not been seen, I crawled from the clearing into the nearby woods.

The scent of bayberry teased my nostrils, tempting me to think all was well. But all was not well, and I felt unless I made it to Abram to beg of his help, all would never be well again. Within the cover of woods, I stood and ran, the light of the moon as my guide.

I never knew such fear. I could be shot by an arrow at any moment. Hands could grasp me from behind. My head could be on a pole by sunrise. 'Tis a wonderful thing to live in peace, to not be frightened for thy life. Until now, I have taken it for granted.

Our plight pushed me forward. I could get to Abram. He could seek help. An army would arrive by tomorrow morn. And perhaps I would be back at the garrison before Caleb realized I had broken my promise to him.

I passed through Goodman Alby's backyard. The dirt road before his house shone in the moonlight. Along with it an unnatural lump on the side of the road.

I could not stop myself from looking.

Oh, but that I had controlled my curiosity.

If I had any innocence left, it fled at the sight of the headless, naked body of John Salisbury, his innards protruding in grotesque bloated form. Up the road I saw several other familiar lumps. I swayed. Sour bile filled the back of my throat.

I made it to the woods, and the small contents of my stomach left me, though the remembrance of the men's bodies never will.

My insides burned with sudden fever-like grip. I pushed through the woods, no longer feeling that anything was certain. One thought remained.

Abram.

The massive rock welcomed me beneath the moonlight. It, at least, never changed. In the far-off horizon, fingers of pink climbed the sky. It had taken me too long to reach my destination.

"*Abram,*" *my voice croaked, unrecognizable. I crawled toward his cave.* "*Abram!*"

His black head poked out and I fell to the ground in relief. He jumped from the cave and ran to me. "*Chickautáw?*" He helped me to my feet and I leaned against him.

"*Philip's men—they have attacked. Papa is dead.*"

Abram massaged my arms. I saw in his eyes that he knew. He knew we'd been in trouble.

"*Why did you not come?*" I asked.

He did not answer right away. When he did, I heard shame in his words. "*It is difficult being in both worlds. . . .*"

I sat on a small rock on the ground. What did I expect? Him to risk his life for me? What could he have done? He would have been killed, if not by the English, then certainly by Philip's men.

"*I failed. I did not learn Metacomet's plans until too late. I went to Church. He says he will go to Taunton to put together an army. I could not do more, Chickautáw.*"

He'd already gone to Captain Church.

And he was correct in saying there was no more he could do. His place was here, working unseen, waiting for and giving information. He was not a fighter, and I accepted that about him.

"*Is there nothing else to be done, then? You know of no one who can help us?*"

Abram shook his head. "*My other acquaintance already helps you.*"

I sniffed. 'Tis likely Abram's other friend was one of the men I'd seen dead in front of Goodman Alby's home.

In the distance, I heard something that traveled up and down my spine with the force of a thousand tiny pricks of a needle. Native war cries. I gripped Abram's arm. "*They are headed for the settlement.*"

"*No, Chickautáw. They come for me. They know of my betrayal. They will want my death before the death of the whites. You must go now.*"

The whoops and roars grew louder, bringing visions of headless bodies and arrows and blood.

The bloated body of John Salisbury.

Papa dead in Caleb's wagon.

"*Come with me,*" I said.

"*And bring more anger upon your people? No. I stay here. You go.*" I'd never heard his tone so firm.

"*Tell me the name of your acquaintance. Perhaps someone will come and help you.*" I knew it to be unlikely, but at least I would be able to give word of Abram's need.

"*Go, Chickautáw.*"

"*Please, give me a name!*"

"*If I give you a name, will you promise to leave?*"

"*Yes—yes, I promise!*"

The name that passed his lips sent me reeling back.

How could it be?

I asked Abram to repeat himself, and the very same name came forth.

Caleb Tanner.

I thought to know so much, and now all quickly unwound beneath me.

Abram pushed me in the direction of the settlement. The war cries grew louder, surrounding me all at once. I stumbled for the woods, tears in the back of my throat.

I could not bring myself to leave. I hid behind a smaller boulder in the distance, certain Abram didn't see me through the thick foliage. Sunshine lightened the area. The massiveness of the rock blocked the light from reaching Abram, still standing on the west side of it.

The first native who reached him seemed surprised he stood without a fight. He grabbed him and waited for others to arrive.

They did, in large numbers. They made way for a plain-looking native with a braid and a single feather in his hair. I wondered if this was the notorious King Philip.

He spoke to Abram. I could not understand his words, but Abram answered calmly.

The sachem looked around and pointed to the top of Abram's rock. He made a motion which I took to mean something falling from the rock. He held three fingers in the air, gesturing with the motion each time. I did not understand.

Two men led Abram up the steep slope. My pulse thrummed against my neck and temples. Would they push him off the top?

When the men reached the top, the two escorts backed away, leaving Abram at the edge.

Abram stood tall and proud. He looked in my direction and I wondered if he knew I never left. The natives started up a chant that swelled, erupted, and then came to a sudden stop.

Then, in one large bound, Abram jumped from the massive height.

I screamed.

I didn't see his body hit the ground. All I saw were natives running in my direction. I turned and ran through the woods as fast as I could, but hard copper arms captured me and dragged me back toward the rock. I fought against them with everything in me, but to no avail.

To my amazement, Abram was still alive. One of his arms was at a crooked angle and his head bled at the side, but he looked at me with sadness etched on the lines of his face.

Philip ripped my mobcap from my head and let it fall to the ground. He fingered my light hair and I shivered, the thought of being scalped causing my legs to tremble.

The two natives who led Abram to the top of the rock before did so again. When he neared the top, I squeezed my eyes shut and looked at the ground, burrowing my head in the rise of my shoulders. As they started up their terrible chanting, the native near me jerked my hair upward so hard I could scarce close my eyes. I braced myself for a knife to be pressed to my scalp. Instead, the native pointed to the top.

He wanted me to watch.

I understood then that the sachem had ordered Abram to jump three times from the rock. I didn't see how he'd survive another leap.

With my neck bent at an awkward angle, I kept my eyes on the man I loved. I wanted him to fight, to refuse such a fate, but again, Abram jumped. This time he didn't manage to leap out so far and I scrunched my eyes half shut to spare myself the sight of seeing him impaled on one of the jagged rocks below.

'Tis a terrible thing to watch, a man plummeting to the ground to meet his demise. A man already injured and hurting. A man I loved.

I heard bones crack, and when I turned my head into my sleeve, certain I would lose the contents of my stomach for the second time that day, the native holding my hair pulled my head up again. I choked on the sour bile in the back of my throat, on the sobs I could no longer suppress.

Abram could not get up of his own accord. The other men helped him. I scarce recognized his mutilated face, once beautiful.

"Chickautáw."

I swallowed the lump of emotion in my throat.

"Jesus meet my heart. And yours."

In that moment, I could make no sense of his words. All I could see was his disfigured body being hauled up the rock a third time.

"Please," I said. "Must you torture him so?"

The native beside me shook me hard by the hair. A clump ripped from my scalp.

When at last they reached the top, they placed Abram on the edge. He wavered, raised a crooked hand at me, and fell forward—this time, it seemed, welcoming death's embrace.

His body slammed against the top of his cave, his head knocking against a sharp rock on top. He fell not far from my feet in a defaced lump.

I prayed he was dead and his suffering gone. I prayed he was meeting his Jesus face to face at that moment. I prayed they wouldn't drag him up the rock again.

I searched his bloodied bare chest for sign of life and saw nothing.

Without warning, a shot sounded through the air. I jumped. The native who held my hair fell to the ground. My hair landed at my shoulders and I pushed it from my face to see what had happened.

Then the whoosh and stick of an axe, and another native beside me also fell. I stood frozen to the ground as another shot sounded and another native fell.

Then, from the thick of the woods . . . "Elizabeth, run!"

Caleb.

He'd come for me. Foolish man, he'd come for me.

I ran in the direction of the settlement, hoping Caleb could follow close behind.

But the natives regrouped quickly, readied their bows and arrows and a few muskets. From what I could gather, Caleb was alone. His single musket and a couple axes could not compete with their many men and weapons.

A path stood before me, calling me to freedom, and I hesitated. How could I leave first Papa, then Abram, and now Caleb to die at the hands of Philip's men?

The hesitation was time enough for a native to grab hold of me. A tussle ensued. Caleb hurled himself at my assaulter. He seemed to gain the upper hand, but more natives fell upon him.

With one last surge of strength, Caleb hurled his musket at one of the natives who held me. I felt the release of hands upon my body, but 'twas not enough for me to make an escape. Quick as lightning, one of the natives loosed an arrow.

"Caleb!" I called as I watched him fall.

More hands upon me, dragging me away, taking me with them, taking me from my proud Abram and my loyal Caleb.

They brought me to their camp, invited me inside their wigwams, offered me their food of ground-nuts and pork. I want none of it.

I am here still, refusing their food and their company.

I hate the beastly lot. How had I ever thought them harmless? They have taken everything from me. There is no future or hope on this side of heaven, and I am not altogether certain there is any hope for me there, either.

I care not if they kill me tonight.

"How's it going?"

I turned from my laptop at the sound of Jill's voice. I shook my head, still in a trance from what I'd just read. "I'm sorry. I didn't realize it was closing time already."

I didn't want to leave Elizabeth in this place of despair. Both the men she cared for were dead. How would passing on this story to Mary inspire anything good?

Jill glanced at her phone. "You still have a couple of minutes, but your son's waiting for you in the foyer. I was curious about what you thought, though."

"Of Elizabeth's story? It's amazing, but sad. Barb seemed to think it would heal or inspire hope or forgiveness. . . . I'm not seeing it yet."

The young woman smiled and opened the case that housed Elizabeth's journal. "Hang in there." She turned to me. "I think sometimes we might not recognize hope until we've been in the darkness."

I pondered her words, feeling their truth, wondering if my own life would ever meet hope again. I thought to affirm that Jill was right, or at least thank her, but no words came forth. All I could feel was anger and resentment, for both my situation and Elizabeth's.

I stood and Jill worked to pack up Elizabeth's pages. I couldn't imagine not coming back for an entire five days. Briefly, I entertained the thought of calling out sick tomorrow, but the picture of Jen and the rest of the team pulling extra weight because of my absence caused me to lay aside the idea.

I packed up my laptop and thanked Jill, telling her I'd be back the next weekend.

Whether hope resided in the remaining pages of Elizabeth's journal or not, I intended to finish it—not only for Barb, but for myself as well.

CHAPTER 25

Jen caught me in the hall the following day. "Is it just me, or are you avoiding me?"

I had been. Though it wasn't her I was actually avoiding, but all of my coworkers. I hadn't told anyone about Matt's mention of divorce. Not Essie, not my parents.

"Things have been busy, that's all. How're the boys?"

"Camden was up sick for most of the night, poor kid. I'm assuming his brother will be next." Another nurse called to her from down the hall. "Waiting for a call from a doctor. Catch up later? Oh, can you check on Mrs. Gordan? She said her stomach's bothering her."

"Sure. I hope Camden feels better soon."

She flashed me a smile and I turned to attend Mrs. Gordon, but slammed into a hard chest covered in a white lab coat.

"Whoa, there. Where you off to in such a hurry?" Pete placed his hands on my arms.

I'd avoided him, too. But here and now, I realized I was glad to see him. "Room 324."

"Mrs. Gordon. Just came from there. Might not be pretty."

I snorted. "I didn't get into this field for beauty."

"Oh, I don't know about that. What you do—helping the patients here . . . I think that's pretty beautiful."

I blushed. This man always seemed to know what to say. "Thanks."

"How's the golf swing? I think it's time we get you out on a real course."

It sounded like an invitation for a date. I'd spurned him too often. And now, with my marriage shattered, what was the point? Matt rode around Newport, Cassie tucked cozy on his bike behind him. With Kyle out of his rental house, who knew what went on.

I shivered.

"Is a course that intimidating? We'll do a small one. I know a good par three course not far from your house."

I forced a smile. "That sounds good."

He straightened. "Really?"

I laughed at his obvious surprise. "Really. Maybe we could grab a bite to eat, too."

His eyebrows shot up, making him all the more charming. "Yeah...yeah, that'd be great. How's Saturday? I'll schedule a tee-off time."

"Sure—ah, sorry, I take that back. I need to finish up the journal on Saturday." Okay, I didn't need to. I wanted to. Surprisingly even more than I wanted to spend the day with Pete.

"No problem, I understand."

Why was I surprised that he genuinely seemed to? Because Matt had never bothered to ask or care? Or maybe because I couldn't picture him even pretending to do so?

But the comparisons had to stop. If I was going to move past Matt, if I was going to allow something between me and Pete, I would have to like Pete for Pete—not because he had proven himself a better man than my husband.

My husband.

Something curdled in my stomach—the same feeling I'd had when reading of Elizabeth watching Abram's last fall from his rock. The same feeling I had when realizing it was Caleb who had come to her rescue, Caleb who had given his life for her.

Unconditional love.

But no one expected me to love my husband unconditionally at this point. The moment Matt had chosen divorce—the moment he'd chosen Cassie over his wife—I'd been excused.

The thought made me feel only marginally better.

"What about Friday night?"

I stared at Pete, not really seeing him. I blinked, shook my head. "Yes—yes, Friday's great."

"Great." He said good-bye and walked down the hall, a light spring in his step.

I couldn't remember the last time I'd made someone so happy.

And the idea of a date wasn't really so terrible. My vows were practically meaningless at this point. Matt had broken them. They were as good as my wedding rings—forever gone, forever missing.

Like poor Abram, dead at the bottom of a rock.

———

Four days later, a divorce petition was handed to me by my mailman. It struck me as odd that it would reach me in such an impersonal way, by courier, the unfamiliar name of a lawyer neatly typed on the certified mail envelope. Shouldn't Matt hand it to me, be here to look me in the eye? I didn't want us to be one of those ex-couples who never spoke to one another, who constantly pitted our child against each other.

No, there was a right way to do this, and it wasn't by mail.

I tore open the envelope. Who was I kidding? There was no right way to go about this. No right way to permanently disconnect yourself from a person you shared a life with.

I sat at the breakfast bar and inhaled the fresh smell of rain on pavement. It trickled lightly outside, watering the grass and flowers, bestowing life upon them.

But it also trailed tears down the windows.

Could something be both good and bad? Could good come from my divorce? I thought of Mrs. Rhinehart. I remembered Elizabeth writing of beauty from ashes. I didn't see how God could ever bless a failed marriage, but certainly he couldn't bless a marriage in which my husband was unfaithful, either.

I looked at the papers. Crisp, black writing contrasted the brilliant white paper. It all looked so neat and clean, but I knew the papers lied. What waited was messy.

I looked it over, the realization that Matt really wanted to go through with this hitting me as hard as the edges of his familiar signature on the petition—the first step in what was certain to be a lengthy process. At the bottom was a request that I file a response—in essence, sign and agree to the separation—within thirty days.

I wanted to tear the neat papers in two. Flush them down the toilet or place them on the lawn and mow them up until they were nothing but shreds.

Instead, I tucked the papers back in the envelope, opened a cabinet on the side of the bar, and placed them beside my cutting boards.

I wasn't ready for this. If I signed, I was indicating I agreed with the divorce. That it was okay by me. I simply couldn't agree to the dissolution of seventeen years with the stroke of a pen.

I slammed the cabinet door closed and took out my phone to play the message from the clock repairman. I jotted down his number and dialed it. He picked up on the second ring. An older gentleman who spoke slow and crackly, like a beat-up old record. I made an appointment for the following week, thanked him, and said good-bye.

I laid my head in my arms and lightly kicked at the

woodwork beneath the breakfast bar, where Matt's divorce papers were hidden.

Outside, rain continued to dribble tears on the panes of the windows.

CHAPTER 26

The challenge of golf is that there are about a million possible directions the ball can go. Far off to the right, in a thick tangle of shrubs. Far to the left, in the wrong fairway. Not far enough, splashing into a water hazard. Close to the green, but off to the side, in a sand bunker.

It takes skill and persistence to get that ball to cooperate. And there's only one shot. If it's not right the first time, the score on the hole is at stake.

Unless the golfer can recover. Unless they can rally their efforts and tenacity and make a good, clean shot on the second stroke.

In golf, the players get a second chance, their opportunity to do things right.

I think that's what I was coming to like about the game.

I took a deep breath, raised my driver, kept my eye on the ball, and followed through until the head of the club connected with the word *Titleist* printed in flowing script on the hot-pink golf ball. Pete had given me a small bag of identical ones before we teed off. I liked them. They were flashy and different from the normal white. They stood out.

Maybe that would help when I needed to search for my ball in the hedges.

I kept my arms poised, my driver aimed toward the white flag flying in the breeze, and I didn't release my stance until the hot-pink blur landed on the green, bounced once, and rolled within three feet of the hole.

"Yes!" I did a small, excited jump—certainly not suitable etiquette for a golf course. I wish my first thought wasn't of how proud Matt would be of me had he seen the shot.

Pete gave me a high five. "Nice. You showed me up."

We gathered our bags and started the 150-yard walk to the green. "I still have to putt. That could be a disaster."

"You're doing great."

"Thanks."

"You getting excited for school?"

Excited wasn't exactly the word. While I didn't regret my decision, I wondered if now was the right time. "Truthfully, I've been thinking about putting it off." I cast a quick glance at Pete. "Matt's asked for divorce." There, I said it out loud. I said it out loud and I was still living. I was still breathing. It might hurt like the dickens, but I was still standing.

"I'm so sorry, Sarah."

"Really?"

We kept walking, and he dragged in a breath that was visible beneath his polo shirt. "No . . . and I'm sorry for that, too." He put a hand on my arm. "I am sorry you're hurting, though."

I swallowed down my misgivings. Matt probably occupied Cassie's yacht right about now. Or maybe they rode the Harley, or shared a drink after a round of golf, or a kiss on the beach.

I sniffed, tried to gather myself.

"I know it's none of my business, but school might be just the thing for you in this season. And I'd be happy to help you study."

I gave him a sidelong glance. "I bet I'd be the only student with a medical doctor for a tutor."

"That's right. It'll be good for your education. We made a great team in undergrad chem lab—we'd probably make a great team getting you your NP license."

I smiled at his willingness to help, but shook my head slightly, not wanting to encourage him too much.

I placed my golf bag off to the side of the green and slid my putter from the bag as Pete removed the flag from the hole.

One thing I hadn't told Pete was how the petition sat in my cutting board cabinet.

I set up for my putt and tried to clear my head. If I made the shot, it would be my first birdie. The ball skimmed the edge of the hole and veered to the left. I groaned.

Second shots weren't always about redemption. Sometimes those were a mess, too.

Pete and I both finished the hole at par. We played five more holes and headed for his Toyota. He drove toward Rhode Island. He must have sensed my tension as we veered onto Route 24.

"We're only going to Tiverton. Is that too close to Newport for you?"

He could read me better than a Kindle screen. "That's okay. I'm up for it."

We parked at a restaurant situated on Sakonnet Bay, the sun's red rays shimmering off the water. I reached for his hand and squeezed it.

"What was that for?" A lazy grin played on his face.

"Just for being here."

"I'll be here all you want if that's what I'm going to get."

I smiled. I found myself doing that a lot with this guy. "I mean it. This has been the worst time of my life, but having you here has made things more bearable."

The smile fled his face. He turned toward me. The radio hummed in the background, too quiet for me to make out the song.

"Is it weird to admit that I had a small crush on you back in that chem class? Of course after I saw your wedding ring, I didn't entertain it, but before I knew . . . well, before I realized . . . you had the best laugh. You still do."

I smiled, but I felt the sadness tugging at its corners.

How would things have been different if I hadn't been wearing Lorna's ring in that chem class? If I was just a struggling single mother trying to make something of myself? Would Pete have asked me out? Would we have dated through college? If we'd married, would we still be happy now? Would we have had children? Played golf together? Worked together? Or would we have grown stale and crusty like Matt and me? Was the problem me, or Matt, or maybe the both of us together?

I reached for Pete's hand and it warmed my insides. "It's not weird. We were young. You probably wouldn't have expected . . ."

He lifted his other hand to my face, brushed a strand away from my ear and allowed his thumb to trail down my cheek. When he leaned in to kiss me, I met his lips.

I'd never kissed another man besides Matt. I couldn't help but be surprised by the newness of it, the electric jolts it sent to my many nerve endings.

And still, it was wrong. On so many levels.

I pulled away.

"I'm sorry," he said. "It's too soon. Just tell me to back off."

I hiked a deep breath to fill my suffocating lungs. "I don't want you to back off, and that scares me. I also don't want to let my marriage go, and that scares me. I still love Matt, Pete. Pretty stupid, huh?"

"If you stopped loving him, it wouldn't be real love, would it?"

I thought of Caleb, persisting for Elizabeth's hand despite her unfaithfulness. Yet that was different. I wasn't in the seventeenth century. Neither me nor Matt would be banished from society over our choices. No one's life was at stake.

Physically, anyway.

I rubbed my temples. "Dumb love is more like it."

"Love doesn't judge well."

He was right. Love didn't know practical thinking. It was a free-spirit sort of thing. Uncalculated, unreserved. That's what made it dangerous. Love couldn't be controlled. I thought of Elizabeth's forbidden love for Abram, of Caleb's unrequited love for her. No, I couldn't control my love for Matt, or his for me.

And yet, if one felt love for someone outside of marriage, weren't they expected to control it? Harness it? Leash it or lock it, whatever felt safest? If those first heady feelings of love were allowed to go where they chose, not a marriage would survive.

Marriage required love, but it also sought faithfulness. Perseverance. Belief in the vow taken seventeen years earlier.

Somewhere along the way, Matt and I lost belief in our love. Now, we flirted with trust in someone else's love. No doubt, someday, that love would also disappoint.

Unless we kept believing.

Matt had stopped believing, but did that mean I must also? If I signed those papers, it would be an acknowledgment of disbelief.

As long as I didn't sign them, Matt was still my husband. I was still believing in us.

"Let's go in," I told Pete. "For now, let's just enjoy each other's company. I can't handle figuring things out anymore. Me and Matt, Cassie and Matt, me and you . . . it's just too much. I want rest."

Pete told me he understood. He ushered me into the restaurant, the water shimmering before Aquidneck Island. On the opposite side of that island lay Newport, and my husband. And Cassie.

My own belief had never gotten me far—my trust in God, my trust in myself, and now my trust in my marriage. My faith in all these things floundered like a fish on the shore, its gills stretching for air.

Because belief needed something else—it needed someone else. Belief didn't walk well alone.

"You don't have to go, honey." I stood at the threshold of Kyle's room, a baseball cap in my hands.

"I know, and just between you and me, I don't want to go. But things have been tense between Dad and I. He said it, too. He wants me to come for one more weekend, clear the air before school starts and cross country takes up all my time."

"Sounds wise. And you know, you can always call me if you want to come home. I have no plans besides the museum and hanging out here."

"Thanks." He smirked. "I almost have enough for that Chevy down the street. Think if I ask Dad to pitch in, he will?"

I wanted to tell Kyle it was the least he could do, but I clamped my mouth shut, congratulating myself for doing so. "It's worth a shot."

He scooped up his duffel bag and followed me down the stairs. From outside the screen door, Matt's engine rumbled. I hadn't heard him pull up.

Kyle pecked me on the cheek. "Have a good weekend, Mom." He opened the screen door. Matt appeared on the step.

"Hey, buddy. I'll meet you in the car, okay?"

"Sure." Kyle walked down the path.

Matt stepped inside. "The lilies look nice."

I'd chosen a more delicate perennial. I'd read somewhere that marigolds were hardy annuals, that they lasted longer than others. I didn't want something strong and temporary there right now. I wanted something that symbolized how I felt— fragile and delicate, but willing to persevere through many tough winters.

"Thanks." I hid my left hand behind my back. I still hadn't taken off Lorna's ring.

Matt raked his own left hand through his hair where his ringless finger pierced my heart. "Hey . . . I figured while I'm here I'd check to see if you have those papers for me."

I rubbed the spot between my eyes. "No, I haven't had a chance to go through them yet. There's a lot there, Matt."

He didn't say anything.

"What's the rush, anyway? You're not ready to marry her, are you?"

"Sarah . . ."

"Right, no arguing. But give me some time, will you? I haven't been the one away for the last two months planning this—"

He cut me off with a curse. "I didn't plan this."

"Whatever. The point is I'm going to need to get used to the idea before I sign anything."

"Fine."

"Fine."

He left without saying good-bye and relief descended upon me when his truck disappeared from sight.

Why did I cling to a lifeless marriage with a man I didn't even like anymore?

CHAPTER 27

June 29, 1675

The natives celebrate every night. With much chanting and roaring and singing and dancing and yelling, their perspiring bodies move around the fire with furious movements. Surrounding them are the remains of horses, cattle, sheep, swine, and fowl which they have plundered from our town. They eat of it, and trade English clothes and dinnerware, which they have stolen from the settlement.

I had thought to find adventure among them, but seeing the viciousness, I am filled with disgust. Yet this bloodlust must not be all, for poor Abram was nothing but kind and gentle. And yet I can no longer think of Abram with tender love, for these heathens have even ruined him for me—both his lifeblood and his memory. When I see one among them who resembles my Abram, I hope for kindness but he only sneers at me as he walks past. A bit of the memory I hold of Abram dissolves. So I cling to the image of him at the rock, telling me I am part of his spirit.

I have trained my thoughts to search for the Lord instead of searching for memories of Abram. All is gone. Papa, Abram, Caleb, even the settlement. I know not if Andia or Goodwife Howland still live or if the natives have attacked, plundered, and killed all. I cannot get the sight of

John Salisbury's headless body out of my mind, of Abram's mutilated form. I am broken. I have only Abram's God, or I have nothing.

I think often of Caleb, of the fierce and tender love he held for me. My hands are stained with his blood. I imagine what would have become of us had I never fled to the woods, had I never met Abram. My heart is indeed fickle, for it is Caleb I mourn with tenacity. Strange how I so often accused him of being a bore, of being content that nothing surprising happens to him.

How foolish I was. All along, he worked with Abram, and likely others, to secure protection for our village. I realize now he kept the secret for our own safety. I think of the arrow he took to spare my life. I think of how he came to find me, to protect me—alone—and how he must have known how such a mission would end.

How I wish to turn back the hands of time to save Caleb's life. Yet why is it I mourn him so deeply? Why does my heart not dwell more on my Abram? I fear it is because of the part I played in Caleb's death. I fear it is because I spurned his ever-giving heart. If it were not for me, he would live.

And yet it matters little whom I mourn. I cannot trust even my own heart. The Wampanoag have ruined it.

The natives I am with—Metacomet's tribe—relocate often. They have joined with Abram's old tribe—Weetamoo's. They set up their wigwams and mats in haste but seem to realize that they will not stay in any one place for long.

I wait for my salvation, or death.

June 30, 1675

The natives trade me. This be my third family. They bid me make shirts for their papooses. One of the wives of my master, who often feeds me strawberries and ground-nuts and other victuals, handed me Abram's Bible today, along with an ink-like mixture I am able to put to use.

I did not realize I lost it in the fray, but somehow she came upon it and gave it to me. 'Tis a kindness I will not soon forget. I am glad to be with this family, who shows more compassion than the others and who even speak a small amount of English.

I suppose it is unfair to group all of the natives as savages, though it is tempting to do so. I oft wonder if Andia's slave boy thinks any differently of the English.

I cannot ignore the stain of blood on Abram's Bible. I know not if it be native or English. Our skin colors differ, but I have seen enough of both sides to know our lifeblood runs the same shade.

Most of the beginning of Abram's Holy Book is stained with the wretched color. It runs red, but dries a deep brown. I am reminded of the animal sacrifices offered up in the Old Testament, whereas the Gospels tell of one sacrifice, and it is the one Abram held most dear.

I wonder what it means for me, a lone girl amid war and ugliness. After my fingers turned raw and numb from sewing the shirts, I was given rest and read from the unstained pages of the Bible. I have read them before, but this time I clung to them. I am drawn to the suffering of Christ. For the first time I feel a kinship with this God of the weak.

I think of Caleb's sacrifice for me, of his love. I am filled with shame.

Over and over I read, and yet one verse I have found my heart clings to. "And he said unto me, My grace is sufficient for thee: for my power is made perfect through weakness."

I read this and shed warm tears, for I cannot deny that the words are like sweet balm to my wretched heart. 'Tis nothing but this. 'Tis nothing but His grace and promise and finished work to see me through. 'Tis all I have left to cling to.

July 1, 1675

The English attempted to make contact with the natives today. A gentleman approached the heavily armed natives. "Church," Weetamoo said. The female sachem was dressed in her English makeup and jewelry, which she usually saved for their rituals. Today, she entertained conversation with Captain Church in her wigwam.

Captain Church wasn't at all how I had pictured him. No older than

Caleb, he looked tired and battle-worn, not the regal bearing I had made out in my mind, but for all appearances' sake, very much a common man. I made it a point to come out of the wigwam so he could see I was held captive. I hoped he would manage negotiations for my release, but to my disappointment he left, leaving me with scarce a nod of acknowledgment.

The English attempted an attack soon after. 'Twas a poor battle plan, however, for the natives outnumbered them greatly and the English did not seem willing to persevere. My master made me hide in his wigwam. I prayed.

At least Captain Church knows I am here. But are there any left to care? Will Goodwife Howland or Andia persist for negotiations for my release? Will Andia insist Hezekiah help me? Do they even know what has happened to me, or do they assume me dead along with dear Caleb? Worse yet, do they assume my betrayal, knowing my friendship with Abram? Perhaps they have it in their minds to leave me with what I deserve.

I wonder if I shall ever be found.

July 4, 1675

A young native approached my master today, his pockets full of wampum and his hands with English goods. He made plain his intent to take me as a wife.

I read in the Scriptures of the Lord knowing our every struggle. I try to find comfort in this truth, and yet I think to be a captive wife to one of these men would be more than I could abide.

I hid behind my master's heavyset form, hoping the cloud of pipe tobacco he smoked within his wigwam would secrete me away. My body took up such a fierce perspiring I thought the scent of my sweat would be enough to bid the young native take his leave.

Yet he did not.

My master looked kindly upon me and refused the offer. When the young native left, I fell at my master's feet and clasped his ankles, thanking him. He seemed uncomfortable with this and bid me go back to making shirts.

I did so with uplifted spirits. I was saved from a worse fate. Surely the Lord does watch over me.

July 11, 1675

We have removed once again a short distance from our previous spot. I know not where we are, but I know the fighting has spread. I hear the war cries from both natives and English. Whatever happened on that Sunday of long ago—could it truly be only weeks?—has spread throughout Massachusetts Bay.

The natives keep up their dancing rituals. My mistress tells me they own many gods, and they call on the name of each one in their pleas for victory. My mistress is partial to Kautantowit, whom she calls the great south-west god. She claims he provides the corn and beans and that all souls go to him at life's end.

When she asked of my beliefs, I speak to her of the God in my book who shares some of the same qualities as Kautantowit. 'Twas nearly pleasant to share a piece of my heart with this woman. Yet she seemed distraught when I tell her that my God died for me. She shushed me and I went back to sewing shirts.

July 19, 1675

There is a certain type of peace that comes in accepting one's circumstances. I cannot say I am happy to be among the natives, but I have come to accept my position among them and be glad that I have kind owners.

I have also come to a place where I no longer regret my friendship with Abram. My only guilt is that of Caleb's demise. I fall asleep each night seeing Abram's lifeless body and Caleb's dancing eyes and gentle smile. They each haunt me in different ways.

July 24, 1675

The young native has returned asking my master for me. He looks at my golden hair as if he cannot wait to have it for his own. This time, he brought skins and mats and double the wampum. I feared my master would not be able to resist such a trade.

When he finally said no, the young native, whose name I gather to be Naveen, left the wigwam in a whirlwind of fury. I did not dare to look at my master. He is kind, but he does not love me, nor do I wish for his love. Soon my worth will be better to him in wampum and English trinkets and I will be owned by the young native Naveen.

'Tis not how I envisioned marriage.

God, my Rock, help your daughter.

July 28, 1675

My mistress has taken Abram's Holy Bible from me and burnt it in their fire. Their dark bodies danced around it and I think for certain the devil must be present.

My mistress took the Bible when I told her my beliefs that there is but one God. She seemed frightened of me and shooed me from the wigwam.

I saw my master enter Naveen's wigwam soon after. When they came out, Naveen was smiling at me as if I were a piece of tasty lamb he could not wait to devour.

July 29, 1675
Morning

A most wondrous thing has happened this day!

Caleb.

Caleb is alive! I could scarce believe my eyes when he entered Philip's camp, an escort at his side. I fell to my knees at the sight of him, tall and strong and well. At first I thought I must have mistaken him for another, but he smiled at me and beckoned his escort allow him to come near where I sat outside my master's wigwam.

I groped for his hand and touched his bearded face. He pulled me to him, kissing the top of my head. I inhaled the scent of woods and musket powder and sweat and cried all the harder.

My tears stuck to his shirt. He asked how I fared, told me how glad he was to see me. I could not speak, though I longed to tell him how my fickle heart ached for him all these days, how I was sorry to have run away that last time.

He whispered into my ear. "All I wish to do is hold you in my arms forever and take you home, but we must not let them see how badly I want you. 'Twill make negotiations more difficult."

I nodded bravely and released Caleb. My master bid him inside his wigwam. I could make out their low voices. Caleb spoke the Wampanoag language well, and I thought once again what a fool I had been to think I knew him when in fact I knew so little.

They came out together a short time after. Caleb confirmed what I thought to know. I had been sold to Naveen. He wished to take me as one of his wives. My master said Naveen didn't want me until my upcoming isolation time was over.

The natives bid the women running their monthly courses into a common isolation tent during this time. I had forgotten my time would come soon, but apparently my master hadn't. 'Tis why I had not yet been given to Naveen.

Caleb told me he would go and speak with the young native. I watched Caleb enter Naveen's wigwam and though I made haste lifting great petitions to the Lord that all would go in his favor, my hopes plummeted.

When Caleb came from Naveen's wigwam, I saw the defeat in his stooped shoulders and grim mouth. They allowed him to approach me, guard in tow.

He ran a hand along my cheek. "I offered him all I have," he said.

"'Tis all right." I kept my tears in. "I am only glad to see you are well. I thought they'd killed you. . . . Please forgive me."

"You are forgiven, little Elizabeth."

I basked in the glow of his name for me. At the same time, I realized that once again, Caleb was my only hope. "I am to be his wife. Caleb, how will I get along?"

He ran his hand beneath my hair and ever so gently—so I did not think that the others noticed—he slipped something rough beneath the collar of my shirt. He pressed it tenderly against my skin.

In a louder voice, for his guard to hear, he said, "I will be back to offer more." He kissed me on the cheek.

And then he was gone.

I told my mistress I would be gone but a moment to relieve myself. When I was alone in the woods, I slipped the rough paper from my collar and unfolded it.

Make for the isolation tent.
Run north when the moon is directly above.
I will be waiting.

My head pounded as I read his words. When I had written them on my heart, I dug a hole in the ground with my fingers and tucked the words inside, so as not to be found.

When I returned to my master's wigwam, I told my mistress that my course was upon me. Soon after, I took up residence with six native women in the isolation tent.

July 29, 1675
Evening

Word has come from Philip that we must prepare to leave this place for another. We will begin our journey tomorrow and I can only pray I will not still be among the enemy.

There is much distraction among the camp as they prepare to go northwest to the land of the Narragansett. The English must be pressing in for the natives to want sudden escape. I know their men will be drunk on feasts and dancing and worshiping their gods tonight.

'Tis a good night to prepare for Caleb's plan. I only must sneak by the six other women in the tent. The Lord be with me.

CHAPTER 28

Mariah let out a low whistle when she entered my house for the first time. "Geez, girl. Your ex left you with all this? Wish mine was so generous." Apparently telling Essie about my impending divorce meant half of Bristol County also knew of it.

I rolled my eyes. "Yeah, generous. But he's not my ex. We're not divorced." I led her to the back patio, where Essie, Katie, and Jen sat sipping champagne. It was Essie's idea to invite them. Pete had asked me to go to a fair with him tonight, but I resisted. Two date nights in a row was too much. Having the girls over gave me a perfect excuse to politely turn down Pete's offer.

Flames crackled in the fireplace, keeping away mosquitoes. The mid-August nights held a chill to them, promising days of apple picking and pumpkins and fall foliage. The kitchen timer beeped and Essie joined me in the kitchen to fetch the stuffed mushrooms and potato skins from the oven.

"This isn't too much for you, is it?" Essie asked as she placed the mushrooms onto a serving platter.

"It's nice, actually. Things have been lonely around here, even with Kyle home."

"You sign that petition yet?"

"Not talking about that tonight."

"Got it." She tapped her hand on a freshly printed stack of papers—Elizabeth's story that I'd transcribed so far—before grabbing up a platter of mushrooms in one hand and a set of plates in the other. I followed her outside.

"Whatever happened with your neighbor?" Jen gestured to Barb's property before serving herself a mushroom. "Have you gotten in touch with her daughter?"

I'd confided in Jen on a break at work one day, weeks earlier. We hadn't talked of Barb since.

"No. I'm actually working on it."

"And spending every spare second you have doing it," Essie said.

I rolled my eyes, thinking I should clarify. "Barb left me a letter in her will requesting I find her daughter and give her the story of one of her ancestors. I've been transcribing it from a museum in Plymouth."

"Sounds like a lot of work." Katie wiped her mouth with a napkin, then tucked it under her plate so the wind wouldn't blow it away.

"It is, but it's interesting, too." I swallowed, not sure how much to share with them, but feeling the sudden need to open up to these women, to feel understood. "Barb thought there was something there worthwhile. I spent the entire day working on it and I'm nearing the end. I think I'm getting a glimpse what it might be."

Essie raised an eyebrow. "And . . . ?"

I inhaled a deep breath. "It's about finding hope when we're at our weakest. About the power of God's love, and our potential to love one another."

The table grew quiet and I wondered if Essie regretted inviting everyone here. My sister sipped her wine. "Wow, Sarah. That's . . . deep."

I wished I hadn't shared my discovery. Reading Elizabeth's journal that afternoon had given me something. That

Elizabeth's history of suffering centered on the rock where I'd lost my wedding rings felt . . . supernatural. And as I read of her journey and her heart change, I had felt mine doing so also. For the first time, I didn't feel angry at Matt—I felt sorry for him. For the first time since the divorce petition arrived, I'd felt that it was all a definite mistake. That love—maybe even if it was just my love—might just be enough to get us through this mess.

But now, looking around at the blank stares of my friends, I wondered if I hadn't just been caught up in an old story.

Jen tucked her foot beneath her. "I think that's neat—and I think you're right, though yeah, we don't go talking about it enough. What about the patients at the hospital? The ones that feel hope and love thrive. The ones that wallow in despair don't."

"But what about when someone can't just up and choose hope, or choose love? What about when the strength just isn't there?" Mariah said.

I nodded. "I was wondering the same thing. And I think that . . . maybe that's when we need someone else to step in for us." Elizabeth saw God as the one doing that for her. Then Caleb. Deep down, it's what I desired to do for me and Matt.

"Time to break out the Ouija board, then," Essie said.

"Stop it."

"I'm serious, Sarah. You could contact Elizabeth's spirit."

"Essie, I don't play around with that stuff."

"Why not, because Mom and Dad say it's against their precious Bible? For goodness sakes, think for yourself for once, would you, Sis?"

"I *am* thinking for myself. And the answer's no."

But her words poked at my heart. *Think for yourself for once.* My own soul-searching was long overdue. What did I believe? How could I wade through life's difficulties without knowing how to gauge the world, my life, and eternity?

"Okay, change of subject," Mariah said, holding her left

hand over the table. A glittering rock reflected the light of the tiki torches. "Rick proposed last night."

Essie and Katie gave the proper squeals. Somehow I had trouble scrounging up joy for her, but I smiled and gave my congratulations.

Mariah leaned back and held her hand out to admire. "Yeah, I'm hoping second time's a charm."

Mariah's second chance.

Above the excited squeals, my cell phone vibrated in my pocket. I went indoors and dug it out.

Matt.

What could he want . . . unless . . .

"Hello?"

"Sarah." His voice was strained, heavy.

"Matt, what is it? What's wrong?" My pulse hammered against my temples, and I put my hand on the breakfast bar alongside Elizabeth's journal to steady myself. There was only one reason he'd call at almost ten o'clock on a Saturday night.

"It's Kyle." Muffled sounds in the phone, like sniffling or crying.

Thoughts of fixing me and Matt with my love alone drained from my being. All I could think about was the terror behind the phone. All I could think about was the most precious person in my life—my son. "Tell me!" I yelled. Outside, I was barely aware of my friends' sudden silence, of the fuzziness consuming my brain.

"He was on the motorcycle—Sarah, he was in an accident."

My world fell. I gripped the cold granite countertop, reaching for something dependable and solid. Everything I'd been agonizing over—the journal, Elizabeth, Pete, even my marriage, fell away. Nothing mattered, nothing except getting to my baby.

"Where is he?"

"They're flying him to Boston. Mass General. I'll meet you there."

CHAPTER 29

Life is fragile. But we don't live like it is. We don't walk around day to day, cognizant of the fact that *this* could be the day. This could be the day it all ends. We don't approach life with a label that says *Fragile, Handle with Care.*

But we should.

Because that's what it is. Tenuous. Unstable. As delicate as a butterfly's wings and, in the life of my son, one hundred times more beautiful.

I placed my hand on Kyle's limp one and squeezed. The whirring of the mechanical ventilator and the steady beep of the vital monitor sounded through Mass General's intensive care unit. The scent of medicines and astringents and Lysol and latex gloves—smells I usually found comfort in—unnerved me.

Kyle had spent the night away from us, the doctors casting bones and running blood tests, CT scans, MRIs, EEGs, X-rays and probably about a million other tests. Now, he lay in a bed, an IV drip and a bag of blood beside him, his head bandaged and his battered eyes closed, a breathing tube down his throat. Everything I'd learned in nursing failed me. Words came and went, each making me more and more frightened. Head trauma. Skull fracture. Swelling in brain. Coma—one the doctors had not induced.

They couldn't tell us if Kyle would wake.

Ever.

I'd cried all my tears. My world was shattered. Nothing mattered except for the fragile body of my son beside me.

Across from me, Matt ran a hand over his own bloodshot eyes and stood, exiting the room. I hadn't been much aware of his presence through the night. He hadn't touched me or tried to comfort, which I was more than okay with.

Now, I was left alone, just me and Kyle and no lifeline except my anger.

A need to blame. And a need for answers.

I squeezed Kyle's hand one more time and told him I'd be back soon.

I left the room and made a couple of turns into the long hallway, the walls closing in on me. A window at the end showed bright sunlight outside. Shouldn't it still be dark? Shouldn't the sun and moon cease their everyday jobs until Kyle was awake and well?

I made one more turn and saw Essie sitting hunched in a cushioned chair. A scattering of people occupied various seats in the waiting room. Quiet grief cloaked the room. All of us— strangers though we were—bound in a state of purgatory, where life could go neither backward nor forward.

Matt stood slouched at one of the vending machines. I walked toward him, solely aware of my fuzzy world and the anchor that was my anger.

Something dropped inside the machine and Matt stooped to pick out a water. He straightened as I approached and held out the water to me. "Thought you'd be thirsty."

I didn't take it.

"What was he doing on that bike?" I whispered the words— hot, sharp, lethal daggers targeted at the man before me.

He didn't answer. His hand hung suspended in the air, the water still held out to me.

I slapped it from his hands. It flew past him, landing on the laminate floor and spinning in crazy circles.

"What was he doing on that bike!" This time my words were loud, uncontrolled. I felt the others in the room staring at me. I didn't care.

"Sarah . . ." Essie's voice from behind. I ignored it.

"I didn't know he took it, Sarah."

"Where were you? You were supposed to spend the weekend with him! Where were you?"

Again he didn't answer, but his silence spoke louder than any words could.

I lunged.

My fists found his chest, his face, anything I could reach. I clawed, I hit, I would have bitten if I'd thought to.

He stood there, taking it. When he backed up a couple of steps, he straightened again, letting me pummel him over and over. I felt Essie's arms trying to calm me, but my anger was no match for them. When my energy was spent, I erupted into sobs. My hits became weak. Matt clung to me tightly, and I leaned my head into him, letting my tears wet his shirt. With a defeated hand, I pounded at his chest.

"I'm sorry, Sarah. I'm so, so sorry."

But sorry wouldn't make any of this better.

I shoved him away. "Go."

"What?"

"Go! Kyle and I don't need you. Go!"

"I'm still his—"

I pointed an accusing finger at him. "You caused this. You started it a long time ago, but we're here because of you. I hate you—hear me? I hate you! Leave. Just leave." I collapsed onto the floor, my eyes burning with more tears.

Essie's arms came around me. She led me to a chair,

smoothed my hair, made shushing noises to me as if I were a small child. I sobbed in her arms until I fell asleep.

When I woke, Matt was gone.

———

Mom and Daddy and Lorna were both at the hospital by ten. Kyle's grandparents took turns visiting him, then set up camp in the waiting area. Pete texted me three times and called once. I didn't return either his texts or his calls. What was there to say?

I sat by the hospital bed, holding my son's hand, talking to him in soft tones. I studied his bruised and swollen face—nearly unrecognizable to me—for signs of life. I prayed out loud, not caring who heard, my words often little more than babble. Eventually I clung to one simple prayer, over and over again.

God, help.

A doctor I didn't recognize came in later in the afternoon, told me they wouldn't know anything for a couple more days. It all depended on the amount of swelling, and if that swelling would accompany permanent—or even deadly—damage. He encouraged me to keep speaking to Kyle, to let him know I was here.

So I did. I spoke to him about anything and everything, taking breaks only to use the bathroom or sip some water. I prayed my two-word prayer with him, over and over. I relived stories of his boyhood, of our special times together at the beach or playing in the sandbox in the backyard. I retold the time he broke the living room window with a baseball. The time we ran our first 5K together when he was only in second grade, how he'd whipped my behind even then.

Always, always, I left Matt out of the stories.

I knew Kyle must have been mad at Matt when he took the bike. The blatant act of going against his father—and the law— was a cry for attention.

I still couldn't think of Matt without immense anger

bubbling to the surface. Why hadn't Kyle's own father been able to see the signs? Why had he been so blind? How could he have been so incredibly selfish?

At suppertime, Essie brought me a bowl of chicken soup, which she coaxed me to eat. I forced it down, but it sat heavy in my stomach.

"I'm going to go home and shower," she said. "I'll stop by the house and grab you a few things, okay? I'll be back tomorrow."

I thanked her and returned to my conversation with Kyle, which had mushroomed into over-exhausted gibberish.

I sensed a tall form at the door and lifted my head. I hadn't expected my reaction to seeing Pete. More tears. I held out my hand to him and his arms came around me. I melted into them, sobbing, shaking my head, telling Pete he shouldn't have made the drive, he shouldn't have come.

"Do you want me to leave?"

"No. I want all this to be a nightmare."

A doctor came in to give us another update and this time I took comfort in Pete beside me, asking questions I hadn't thought to ask, hadn't known to ask. He gave off an air of authority while not taking his hand from my shoulder. I leaned into him when he asked the doctor what Kyle's GCS number was.

He seemed disappointed when the doctor told him four.

"What's that? That number?"

The doctor and Pete exchanged a look.

"It's a number that lets us know how deep the coma is," Pete said.

I didn't ask what the lowest number was—from Pete's reaction, four was low enough. The doctor said it was a matter of time, of seeing if the swelling in the brain reduced . . . or not. They'd continue with the CT scans to monitor.

We were just finishing with the doctor when Matt came in. I watched his gaze travel first over Kyle, then to the doctor, then finally to me and Pete. His eyes landed on Pete's hand on my shoulder.

"How is he?"

The doctor gave a summary of all he'd just told Pete and me, then left with a promise to be back in the morning.

The silence in the room grew thick and hot. I wondered if Kyle could sense it. Surely it wouldn't promote his recovery.

"Who are you?" Matt finally asked of Pete.

Pete held out his hand. "Pete Keller. I work with Sarah. Nice to meet you."

Matt didn't take Pete's hand. "I don't think my son needs you here," he said.

"What do you know of what your son needs?" I spat out.

Pete backed away from me. "No, he's right, Sarah." He dug in his pocket, slid a card into my hand. "I got you a room in the hotel next door. You're booked for the week. You should head over there and get some sleep while—" he looked at Matt —"while someone else is with Kyle."

"His father." Matt leaned over Kyle, snatching the card from my hand and throwing it back at Pete. "And I can take care of her accommodations, thanks."

Pete shrugged, slipped the card back in his pocket. I knew he didn't want to make this harder on me than it already was. "I'll call you tomorrow, okay?"

"Okay. Thanks, Pete."

Pete left and I massaged my temples.

"He shouldn't have come."

"Great time to be jealous, Matt."

"You don't see me bringing Cassie here, do you?"

"Don't you dare speak her name in this room."

Matt sighed loudly, sat in the chair opposite me. "Look, no more arguing, okay? For Kyle's sake."

My bottom lip quivered. "Agreed."

"He's right, you know. You need some rest away from this

place. It'll be good for you, and Kyle, too. I'll stay with him tonight and I won't leave until you get back. I promise."

I wanted to ask him how good his promises were, but I kept my mouth closed. For Kyle.

"I'll call and get you a room," he said. "I *will* call you if anything changes."

"Really?"

"Yes."

Foolish or not, I believed him one more time.

CHAPTER 30

I woke late in the hotel room the next morning, swigged down a cup of strong coffee, took a shower, and walked back to the hospital. None of the family was in the waiting room, and I rushed to Kyle's room.

Matt's head lay in his hands, and he whispered words I couldn't hear. I cleared my throat.

"Hey." He blinked. A thick growth of stubble shadowed the bottom half of his face. I hadn't seen him this unshaven since he'd grown a beard when Kyle was two.

"No change?"

He shook his head. "The doctor just came in, said they plan to run additional tests today. He said they might be able to tell us more by the end of the day."

I sat in my chair by Kyle's other side, kissed his cheek. The bruises looked worse today, a sign of healing. I wondered what went on inside his head, if anything. "Everyone leave?"

"Your parents drove my mom home. They said they'd be back later. They all took turns in here with him, my mom telling him trailer park stories, your mom praying, your dad reading to him."

"Hmmm."

He stood. "I'm going to check in next door, too. Get some shut-eye. I'll be back later. Call me."

I agreed. There was plenty to still be mad about, but Matt was right. None of it would do Kyle any good right now, especially if he could hear us.

Essie came in close to lunch with a bag of my things and a few of Kyle's. I picked out his team track trophy they'd won against D-R the year before and placed it on the side table.

"Thanks, Essie. When he wakes up, he'll be glad to see this."

Essie squeezed my hand. "He *will* wake up, Sarah."

I pulled out the stack of papers I'd printed with Elizabeth's story. "What am I going to do with this?"

She shrugged. "You lit up when you were talking about her the other night. When you were talking about hope. I thought maybe you could use it. Or maybe read it to him if nothing else. I'm sure you've exhausted his childhood stories."

I smiled for the first time since Matt had called with news of Kyle's accident. "Yeah. Thanks."

She sat in Matt's empty chair. "I've never prayed so much in my life," she said. "I wonder if it's doing any good."

I made a noncommittal sound and thumbed through Elizabeth's journal.

"Dad says God works out good for those who love Him. What about those of us who don't know Him? Does He leave us out of that circle?"

"I don't know, Essie." I wasn't in any condition to think through big philosophical questions right now.

"Sorry. I've been thinking too much I guess. Trying to finagle God into doing what I want, into making Kyle better. No amount of t'ai chi's gonna accomplish that."

"Well, if you figure out the formula, let me know. I've said about a hundred sinner's prayers in my life, and look at the good it's done me. I gave up praying that prayer. I have one now, and it's my lifeline."

"What's that?"

"Lord, help."

We shared a sad smile.

"Maybe no one has all the answers," she said.

"Maybe." I placed Elizabeth's journal on Kyle's nightstand.

Essie stayed a few hours, then left me alone again. I looked at Kyle, his lips dry and cracked around the breathing tube, his skin pale where black-and-blue spots weren't present.

"Why did you do it, Kyle?" I whispered.

Yet I couldn't blame him. I'd already cast the blame on Matt. And where did I fall in the big scheme of things? Surely I was also culpable in some way. Unless my failed marriage was completely Matt's fault. Unless I had truly been a perfect wife all these years.

I ground my teeth and swept up Elizabeth's journal in my hands, the sight of her words on bright paper in legible print both foreign and comforting. I flipped to the later entries, feeling the need to bond with her in our suffering. Whether or not the events had happened hundreds of years ago, she had found herself in darkness. Like me, like many in the world. Yet she *had* found hope. Now, more than ever, I needed to catch a glimpse of it.

I read her story aloud to Kyle. And when I came to a paragraph I hadn't remembered transcribing that stuck out to me, I clung to it, reading it aloud again.

Over and over I read, and yet one verse I have found my heart clings to. "And he said unto me, My grace is sufficient for thee: for my power is made perfect through weakness."

I read this and shed warm tears, for I could not deny that the words were like sweet balm to my wretched heart. 'Tis nothing but this. 'Tis nothing but His grace and promise and finished work to see me through. 'Tis all I have left to cling to.

I finished the words, their cadence still stirring in my soul. Elizabeth's sorrow collided and embraced my own. I felt as if she spoke to me through the channels of time.

In the moment Elizabeth's last words passed my lips, I

realized I'd been drowning in a swollen black sea of my own weakness.

What if I chose to believe these ancient words? What if I chose to believe in God's strength and not my own? That only by reaching the end of myself could I see what God was capable of?

I clutched the promise close and did not let it go, trusted that it was for me, that God called me in that moment, that He knew my suffering and was promising something undeserved. Love. Mercy. Hope. And all-sufficient grace.

"The last CT scan shows a reduction in swelling." I couldn't recall this particular doctor's name. It didn't matter. The words pouring from his mouth stirred a lightness in my heart.

I glanced at Matt, who licked his lips surrounding the thick growth of stubble. Bags beneath his eyes made him look older than his thirty-five years. "That's good, right?"

The doctor nodded and stared at us from above his glasses. "It's what we hoped to see, Mr. Rodrigues. Unfortunately we're far from out of the woods. We won't know how much damage was done to Kyle's brain until he wakes...if he wakes."

I asked about his GCS number.

"It's still a four. I'm afraid he's not responding any more than when we first brought him in. Only time will tell."

I nodded and thanked the doctor. Matt's phone rang as soon as the man left. He looked at it and stepped out of the door, still within earshot.

"Hi. . . . No, no, I'm not coming home. . . . Louis has it under control." A curse. "He's my son. . . . I don't care, fine. . . . I hope you do." He hung up and paced the hall before coming back in and sitting.

We didn't speak. I knew if Kyle didn't wake soon, life would have to go on. Matt would have to see to his business and the house. I pondered Kyle staying in a coma for weeks, or months even. I thought about him waking up, if he'd be the same Kyle I knew and loved, or a small fraction of the young man I'd called my son. With each passing hour, chances grew slimmer that Kyle would wake without lasting harm, slimmer that he'd wake at all.

The tears were always there, right at the surface, burning my corneas, ready to erupt. At the thought of Kyle waking into a different person, they spewed forth. I hid my face in my hands.

My grace is sufficient for you . . .

Even in this?

My grace is sufficient for you . . .

Matt's arms pulled me toward him, and I didn't resist. I cried harder. I couldn't summon anger or my jealousy in that moment. For now, I allowed him to share the burden of my sorrow. If anyone knew how I felt, it was my husband.

"I will do anything to make this up to you, Sarah. Anything. I'll come home. Forget Newport. Forget divorce papers. Forget the Watermans. Forget Rodrigues Landscaping. When Kyle wakes up, I'm going to work off the rest of my days showing you guys how sorry I am."

I released a sad laugh. How badly I'd wanted to hear these words just a week ago. Now, when they lingered between us, I recognized them for what they were. Penance.

"You can't fix it like that, Matt. It's too late." The words didn't accuse. They stated fact. "And what good is our marriage if it's only to pay off your guilt? What good is it to me or you or Kyle? What if Kyle doesn't make it? What then? Are you going to live in chains bound to me, trying to make amends for this past summer?"

He released me, rubbed his crooked nose. Sometimes, he still felt like a stranger to me.

"You're tired, Matt. You're not thinking straight, I get it. But do me a favor and don't say anything else you'll regret, okay?"

I left the room, my body quaking within. I had to get away,

at least for the moment. There was too much pain. Too much history, too many what-ifs. Neither of us thought clearly. We were running on regrets and emotion.

I wondered if mercy and grace were really boundless, or if one day soon they too would run dry, along with my failed marriage and my son's shriveling brain, along with my deferred hopes and pointless dreams.

I pushed the hospital doors open and gulped in fresh breaths of air. The sound of cars and honking horns alerted my senses.

I couldn't let my guard down with Matt. Kyle needed me. He needed me strong. Matt was a volatile explosion of emotion waiting to happen. And for certain, I would be the first one hit.

CHAPTER 31

Ten days. Ten days since Matt first called me with news of Kyle being in an accident. My hope that our son would wake well diminished with each passing hour.

Our family had become pale vestiges of our former selves— me, Matt, Kyle. We crammed into Kyle's room every waking hour, spending more time together than we certainly ever had.

Our parents and Essie came less. Lorna had even gone the entire day yesterday without coming. Like everything else, time went on, sweeping up people's lives with it.

"When do we stop this?" Matt asked me that afternoon.

I knew what he meant. When do we stop clinging to hope that any hour, any minute, Kyle would wake up. I couldn't give him an answer. An answer would mean defeat.

"I can't leave him." God had given me stretches of peace in this time, but I also felt I battled for my son in prayer. If I left his side, I'd be giving up. "If you need to go back, I understand."

"I don't want to." Matt scratched at his clean-shaven cheek, another sign that time moved on. "Part of me feels like if I walk out that door, even for half a day, I'm giving up on him."

I swallowed. "I know what you mean." I slid my hands into

Kyle's and squeezed. The steady beep of the vital machine sounded from beside me, assuring that somewhere in my son's ravaged body lay a heart still beating and desiring life.

"Don't leave yet," I whispered to Matt. "Give it a few more days."

He nodded and his eyes grew wet. "I'm not going anywhere unless you want me to."

Our gazes met and we shared grim smiles. He slid one of his hands around Kyle's and reached for mine with the other.

I didn't resist his touch.

My fingers twitched at the slight movement beneath them. I put down Elizabeth's printed journal I'd been reading to Kyle on top of the bed and leaned forward. Matt had gone to the hotel to get a few hours of sleep. He usually stayed with Kyle nights, so he often slept in the day while I stayed with Kyle, talking to him, praying for him, reading from Elizabeth's journal. I studied Kyle's hand in mine. So many times I'd wished for a response, a movement, anything. I wondered if it was not a product of my imagination.

"Kyle, honey, can you hear me?"

Another movement. A press of my fingers. This time I knew I didn't imagine it. I called for a passing nurse, who called for the doctor down the hall. Dr. Larson examined Kyle's pupils and checked his pulse. When he did so, Kyle's foot moved slightly beneath the sheet.

"Did you see that?" I asked.

Dr. Larson smiled, the specks of gray at his temples shining beneath the hospital lights. "I did. No doubt Kyle is beginning to rouse from the coma."

I clutched his hand tighter. Warm tears brimmed at my lids. I fumbled with my cell phone in my other hand.

There was only one person I wanted in the room with us when Kyle woke.

———

Matt entered the room not five minutes after I called him. His hair stood out in all directions, the white T-shirt he'd slept in crinkled and twisted, his eyes bright with hope.

"Anything more?" He sat in his usual chair, but pulled it closer to Kyle's bedside.

"Just a lot of twitching toes." I looked at Matt, knowing his thoughts must echo mine. "I'm scared, Matt."

His Adam's apple bobbed up and down, slowly. He licked his lips. "Me, too."

It was the first time my husband ever conceded fear to me.

All we'd been through up until then paled in comparison to the precipice we hung on now. Here, on this side of Kyle's coma, there was still hope of complete recovery. On the other side, if things didn't work out as we wished—if Kyle didn't wake as the Kyle we'd known him to be—could I cope with that new reality?

But we couldn't stay in this in-between place forever. We needed to move forward.

Matt slid his hand into Kyle's. "Hey, buddy. We know you're in there, waiting for the right moment to wake up, but you're giving your Mom and I a good scare, here. We'd sure appreciate it if you'd wake up. I—I need to talk to you, Kyle." Matt's voice quivered and I inhaled deeply to keep my emotions in check. "I really want to talk to you, kid."

Kyle's hand moved under mine. Beneath the bandages wrapped on his head, his eyelids fluttered.

My breath hitched. "Matt . . ."

Dr. Larson stepped forward, speaking in a calm tone, explaining to Kyle that he was in an accident and that he had a breathing tube down his throat but that it would come out soon.

"That's it, buddy. Nice and easy now." Matt took up Dr. Larson's encouragement.

Kyle's eyes opened. He stared blankly at the hospital ceiling. He closed his eyes. They opened again, expressionless.

Defeat shot daggers at my heart.

"Hey, kiddo. It's been too long." Matt's voice remained steady and I was thankful for the rock he was in that moment. For Kyle and for me.

Slowly, Kyle's gaze moved to Matt. His dry lips worked around the breathing tube and then with a sudden motion, his hands flew to his throat.

Matt and Dr. Larson kept Kyle's arms by his sides. "We're going to take that out real soon, buddy," Matt said. "Just want to make sure you're breathing okay on your own. I think that's how it goes, anyway. I'm not a nurse like your mom."

I marveled at Matt's ability to remain calm in this, such a telling time for how the rest of Kyle's life may play out.

Dr. Larson worked with Kyle as he unhooked the breathing tube from the ventilator. Hollow breaths came through the tube, indicating Kyle breathed on his own.

Kyle looked at me, and I saw something wonderful.

Recognition.

My heart sang.

After ten minutes of continuous monitoring, Dr. Larson called for a nurse to assist him, and I looked away as they took the tube from Kyle's throat.

Kyle licked his lips and mouthed a word that caused the last of my strength to wilt. *Mom.*

"Thank you, Lord." Grateful tears came forth, and I didn't bother to stop them. "Oh, honey."

He looked at Matt and mouthed, "Dad."

"Hey, kid. I'm here."

Then another word. We couldn't make it out and asked him to mouth it again.

My bottom lip trembled when I realized what word he wanted to convey to us.

Sorry.

Matt's chin quivered. I knew he was having trouble holding it together as much as I was. "I'm sorry too, Kyle. I—" he glanced at me—"I am so sorry."

CHAPTER 32

Kyle's recovery proved slow, but hopeful. Three days after he woke, his doctors moved him from ICU to a recovery room, where I was allowed to be more active in his care. The nasal feeding tube came out, bandages came off. He took short walks around the room. Matt and I continued to take shifts. Kyle slept often, and I read Elizabeth's journal to him while he dozed.

I read the last passage I'd translated just as Matt came in for the night.

"Everything okay?"

I placed the papers on the stand. "Yes."

Sort of. I was feeling that hope again. That chance for mercy and new beginnings. Despite all Matt and I had gone through, I still wanted him for my husband. I didn't want to give up on him, but I couldn't bring myself to tell him as much. I was too scared. Scared of rejection, scared he'd want to come home and things would just settle back into the way they'd been before, scared he would only want to be with me as a means of atonement for all we'd been through.

"Any news on next steps?"

"Dr. Larson came down today. He—"

A knock at the open door of Kyle's room. Matt's face paled.

I turned and saw Cassie—fresh as a spring daisy in a form-fitting dress and high heels.

I realized then that none of this had been real. Here, in the hospital with Kyle injured and now recovering had been torture, but it also served as a sort of cease-fire. A fantasy peace, where we could put our own selfish problems on hold for the sake of our son.

But it wasn't real. Cassie's presence proved it.

"Cassie." Matt stood and went to the door. Once in the hall, he closed it just short of clicking.

"Matthew."

"I told you not to come."

"I couldn't stay away—I haven't seen you for weeks. You haven't called . . ." Her voice sounded pouty. They could at least walk down the hall. I didn't want to hear their conversation. I didn't. And I did.

"He's better now, isn't he?"

"Yes, Kyle's doing well."

"Good." But it didn't sound like she was happy for Kyle's sake, or for Matt's sake, but for her own. "You can come back to Newport sometime then, yes? Mommy and Daddy are talking about redoing the landscaping on the guest house. They want to know your ideas."

"Cassie—I'm here now. This comes first. My family . . . my family comes first."

I choked down a half sob, half laugh over his statement. He sounded sincere, but I couldn't trust it.

"Before your work, yes, but before me? We were just starting things together."

A long sigh. "Look, now's not a good time. When we're out of this, we'll talk."

My hope deflated. What had I expected? Him to run back home to our empty marriage after a few trying weeks? For things to be how they were before? Better even?

I was a fool.

I heard her heels click against the hospital floor until they echoed out of sight.

Matt came back in the room. "Sorry."

I didn't say anything. I knew if I did, it would come out bitter.

I stood. "I'll be back in the morning. Dr. Larson suggested moving him to rehab in the next day or two. Someplace closer to home."

Matt nodded. "Sure. Good." He waited until I was at the door. "I am sorry, Sarah. She shouldn't have come."

I left the room. Matt was sorry a lot lately, but frankly, I didn't know if it would make one iota of a difference.

On impulse, I drove home for the night. I was sick of hotel rooms, and Cassie's visit renewed my anger.

I wanted my marriage. Despite the hurt, despite the threat of failure, I wanted to fight for my husband as Caleb had fought for Elizabeth.

I opened the door of our house. It smelled stuffy and stale, and I pushed up all the windows. But silence didn't loiter in my home. A wonderful steady tick came from the grandfather clock.

Night's shawl hovered above the last of the sun's rays as I stood in the living room, basking in the persistent resonance of the old antique. Had it roused to life on its own? It didn't matter. It was back, faithful once again.

There was a note on the counter in Essie's handwriting.

Hey Sarah,
I hope you don't mind but I was grabbing some of your stuff when that clock guy came. I let him fix it. Didn't want to bother you with this until you were home.

I mentally thanked Essie and focused on my next task. I ran

upstairs to pull on a pair of old sneakers and jeans before returning downstairs.

I opened the cabinet beneath the breakfast bar and pulled out the divorce papers. Unless I was wrong or filled with pathetic hope, something had changed in Matt the past couple of weeks. If he truly still wanted a divorce after what we'd been through, he'd have to visit his lawyer again.

I slipped onto the back patio as the clock released seven beautiful chimes, cheering me on. I headed for the shed. I dropped the divorce papers on the freshly-trimmed lawn and hauled the old lawn mower out. It was one of Matt's firsts. A push-mower that didn't even propel forward. I don't know why he kept the thing. It was one of the few old objects he cherished.

I poured some gasoline into the mower, the rich, oily scent churning my stomach. I pulled the cord once, then twice, my arm protesting the effort. The engine stayed quiet.

I took a deep breath, and yanked it once more, as hard as I could. It rumbled to life, and my heart lifted, my aim on the neat papers before me, Matt's signature at the bottom.

They were gone in four seconds. The mower's hungry blades chewed the papers into small shreds that fed into the mower's bag. When not a white speck remained on our vibrant green grass, I unhitched the bag and walked toward the stone wall. Tall, unruly grass beside the rough trail brushed at the legs of my jeans. I saw the pile of lawn clippings Louis and Greg had tossed there and kept walking. I wanted the shreds of paper as far away as possible—the dirtiest, most useless of lawn refuse this family had ever known.

When I found a spot I deemed suitable, I dumped them. White confetti dropped from the bag and when every last shred had fallen, I scraped the spot with my shoe. I turned toward the house.

Yes, a lot of the future of my marriage was determined by Matt. But our union was made up of two, and I had half the say in how our marriage would go.

The following Monday, Kyle was transported to a rehabilitation center down the street from our home. I moved back into the house and stayed with him during the days. I effectively deferred my school enrollment to January. Matt returned to Newport and his work, visiting the center every night.

I felt us drifting back into the life we'd lived before the accident. I wondered if Matt sought Cassie's arms after he left the rehab center.

The thought sent fresh grief to the core of my being.

I wrestled with God a lot. I didn't push Matt. I talked to Jesus. I didn't goad my husband into arguments. I poured my grief-ridden heart out to God, tried to wrangle a blessing, tried to fill up the great chasm I felt in the core of my being—a great chasm that I was beginning to realize only He could fill.

One day, I drove to Plymouth instead of spending the day with Kyle in rehab. Yes, I needed to fulfill my request to Barb, but right now, with things finally settling down with Kyle, I wanted time alone—time to finish Elizabeth's story.

Jill hugged me after the receptionist called for her. Sometime in the first week after Kyle's accident I thought to send her an email explaining my absence.

"How is he?"

"Good." I tried to keep my grateful tears in check. "Really good."

She led me to the Steinway Library, where she'd already set up Elizabeth's journal. In some ways, the sight of the yellowed pages felt like coming home to an old friend. I stood above the journal, reflective. "She helped me. In the hospital, I mean. That hope we were talking about? Elizabeth helped me find it."

Jill smiled, and I felt she understood—perhaps more than my sister and friends, perhaps more than anyone, even. It would make sense that someone who had a passion for history, a passion for the people represented by the artifacts in this room, would understand.

She left me to my work, and I carefully went to the page where I'd left off weeks earlier, remembering how Elizabeth was in the isolation tent and had planned an escape. I read and typed, sinking slowly back into her words and story.

July 30, 1675

I waited until all the women in the tent fell asleep, then made for the site in which we relieved ourselves, my journal the sole item in my pocket. Smoke encompassed the camp—heady fires now dying, its occupants drunk with heavy sleep and full bellies. I walked calmly in the woods, yet as soon as I was out of sight, I ran.

Seemed too simple to escape in such a way. And it was.

I heard footfalls behind me. I stumbled upon a hole in the ground. My skirts caught in brambles. I turned, hoping to see Caleb as the owner of the footsteps. Yet by the moonlight, I could not mistake the black hair and proud stance.

Naveen.

I ran all the faster.

If I were to ever make it out of the camp, 'twas now. After tonight, Naveen would not let me from his sight. He would take me for his wife and I would be bound to him in every way.

The thought of sharing his bed propelled me forward. Naveen's footsteps drew closer. I ran into something solid and felt hands at my sides. I fought.

"Elizabeth, 'tis me."

I gave a small cry and clutched at Caleb's shirt. "He comes."

Caleb pushed me to the side. A shiny knife in his hand glinted in the moonlight.

I turned away and crouched in a bayberry bush. I could not bear to see my dear Caleb take another life, even if it be one as horrid as Naveen's.

The struggle did not last long. Naveen did not expect Caleb.

Caleb took my hand in his own, still wet from Naveen's blood. I allowed him to lead me, running, through the thick bushes until we met the water's edge, where a small rowboat waited. He lifted me inside, as gentle as if I were a lamb, and rowed with strong strokes to the large island called Aquidneck.

When we reached its shores, he took me in his arms and I near melted for the feel of him.

"You are safe, little Elizabeth. 'Tis safe here."

I put my hand on his bearded cheek, and when his head lowered to mine, I did not resist him. For a slice of time, I forgot everything, save what felt like my betrayal to Abram. I pulled away. Caleb's protective arms did not leave me.

He pushed a lock of hair from my eyes. "I love you, Elizabeth."

This man had done so much for me, I thought to return his words. Yet still, I cannot trust my heart. I will not speak words that I am not certain.

August 1, 1675

Caleb wasted no time in securing our marriage. He told me he wants to ensure my place as a widow if something should happen to him when he goes to fight.

He will leave me soon.

'Tis more than I can bear, for being connected by marriage now and having shared his bed, I am bound to him in a way I never expected.

Before now I did not realize the ferocity of marriage. It binds with the gentleness of a sweet dove, but protects like a vicious, roaring lion. Beneath its canopy, I find it easier to relinquish Papa to heaven. I can heal from the horrid images I have seen due to war.

I trust the Lord to give me strength in this hour that Caleb should depart from me.

I find comfort in renewing my ties with Goodwife Howland and Andia. They have been at Aquidneck for weeks. Our settlement at Swanzey is gone. If ever this war should end, we will have to rebuild everything.

Andia mourns Hezekiah. He is one of the lost. I can understand her deep sorrow. I keep her company but do not offer up too much advice or words of comfort. These are like daggers to an already broken heart. If she talks, I listen.

I asked Goodwife Howland if she thought beauty could come even from the ashes of our burned settlement. She told me it was not for us to know how God's hand works. That beauty would come in time, if not for many years, when our bodies lie buried beneath the ground.

Caleb will leave tomorrow. I share his bed tonight with tender knowledge that what we have is precious and fragile. I savor his love tonight and will hold it in my heart until he returns.

September 26, 1675

I have busied myself preparing for the small harvest on this sandy island. The crops are not as plentiful, and we realize the winter will be hard.

I wonder if the little one that grows within my womb will survive such conditions.

News of battles throughout Massachusetts Bay and Plimoth Colony reach us. The number of dead strikes my soul, and I pray Caleb is not among them.

I ache for my husband. I regret not telling him of my love. I have lived in guilt and regret too long. Surely Abram would not approve of this frame of mind.

I spend many nights pondering my feelings for Abram, pondering my feelings for my husband. I have realized that love takes many forms. I loved Abram, but I was perhaps more drawn to the adventure and promise he represented to me.

Now, I am certain. I do love Caleb. 'Tis not wrong to love someone because they first loved you. For isn't that how we express our love for God? He hath loved us first, showing that love with ultimate measures as Caleb hath shown his love for me. And now to the one who has done battle for me, the one who never gave up on me— I willingly give my entire, eager heart.

Both my sweet Jesus and my sweet Caleb.

December 23, 1675

News has come to us of a great fight across the bay against the Narragansett. 'Tis the worst fight yet. We are told it is a great victory for the English, but with so many dead on either side I wonder who is truly victorious.

I think of Andia's native boy, another living in two worlds. He seems to have acclimated well. Andia even offered him a way back to his people and he refused. One night, I saw his shadow at the edge of the water. He made sounds I did not understand—sad, mourning sounds of his people. Andia waited at the top of the beach, and when he was finished she wrapped him in a hug. She treats him as a son, for he is the only child Hezekiah has given to her.

Sometimes, even in the ugliness of war, we can break through to the other side. That blessed side where neither skin color nor background are of import. 'Tis not common. But I see it with Andia and Samuel and I am reminded of a time I saw it briefly before, between myself and Abram.

The women keep busy tending the fires and splitting wood. 'Tis strange with so many of the men gone and but few to guard Aquidneck. Yet the threat of attack from the Wampanoag is indeed slim. They have been run off in the land of the Narragansett, and now it appears even this mighty tribe is being defeated.

I hope it ends soon. I hope Caleb's lifeblood still flows strong within him. I hope I can tell him of my love for him. I hope he comes home to me and the wee child growing rapidly in my womb.

April 24, 1676

I gave birth to little Michael Caleb last night. In the distance, we saw the fierce fires of a waging war off Aquidneck. I wondered if Caleb fought against the continued plundering of nearby towns. I think it strange he has not come to see us if he is close.

Through the night and billowing clouds of smoke far off, I gave birth to our son. He be such a sweet thing. Goodwife Howland and Andia helped me push him from my womb into the world, where he gave lusty cries.

I am struck by this love I have for him. 'Tis another sort of strange love, both protective and sweet.

The weather warms. We have made it through the winter. I nurse my babe in hopes that his father will soon be with us.

May 9, 1676

Caleb has returned to us. He walks with an injured leg, but it is the least of the evils done him I think. He cried when he saw Michael. He does not let either one of us from his sight and fears when I am gone longer than usual to the privy.

My husband is not the same man who left us. Often I see him gazing blankly at the wall and I must call to him thrice before he realizes where he is. He shares my bed with vigor. And though I can't say I haven't enjoyed his intense affection, I feel he attempts to drive away the evils in his head with his love for me.

I sat up with him the whole of his first night home. When I told him I loved him greatly, his eyes seemed to lighten. I see hope there. I pray the Lord grants us mercy.

I am patient with him, and with little Michael, who often fusses. I rise each day with renewed purpose. I wonder at how I ever thought there was anything more worthy to do with my life than take care of a man I love and a son I cherish. What adventure could be greater?

June 11, 1676

Captain Church visited us today. When he left, Caleb went down to the shore for a long time. I fear the captain has asked my husband to return to the battles.

I want to keep him here. I want to never let him go again.

And yet I know he will go. He feels 'tis his duty, and part of me wonders if he has unfinished business; if he goes and comes back, perhaps he will arrive home a whole man?

I cried when he confirmed my fears. I asked him if he wished Michael to grow without a father as I did without a mother? We fought, but at the end of the night I allowed him to take me in his arms.

'Tis no use fighting with a man as stubborn as a mule. He will go. And I do not wish his last memory of us to be a foul one.

July 15, 1676

News of English victories come to us from across the river. Little Michael grows. When he smiles at me, he reminds me of his father.

August 7, 1676

News comes of Wampanoag defeat. The body of Weetamoo was found washed ashore at Swanzey, likely not far from Papa's old home. Her head was mounted on a pike in Taunton. As much as I want this war to end, I cannot help but feel sorrow for her.

King Philip still eludes our warriors.

August 9, 1676

Caleb has returned! He and Captain Church's troops rest on Aquidneck. My husband fares well and his mind has seemed to clear some.

We sat outside as Michael slept and I asked him to tell me all the horrors he has seen. I asked him to share his burdens with me so that I could make them lighter.

Caleb tucked me close and I nestled my head in the crook of his neck. The island cools quickly at night and I found my husband's warmth comforting and enticing, as I had again been without it for weeks.

He spoke into my hair. "You once told me I may not wish you innocent if war came to us. Do you think what you have seen of war has better prepared you for the life you wish to live?"

I thought of Abram's mutilated body, falling and spinning off his rock. Of the headless, naked body of John Salisbury. Of the fierce painted faces of Wampanoag warriors. Perhaps innocence was not such a bad thing. I could not admit that to Caleb, though.

"I wish to help you. Let me help, Caleb."

He smiled. "I still love hearing my name on your sweet lips."

"Will I be less sweet if you share the burden of your heart with me?"

He was silent for a moment. "What my mind sees is poison to the heart. I can no more poison you than I could stop loving you. Let it lie, Elizabeth. I seek the Lord with my burdens and He supplies me with mercy by the day."

I did not press him. He has always considered it his duty to protect me. This time, I will allow him to do so.

August 11, 1676

News came to the island today that one of Philip's men is willing to lead the English to his camp at Mount Hope. Caleb once again gathers powder horn, bullet pouch, musket, and balls to take up the fight against the natives alongside Captain Church.

If they catch Philip, this wretched war will be near an end. I pray it is so.

As I hold Michael, I feel sorrow for the needless lives lost on both sides. War is an ugly thing. I do not see why both sides could not live together in peace. Perhaps that is the innocence within me that Caleb says I still own. Perhaps that is the innocence that killed Abram.

Either way, I pray better things for my son.

August 13, 1676

Philip has been captured. Already Caleb returned home this night. He says the battle is not yet done, but that he will stay on a few more weeks to help with the harvest.

We work together, side by side, and I find satisfaction in our common toil by day and our common rest at night. I think of Papa, of his desire to see me provided for. I think not of his dead body, ravaged from sickness and natives, but of the life he gave me as a child. I speak of him often to Michael, and although my son does not understand my words, I know he will grow to know who his grandpapa was.

October 19, 1676

The pages of this journal draw to an end. I will have to ask Caleb to obtain paper when next he is near Plimoth. But for a few small skirmishes, the war is over. We have migrated home, though little is left. One of the only buildings that stand is the garrison we hid in many moons ago. I cannot bring myself to look upon it again. I wish to move forward, and the past is still too painful to think on, especially now that we are here upon this ground.

Caleb insisted we visit Abram's rock. I voiced my fear of finding Abram's bones at the bottom and so he visited first and assured me the place was clean of the past, save for a few trinkets hidden in the cave.

Andia watched Michael for us and we left together. My skirts now hide a stomach once again blooming with life. I remember how I used to run from Caleb into these woods and I am grateful that we can now walk into them together. Caleb knows me truly and deeply—inside and out. He knows my rashness and my temper. He knows how I loved another before knowing my love for him. And still, he persists in loving me.

He believes I am the one who needs to see the rock again, as a sort of final good-bye to my native friend. I believe he is right.

It stood the same as I remember, perhaps even more beautiful framed by the changing foliage around it. We looked in the cave, where one of Abram's tin cups still lay on its side. Caleb asked me if I would like it and I told him no.

We walked to the top of the rock and Caleb held me as I shed tears at the memory of Abram's falling body.

"He wanted peace," I told him. "He longed to meet God."

"He received his longing, then," Caleb said. "Remember his life, not his end, Elizabeth. His faith."

"I know," I whispered.

Caleb nodded. "He was a blessing to me for the short time I was his friend." He placed his hand on the small bump of my womb. "If we have another son, I wish to name him Abram. Does that suit you?"

"Yes." I looked into my husband's hazel eyes, ran my hand over his honey beard, and kissed him fully.

'Tis a blessing to know I belong to a person so intimately, and he to me. As we stood on the top of the rock, I realized that were it not for Abram, I would not have loved Caleb with the intensity I do. Even as love is an object of but two people, it is shaped and formed by others, by the circumstances that surround it. It can grow, or it can shrivel. Had Caleb and I not suffered the times of adversity, we would not have grown together, into the man and wife we are today. I am thankful he did not give up on me. I am thankful he persisted in showing me the beauty of love.

A single tear fell from my eye as I finished Elizabeth's story. Something sealed within my heart at that moment. The somewhat hazy hope I'd clung to seemed to come full circle. I couldn't fathom how Barb knew how much I needed this story at this time in my life.

But of course, the simple answer was that Barb hadn't known—God did.

I closed my eyes, thinking of Elizabeth's words—or Goodwife Howland's, rather—that I'd read a few passages back.

I asked Goodwife Howland if she thought beauty could come even from the ashes of our burned settlement. She told me it was not for us to know how God's hand works. That beauty would come in time, if not for many years, when our bodies lie buried beneath the ground.

I thought of my hometown's history. The rock where I'd lost my rings—Abram's. And I wondered—hoped—that maybe, just maybe, part of this beauty was taking form in my life, in my heart.

I dug a tissue from my purse and blew my nose. I would print out the entire story, maybe see about having it bound. Then I would contact Mary and hope Barb's wish hadn't been for nothing.

CHAPTER 33

I hadn't taken the quilt off Barb's bed. While most everything besides furniture had been packed away, the quilt on Barb's bed remained. I now knew why my neighbor had made it. It was a likeness of the one Elizabeth had created. I could picture Barb tucking herself beneath it every night, remembering her ancestor, reminding herself that love had the power to conquer. Reminding herself that perhaps, one day, Mary would forgive whatever she'd done.

I sat on the quilt, ran my fingers over the appliqued finger of Abram. Then I dragged in a deep breath, catching the faint scent of pine through the open window, and pressed numbers on my cell phone. Numbers that would connect me to Barb's daughter.

My breaths turned tight in my chest as I listened to the ring echo on the other line. I would need to tell Mary her mother died. Somewhere along the way, she'd find that Barb had given everything to me. I wasn't sure how it would all sit with her.

The voice mail picked up and a pleasant voice came on. "Hey, you've reached Mary. I'm not able to get to the phone now, but leave a message . . . unless you're selling something. In that case, just hang up."

She didn't *sound* intimidating. I gathered my fortitude as the beep sounded. "Hi, Mary. My name is Sarah Rodrigues. I have news of your mom, who was my neighbor. I realize you two haven't spoken, but could you please call me back? Any time is fine." I left my number and hung up, already wondering how persistent I would have to be in reaching her. If it came down to it, would I have to travel across the country and knock on her door to speak with her?

I leaned back on the quilt, closed my eyes. Barb was wrong to leave this unfinished. But that didn't change the fact that I would do everything I could to help her make amends with her daughter—even in death.

Kyle's improvement proved rapid. September rolled in without word from Mary, despite two more messages left. Soon, I would go back to work. Matt's rental agreement would expire. Kyle would return to school.

What did our future hold?

Matt didn't ask for the divorce petition. I thought he probably bided time for the sake of being tactful. I braced myself for "normalcy" and for Matt to ask the dreaded question.

Part of me regretted shredding the papers. Matt was in the wrong. What he did to our family was unspeakable. I should be kicking him out of my life.

But a gentle knowing prodded me into the uncomfortable, reminding me of my own faults, of real and enduring love, of the beauty of mercy. Just as Elizabeth knew she couldn't blame the native people for the whole of King Philip's War, neither could I cast the full blame of our failed marriage on Matt.

One night I took a long soak in the tub. The late summer air and shorter days cast a coziness on the house, and I lit a few candles and ran a bath to enjoy some overdue relaxing. The scents of lilac and bath salts soothed my frayed nerves.

I was anxious to get back to work, to have Kyle home, to start helping him plan for college and fill out applications and other normal things mothers of seniors did.

When my phone rang, I scooped it up quick as I always did, half expecting it to be a doctor from the rehabilitation center telling me some unforeseen news.

"Hello?"

"Hi, Sarah."

"Pete."

"Yeah . . . how's it going? Just figured I'd check in on things."

My stomach quivered. I hadn't talk to Pete in weeks—not since Matt had told him to leave the hospital.

"I'm sorry; you must think I'm awful for not calling."

"No—no, I could never think that." I heard the longing in his words and my heart ached for him. "How's Kyle?"

"Good. Perfect. He should be home next week. He's at a rehab center not far from home, so we're settling in. I'll be back to work soon, if you guys'll still have me."

"We've sure missed you there." Awkward silence clung to the invisible waves that connected us. I swirled the bubbles with my fingers, popping a few. "I've missed you."

"Pete, I'm sorry. I know this is unfair, but I think we got too close, too fast. I'm—"

"He's coming back to you, isn't he? Matt?"

"What? No, no. We're still separated."

"Oh."

"I just—I can't rush into things. I'm still married."

"You haven't signed the papers." His tone reflected defeat.

"No. I haven't. He's my husband, Pete. And this thing with Kyle really threw us for a loop. I'm sorry."

A long sigh. "Don't be. I want you to be happy, Sarah. And if things don't work out, well . . . you know where to find me."

I smiled into the phone. "Don't wait, Pete. Please. Go on with your life. You—you're a good guy."

From outside the window and coming from below, the sound of a guitar reached my ears. Someone's car radio? No. Nothing on the radio would sound this bad.

Then singing drifted up to me. Loud, slurred, off-key, horrible singing. "Wise men say, only fools rush in . . ."

Matt?

"I'm sorry, Pete, someone's at the door. I'll see you next week, okay?"

"Sure. Bye, Sarah."

I put the phone down and stood in the tub, dripping wet. I patted myself with a towel and wrapped a robe around myself—a light silky thing Matt had gotten me from Victoria's Secret ages ago.

More singing. "Shall I stay? Would it be a sin?"

I knotted the robe and wiped my feet dry so I wouldn't slip on the tiles of the master bathroom. The grandfather clock sang out ten chimes.

I peered out the window to see Matt on the front lawn, strumming a guitar whose strings couldn't have been tighter than the ones around my heart.

I hurried down the stairs and opened the front door.

Matt's gaze landed on me and stayed there, even as his body swayed. He strummed a few more off-beat chords with no words. Took an unsteady step forward. "Sarah."

"Matt. Are you . . . drunk? Did you drive?" A drunk Matt was as foreign to my mind as a slow Dale Earnhardt. An awkward Taylor Swift. It just didn't meld.

He stumbled toward me, not bothering to sidestep the phlox. "I had a few. Used an Uber." His voice slurred and when he reached me, I could smell his breath, heavy with alcohol.

I led him inside. "I thought you were visiting Kyle."

"Did. Then I stopped at that restaurant . . . what's it called? Heck, I can't remember." He closed the door and became surprisingly steady for a moment as he looked at me. He pulled the guitar strap off his neck, and I thought he'd topple over.

"Easy there, Elvis." I took the guitar from him, the neck still warm where he'd held it.

He spread his feet to steady himself, looked at me hard and long. "Now, what I came for."

He lifted his hand to cup either side of my face. With gentle strokes, he brushed my damp hair from my shoulders and ran his fingers down the curve of my neck.

My brain hummed so loud and quick I thought a hummingbird's wings flapped beside my ear. My stomach jumped and twitched, sending pop rockets to every part of my body.

Matt stepped closer and lowered his lips to my neck and then up to my ear. "You're so beautiful, my wife."

My body quaked, and I stifled back a quick sob.

His eager fingers slid beneath my robe and lowered it off my shoulders.

I wanted to sink into his touch, pretend this was the beginning of a right step for us.

But we'd been here before. And even as I sought to enjoy the moment, harsh images entered my mind. Matt's lips on *her* neck. His hands on *her* . . .

I pushed him away gently. "No. This can't be how it happens. We can't—we need to talk. A lot. When you're sober."

"I'm not that drunk." But his eyes skidded over me. "Is he here? That doctor?" He headed into the living room. "If I find him, he's gonna wish he was never born."

"There's no one here but us." I grabbed his arm and pulled him toward the stairs.

He went willingly. When I entered the guest bedroom and pulled down the sheets, he didn't protest. I untied his sneakers and pulled them off, along with his socks.

With a lazy grin he unzipped his pants until he stood in his boxers. He collapsed into the bed and I pulled the covers over him. "Want to join me?"

I shook my head, even though it was a lie.

He gripped my hand. "You're a good nurse. I ever tell you that?"

"No." I sat on the floor, my hand buried with his beneath the covers.

"I thought it. Every day when you—when you were in the hospital with Kyle. You took good care of him." He crushed his hand to his forehead, but the action didn't suppress the quick tears springing from his eyes.

Another first from my husband.

The sobs broke loose then, and seeing him in this pathetic state served to undam my own tears.

He cursed. "I'm sorry, Sarah. I'm so, so sorry. I want things to be like they used to be—before this summer. Can they, baby? Can we go back?"

I shook my head through my falling tears. "We need to go forward."

Forward. We couldn't undo what had been done. Elizabeth's own journey reminded me of that. There were layers of hurt and pain to wade through, and I didn't know where to begin.

But I knew it wasn't here, in our guest bedroom with a drunk husband.

I stood and kissed him on the forehead. "We'll talk in the morning."

I think he passed out before I made it to the master bedroom, where I curled under the sheets and wept. Did Matt really want to come home? Was he through with the idea of divorce? Of Cassie? Did he want me and our marriage, or was it a way of paying a debt he imagined in his mind? Was it the alcohol speaking, and not really my husband? Would he wake tomorrow and regret coming here?

I turned toward the window and burrowed deeper in the covers. Even if Matt wanted our marriage, how could I ever be with him when he'd been with another woman? How could I ever enjoy his arms again and trust that he totally and completely belonged to me? Would the images fade with time or would they haunt my remaining days? Whenever Matt had a job to do in Newport or a night meeting, I would likely torture myself with doubt and disbelief.

I wanted to forgive. I wanted to show mercy. But the question still remained: how could I ever trust my husband again?

CHAPTER 34

I woke the next morning to the sound of retching in the bathroom down the hall. I dressed and went downstairs to make coffee and toast, my stomach fluttering with the force of a hundred butterflies' wings.

My head swam when Matt joined me, clad in an old pair of jeans and a gray Rodrigues Landscaping T-shirt, his hair damp from the shower.

"Now I know why I've stayed away from that stuff," he mumbled. "Thanks." He popped two ibuprofen in his mouth and swigged a gulp of coffee.

"Toast?"

"Sure."

I slid a plate of two whole-wheat buttered toasts over the breakfast bar to him. I went to the fridge to get the strawberry jelly. I clasped the jar tight to still my shaking hands.

"You don't have to do this."

I looked up from the open fridge. "What?"

"Serve me."

"You don't feel well." It's what I'd done all these years. Take care of my family. And despite what Essie and Mariah might say, I thought it to be one of the most worthy things I'd done with my thirty-five years. Even if I hadn't been well compensated these past few months. Even if Matt and I never "fixed" our marriage. Even if he served me another round of divorce papers.

"I don't deserve this," he said.

"What do you deserve?"

He raked a hand through his hair. Behind him the rays of sun streaming in through the slider showed droplets from his wet locks splattering into the air.

"To be hanged, drawn, and quartered, maybe."

"That wouldn't do on the rug—too messy."

"Seriously? You're joking about this?"

"What else do you want me to do?" I pushed the jelly at him. "I don't know what to do, Matt. Where do we go from here? I mean what happened with her? What happened before her?" I leaned over the counter and rubbed the palms of my hands over my eyes. This was work. I didn't know if I had the stamina to drag myself through the roiling emotions, intense anger and crazy jealousy. My stomach churned, and I looked away from the toast, my appetite all but gone. "I feel like you've never shared your heart with me—the whole of it. I don't know what you've been thinking the past few months . . . maybe the past seventeen years."

I didn't voice my other thought out loud.

He hadn't truly said he was sorry.

Sure, he'd said it under a thick, foggy blanket of alcohol and in the hospital, beneath a heavy cloak of grief and guilt. But I wanted to hear it with just us. I wanted to know if he really regretted breaking our marriage vows. If he wished he could take back the hurt he caused me.

"I'm trying, Sarah. I'm willing now. Just tell me what you want our next step to be and I'll do it. Anything. You want to see a counselor, I'm there. Please." He reached toward me, his fingers playing with mine. If only he'd agreed to see a counselor at the beginning of the summer, we might have been able to avoid this whole mess. "Still wearing my Mom's ring, huh?"

I grabbed up my hand and fiddled with the metal. "You know, since we need to open up and all, I'll go first." I dragged in a breath. "I lost my wedding rings. Off a large boulder."

He grimaced. "How'd that happen?"

"I was taking a hike after you first told me you wanted to move out. I ended up at the top of a big rock. I was thinking about what it would be like to not have the rings on if you, you know, wanted a divorce."

He breathed deep. "Ouch."

"Yeah. Well, I dropped them. Not on purpose. I've looked for them for hours, but they're nowhere, Matt. I'm sorry."

A moment of silence. Then, "You didn't mean to lose them."

Wow. An understanding husband. I could get used to this.

I sipped my coffee while he picked at his toast. "Your turn."

He looked up from the red jelly smeared on the crust of his breakfast. "What?"

"Tell me something."

He pushed his uneaten toast aside. "I'm an idiot."

"Something I don't know."

He smiled, but it disappeared quickly beneath the weight of his thoughts. "Can we just chalk this whole thing up to a pre-midlife crisis or something? I've never been good at getting out my feelings and all that. I'm not even sure what they are myself."

I turned to the sink and opened the dishwasher to load the few stray pieces of silverware. I ran the water to drown out the need for conversation.

He didn't get it, and I didn't want to be difficult. But I did want us to grow. We couldn't just hop over the past couple months like a skipped stone skids over the surface of a lake. We needed to dive in, take the plunge, and figure out why it happened so we could move forward with a healthy marriage.

But Matt needed to want this as much as I did. I couldn't push him.

He tapped the pile of papers titled *Journal of Elizabeth Baker* on the side of the island. "Did you finish?"

"I didn't think you knew what I was doing."

"Kyle mentioned it to me one night at rehab. He only caught pieces of it while you read I guess, but he said it sounded interesting."

I raised an eyebrow. "Yeah?"

"Yeah."

"It belongs to Barb's ancestor. She asked me to get it down on paper for her daughter."

It grew quiet between us again, tense. He got off the stool, came closer. I felt my defenses rise. He'd hurt me. While I may not want our marriage to end, his actions had trained me to be on guard.

"Sarah, I want you to tell me things. I want to know about you. I want to start over."

I clung to those words. He was inviting me in. Listening. Really listening.

I wondered what he'd say to the truth. "I mowed up the divorce petition," I whispered.

"What?"

"I mowed it up. Shredded it. Dumped it behind the stone wall."

He turned to me, put his hands on either side of my elbows. "You don't want a divorce, then? After all this . . ."

"What do you want?" I whispered.

He slid his hand down my left arm and raised my fingers to his lips. "I want to spend every moment of the rest of my life making up for the past several months. I want to wake next to you every day, tell you over and over again how sorry I am."

His words lingered sweetly in my ears. He pulled me closer and kissed me gently, capturing my bottom lip within his own. I felt the urge to give in. He'd apologized. I could easily fool myself into thinking that's all we needed. I would have let the kiss deepen if I could have forgotten about her.

I stepped back. "We need distance if we're going to work this out. We need to talk without the bedroom."

"Okay."

"Maybe you should keep the Newport rental for another month."

"I'm done there. I'll get a place close by here. I want to be near you and Kyle."

"I—I have to know. What changed? Was it Kyle's accident? Was it something she did? I need to know what we're basing all this on."

He went and sat on a barstool. "It started before the accident. The minute I had my lawyer draw up the divorce petition, even." I knew each word cost him something and I stood still, unwilling to tarnish the moment. "You were right, you know. About why I was drawn to Cassie. It was all the superficial things you accused me of and more. I was running, Sarah. I have been forever, in a sense. Running from my childhood, running from what my father did to us. Running away from poverty and my mother and her boyfriends. Running to everything that meant success and happiness to me. Newport . . . the Watermans . . . . Crazy, but I've wanted that life since I was in high school."

The words poked with the intensity of a hundred needles. I'd wanted honesty, but I'd forgotten how the truth could hurt.

I hadn't been enough for Matt.

I was his wife, and I wasn't enough.

"More than anything, I wanted that kind of life for us." He sighed long and slow. "Only you never seemed to want it. You'd be content in a six-hundred-foot fixer-upper if it's all I could give you. You were content with me, and I—I fell short."

I opened my mouth, then closed it, unsure what to say.

"I always pushed for more. More business, more employees, more clients. Bigger, bigger, bigger. Like my whole life I've been in a race I didn't know I was part of, and in Newport, I felt like I'd won that race." His eyes glistened, and he swallowed, hard. It didn't stop his words from cracking. "Only I lost. Big time."

He didn't look at me as he spoke, and I was glad of it. "Since we were teenagers you always encouraged me to go after what I wanted. I clung to that. The belief you had in me. But somewhere along the way I lost your belief."

I sat next to him on a stool. "I didn't think you needed it anymore. Everything you did, you did well. Do you remember the night of our wedding . . . what you said to me?"

He stared blankly at me.

"You told me I saved you. What did I save you from, Matt?"

A small smile crept to his mouth. "From myself. From living day after day without purpose, wondering if I had what it took to be better than my dad, wondering if I had what it took to support you. With you and Kyle, I knew I didn't have a choice. I'd provide for you both if it killed me. There was no more wondering. There was only one way—work hard and don't take no."

"Will you tell me about your father?"

My words hung in the air.

Finally, he said, "Yes. But not today." He stood, kissed me on the cheek. "Thank you. I'm going to clean out the Newport house, find a place to stay around here, check on the guys."

I swallowed. I suppose it wasn't reasonable to heal our marriage in a single morning.

"Can I ask you one more thing?" I wanted to cling to this moment where he'd made himself vulnerable, scared that if he walked out the door it would be gone forever.

"Sure." He stood in front of me, patient.

Listening.

I wanted to ask him if he'd married me only because of my pregnancy with Kyle. I wanted to ask him if he'd married me because he was scared of my father, of not doing the right thing. I wanted to ask him if he'd married me only out of obligation—if he wanted to fix our marriage for the same reason.

"Never mind; we'll talk later."

"Okay. I'll call you."

"He didn't make a fuss over the rings?" Essie stood in Barb's bedroom staring at the quilt I'd carefully folded. I planned to take it over to my house today.

"No. He really seems sorry. He's changed. Walls are coming down. I'm almost scared to hope."

"Just be careful."

I tried not to be annoyed at Essie's words. "Shouldn't I give my husband a second chance?"

"Of course. I just don't want to see you get hurt all over."

I began to strip the sheets off Barb's bed. One of the fitted sheets caught on the mattress, pulling beneath my fingers. "It *is* risky. I could get hurt again. I'm hoping my marriage is worth the risk."

Essie grabbed the other side of the sheet and tugged it from the mattress. "Do you think love changes? Like maybe we could fall in love with someone at one point in time, but if we met that same person twenty years down the road, we wouldn't end up falling?"

"You're awful reflective lately, aren't you?"

She shrugged, gave me a sheepish grin.

"I suppose that even if that were true of me and Matt—if we met now instead of nineteen years ago—well, I think it's a moot point."

"How so?"

"He's my husband. What we've been through the last seventeen years has shaped us. Whether we've grown apart or not, I have to believe that our marriage is real. That it's worth the work, and even the hurt. Marriage . . . it's belief in another person's love. And that's what hurt—the moment Matt walked away, the moment Cassie turned his head, he began to stop believing. His faith in our marriage faltered."

But I couldn't pretend mine had stayed strong. I'd let Pete get too close. I'd found comfort in his presence, in his touch, and even in his kisses.

I'd stopped believing, too.

My phone rang and I glanced at it, the name causing a small shriek to climb my throat. *Mary Dawson.*

"What? Who is it?" Essie came around the bed.

"It's Barb's daughter."

"You've been waiting. Answer it, silly."

I gulped in air from deep within my being, and slid the button on my phone to accept the call.

"Hello?"

"Hello. Sarah?"

"Yes . . . Mary?"

A moment of silence. "I'm sorry it took me so long to get back to you."

"No . . . no, that's okay. I'm glad you called." I walked into the living room, sat in Barb's old rocker. Words failed me and more awkward silence clogged the line. I had called her. I was supposed to spearhead this conversation.

"She's dead, isn't she?" Mary asked, surprising me.

"I'm sorry," I whispered.

A wobbly sigh. "She told you all about me, I suppose." It didn't sound like a good thing.

"No—no, I mean, I knew she had a daughter, but I didn't realize you weren't close until after her heart attacks."

"I'm at Logan. I honestly don't know why I came. Closure, maybe. Is it okay if I come to the house?"

My mind whirled. Barb's daughter, here. I hadn't expected this. What would she want? Quite suddenly, I felt threatened. Barb's home, her request that I transcribe the journal, Elizabeth's story—so much of it had become a safe haven for me the last few months. Now, I would share it all, as Barb had asked.

"Yes, of course. Do you need a ride? I could come and—"

"No, I already rented a car. Will you be around in another couple of hours?"

"Y—yes."

"See you soon."

I hung up, a million questions vying for precedence in my mind. "She's here," I said to Essie, who stood in the bedroom doorway with Barb's sheets in her hand.

"Where?"

"At Logan. On her way here." I looked at the house, packed away in boxes. "What will she think? This place is a mess. She doesn't—"

Essie knelt beside me, grasped my hands. "Sarah, you have nothing to be ashamed of, hear me? You are not responsible for Barb's relationship with her daughter. Barb left *you* everything, and you've been taking care of things as best you can. You've been trying to reach her for days and she springs this on you? Don't let her intimidate you, okay?"

I pressed my lips together before answering. My sister had changed since Kyle's accident. She was more contemplative, more fiercely protective of me. "Thank you. I do want to help, though."

Barb had entrusted me with this last thing, this important message. I felt that, with all that had happened lately, renewal was possible. In Kyle's health, in Barb's relationship with her daughter…maybe even in my broken marriage.

CHAPTER 35

I wished Essie could have stayed. I wished the rehab place would have called me saying Kyle needed me. But no one stayed or called and I found myself running a load of laundry to wash Barb's sheets, convincing myself that this is what I'd been waiting for—to speak to Mary.

I'd brought over Elizabeth's journal, placed it on Barb's dining room table. I'd print out another copy for myself, but this one belonged to Mary.

When a car pulled up Barb's drive, I opened the screen door for the middle-aged woman walking up the path. She had on tennis shoes and her hair was dyed a platinum blonde. I held my hand out to her and introduced myself, inviting her in, a flowery scent trailing behind her.

Her gaze darted around, taking in the many boxes. "Maybe we could talk outside?" she asked.

"Certainly." We went on Barb's small porch, sat in the two rockers with chipped white paint.

"Place is almost the same." Mary's gaze landed on me and I saw that her skin was loose at her neck, and her eyes . . . they were the same shade as Barb's.

"I'm sorry I couldn't tell you right away. I didn't know how to reach you, and your mom . . . she asked me to prepare something for you that took most of the summer."

"Oh?"

I went back in the house and grabbed up Elizabeth's journal. When I returned, I held it out to her. "Her ancestor. Your ancestor. Barb wanted you to have it."

Mary stared at the folder for a long time. "Unbelievable." She let out a small snort. "I finally decide to come home and this is what I get. A story. Figures."

I tried not to be taken aback by her suddenly hostile tone, by her casual attitude to the precious gift. "Your mom cared about you. Her final request was that you be found. That I give you the journal and tell you that she loved you. She loved you and she said she was sorry."

I thought her gaze softened for a moment, but then it was gone. "Well too bad sorry don't bring the dead back to life or wash the blood off her hands, Ms. Rodrigues."

I'd known Barb's sins had been great, but I hadn't realized someone had died because of her actions. All I could think of was Abram's body falling off the rock. Death. Done, permanent. But Abram had believed life would go on, that eternal life could be found in his God. And Elizabeth had believed that as well. She had found hope in the darkness. Would Mary see that hope from the journal, or would her pain blind her to it?

"My mother tell you what she did?"

"No." A part of me didn't want to know.

"She made our lives miserable, that's what. Always harping on Daddy to give up the bottle. When he finally did, she still didn't think him good enough. Always demanding he go play his guitar at soup kitchens or dress up nice for church or some other agenda. And I wasn't far behind. I could never do anything right for that woman. But I got old enough and I got to leave. Dad . . . he found another way to leave. We woke up one morning to find him missing, keys still on the nightstand, car in this very drive. The search team found him in the back woods, hanging from a tree. I left for good the day after his funeral and I vowed never to come back here until she was gone, too."

My bottom lip trembled as I listened to Mary's story. My heart went out to her, and Barb. "I'm so sorry," I whispered.

Mary leaned back in her rocker, closed her eyes. "Yeah, well it wasn't your fault. And I don't mean to take issue with you. I just wonder if my mother wasn't playing you like she tried to play me and Daddy."

I sniffed, shook my head. "I have to admit, I've had my moments of anger toward your mother. I wondered how she could strap me with such a big request, one I didn't even know the details behind. But, Mary, please believe me when I say your mother changed. I don't think I ever saw a judgmental bone in her body. She served in any way she could, yes, but it never seemed to be out of guilt or obligation. I have to believe she changed." I placed my hand on Elizabeth's journal. "I'm not certain, but I think what she read here helped her as well. I think we all make horrible mistakes—mistakes we wish we could take back." I thought of the marriage I'd taken for granted. I thought of Matt's choice to abandon us, of me allowing Pete to get close. "But I also believe there's always hope of reconciliation too. Even now, with your mother buried. I think that's what she wanted to offer in this . . . though now, it's up to you."

Mary snorted, but I counted it a small victory that no fighting words came forth.

I swallowed, thinking something more was needed to open Mary's heart. Maybe this time, it was up to me. "I think she knew how painful this place was for you, and that's why she didn't give it to you, but I think she'd be pleased if you'd accept it."

"The house?"

"I was surprised when she left it to me, but I'm wondering if she just didn't want me to hold it for you."

Mary shook her head. "I don't want this place. You're right —it is too painful."

"Then sell it. Do you have any kids?'"

Her face softened. "Two children, three grandkids."

"I think Barb would be happy if you blessed them with it all somehow." In that moment I was certain I'd just been the caretaker, that Barb had known I would make this decision, and it felt . . . right. I didn't mourn it for a minute.

"She left you the house, but you're giving it to me? You have some screws loose?"

"I think she intended for me to be only the steward all along."

Mary rubbed her eyes. "I don't know what to make of all this."

"Read the journal," I said. "Stick around and go through your Mom's stuff for a couple days. Maybe then things will be clearer."

She rocked, her tennis shoes pushing off the floorboards of the porch. "Okay, I'll try. Ms. Rodrigues, you sure are different than I thought."

"I think . . . I think I've changed a lot, too."

Kyle and Matt and I slowly eased back into family life at the rehabilitation center. We brought Kyle pizza, and his spirits lifted when he heard that Matt rented a house in town, less than ten minutes from our home.

"The physical therapist says I'll be back to running in another month. I might not be first on the team for cross, but I'm going to train over the winter for track. She says I'll be good as new by spring."

"That's great," I said, juicy pepperoni bursting on my tongue.

"Big man on campus this year. Can't believe you're a senior." Matt studied Kyle, pride lining his face.

There was something different between them. The fissure closed. Matt had told me on the phone last night that they'd had a good talk that day. He hinted there'd been confessions and apologies and more than a few tears.

I woke with nervous excitement each morning at the prospect of restoring our marriage and our family. I also woke with doubts. Doubts over whether I'd ever be able to trust Matt again. Doubts if I'd ever be able to enjoy his touch without thinking of his betrayal.

We said good night to Kyle and left the rehabilitation center together. He opened the driver's side door of the Mercedes for me.

"I'll call you in half an hour?" We'd fallen into a comfortable ritual of nightly phone calls.

"Sure."

He pecked me on the cheek and walked to his truck.

I went home, took a shower, printed out the last entry of Elizabeth's story for my own copy, and snuggled into our king-size bed, the phone by my side.

Mary had been next door longer than three days, and I started to worry. Was her heart softening toward Barb at all?

My stomach jumped when the phone rang, and for a moment I felt like we were dating again. Only our conversations these days were more than getting to know each other, though there was a sense of that too.

"Can I come home yet?" Matt's husky voice came over the line five minutes after we'd greeted one another.

"We have to talk about her at some point, you know."

A long sigh. "I know."

"You ready?"

"Tell me what you want to know."

Man, this would hurt. But I needed to know, I needed to hear it from his lips.

"You slept with her, right?"

A muffled sound. I felt the temptation for my husband to lie, to tell me what I wanted to hear to make things easier. But I knew him. I knew the truth before I even asked. We just needed to get it out into the open.

"Yes."

The word drilled into my being. Knowing the truth and hearing it from him were two different things.

Renewed anger bubbled up inside me, threatening to tear me at the seams. Unwanted images came to my mind's eye. "Was she good, Matt? Experienced, I'm sure, hot young thing. Nothing like your homely wife you've been with for—"

"Sarah—"

I hung up the phone and flung it across the bedspread. I huddled deeper into the covers and let my tears wet the pillow.

This wasn't worth it. I didn't see a way out of the maze of hurt Matt produced in his admission. Maybe it would have been better if he'd lied. I may not have believed him, but at least I could have tried.

The bedspread muffled the ring of the phone. I thought about ignoring it, sleeping on my hurt, hoping it would numb with slumber.

But I claimed I wanted to work on our marriage. And now when the labor presented itself, would I walk away?

I scooped up the phone and clicked it on without saying hello.

"Sarah, I'm sorry. You don't know how much I wish I could take back what I did. Over and over, I want to turn back time."

"How am I supposed to live with this? How can I even hope to compete with her?"

"There's no competition," he said.

"Don't lie to make me—"

"Doggone Sarah, it's true. When I was with Cassie it was new and hot, I'll admit that. But it wasn't real. It was shallow. It wasn't what we had. Have. Sarah, there's always been electricity between us. But there's something else, something more. I didn't realize it until I didn't have it. I can't even describe it. You own my heart."

His words softened the hurt. Just a little. I let them sink in for a long moment of uninterrupted silence. I knew what he meant. We'd been bound together for years. We'd shared too much together. We couldn't just walk away from the love we had.

"You still there?" he said.

"What changed your mind about her?"

"You know how you used to listen to me when we first dated? You stood by me and my stupid, crazy ideas. When I talked to her, it was like an evaluation. Like she was taking what I said and trying to assess how she could change me to her liking. I began to realize it after I drew up the divorce petition. Then when Kyle had his accident, I realized the extent of her selfishness. All I could see was you all these years putting your dreams on hold for me, putting me and Kyle before every other thing you did, every decision you made. I was ashamed. I thought providing for you was enough, but I never supported you like you did me. I'm sorry." He dragged in a quivering breath. My eyes burned. "I want that to change, Sarah. *I* want to change. You should go after your dreams—go back to school. You should have a long time ago. I never should have discouraged you. I should have believed in you, like you did me."

I bit my bottom lip until I felt a two-teeth indent. "Thank you." Silence. "What happened the night of Kyle's accident?"

"Getting all the tough questions out tonight, huh?"

I didn't answer. I didn't need to.

"I'd told her I wasn't going to see her that weekend. I wanted it to be just me and Kyle. I thought we could make amends before he went back to school.

"We were about to head to the golf course when she called. She asked me to come to the house, said her parents were real excited about some new ideas for the fall." I heard him swallow over the phone. "I should have said no. I knew she was jealous of Kyle—crazy, huh? How could I think I loved a woman who's jealous of my own son? Anyway, I told Kyle I'd be back in half an hour. I asked him if he wanted to come, but he was mad. He said he'd wait. When I wasn't back in half an hour he took the bike. It was a stupid thing for him to do, but not stupider than any of the other crappy decisions his father made the past few months. He wanted my attention. Well, he got it."

I wondered how things would be between Matt and me had Kyle not survived. "This can't be about penance, Matt. Us fixing our marriage. You get that, right? It's not like going to confession and saying a bunch of Our Fathers and Hail Marys."

"I *want* to fix our marriage, Sarah. Believe me. It's not about guilt, though I'm sure there's enough of that on my shoulders now as well."

My hand grew sweaty around the phone. "While we're confessing . . ."

"Yeah?"

"I have to tell you I did get close to Pete while you were away."

"Okay." His voice sounded strained and heavy. "How close?"

"More emotionally close than physically, although I did kiss him."

I heard Matt grinding his teeth over the line. "Ever think how different your life would be with someone like him?"

Definitely the night for tough honesty. "Yes. But I think I know what you mean when you said it wasn't the same with Cassie. *You* are my husband."

He sniffed hard into the phone and I could tell he tried to keep his emotions in check. "And you are my wife . . ."

More silence. We spent just as much time between confessions as we did talking. We both needed time, time with one another being quiet. Time to process all we told the other.

I was the one to break it this time. "One good thing might have come out of my time with Pete, though."

"What's that?" Again, hesitant.

"My game of golf."

"You golfed with him? Talk about betrayal."

I laughed. "I went to the range after you made that cruel joke about me not knowing the difference between an iron and driver at your employee dinner. He happened to be at the range."

"Ouch."

"I suppose I supported you all these years in your business, but I was stubborn when it came to how to spend our time. I didn't even try to like golf. Or motorcycles. Or sailing. I want that to change. I want to get past my fears. I've already been praying about it. And I want you to help me."

"Well, I think I'm done with motorcycles if that's okay with you."

"Sure. But maybe next time you and Kyle head to the golf course, you'll invite me along?"

"No doubting it. I'll teach you everything that doctor didn't." His voice sounded hoarse again, and I knew I hurt him, too. My betrayal may not have been as extensive, but unfaithfulness hurt—no matter how it was cut.

"I'm sorry, Matt."

"You don't have to apologize—"

"Yes. I do."

"I forgive you," he said. "Do you—can you think about forgiving me?"

I opened my mouth to reciprocate the grace, but my tongue felt dry. "I'm getting there."

It was something.

CHAPTER 36

I snapped a lid onto my salad and put it in the refrigerator for my lunch the next day. I would work in the morning, then go to Kyle and begin talking to the staff about his transition home.

Home.

Matt and I continued our nightly talks. They got easier. Like a bad paper cut in the crook of one's finger, each bend hurt less and less. I could see a path ahead for us. Not an easy one, but one bright with hope.

The doorbell rang and I went to it, surprised to see Mary on the other side. We hadn't seen one another since our first meeting, but I often saw her rental car coming and going from the drive, so I knew she was around. I'd wanted to give her space and time to think. I prayed that God would work in the mess.

"Hey."

She stood on my porch looking smaller than I remembered. "Hey."

"Would you like to come in? I could fix us some coffee or tea."

"I'll come in, but no need for coffee. Thank you."

She stepped inside and I led her to the living room, where we sat. Beside us, the grandfather clock punctuated the silence.

"I've been trying," she started.

I nodded, as if to prod her onward.

"I read the journal, along with some letters Mom and Dad wrote each other when they were dating. I even went to her church if you can believe that. I think . . . I think I'm beginning to see some things."

I didn't want to push her. It wasn't my place.

"I have to tell you that I resented Mom's religion most of my life. It just seemed like a way to prove herself to God, prove herself to herself."

I nodded, understanding probably more than she knew.

"And I think that is how my mother thought. But you know, reading about Elizabeth . . . about Caleb pursuing her . . . I had this odd . . . thought. Like maybe that's what God does. Pursue us."

I smiled.

Mary laughed. "Yeah, I could be way off."

"I—I don't think you are," I whispered. I was coming to see that God *did* want our hearts. Maybe He even pursued us. Even when we were rebels, like Elizabeth.

Mary smiled, and I noticed a peace about her I hadn't seen the other day.

"Never thought I'd be talking about God with a near stranger, much less my Mom's neighbor."

We laughed.

Mary stood, seeming uncomfortable all of a sudden. "I'm a long way from forgiving everything, but I'm glad I came. I'm glad we talked." She wiped her hands on her jeans. "I don't feel right taking the house. Mom said she wanted you to have it, so I think that's how it should be."

I swallowed. "I understand, but I'm going to sell it. I simply don't need two houses. . . ." Out of nowhere, an idea came to me so swift and perfect, I felt Barb herself had plucked it out of thin air and sent it to me. "Wait . . . what if, after we sold it, we donated some of the proceeds to the historical society? Maybe we could have them publish Elizabeth's story, maybe they could do something special surrounding the King Philip's War, considering it started right here. That is, if they don't have something already."

Mary nodded. "I think that would be fitting." She held out her hand, and I grasped it.

"I needed this closure, Sarah." She looked off to the wall where the grandfather clock ticked steadily. "I wish I'd realized it sooner."

Barb's daughter hugged me, and in that moment, with her warm arms around me, I felt I had completed Barb's mission, and that if she could, she was smiling upon us from heaven.

The following Tuesday Kyle and I heard the good news that he'd be released from rehab the next day. We called Matt to celebrate, and after I shared lunch with Kyle I left the center to purchase groceries.

When I returned to the rehabilitation center, Kyle lay sleeping in bed and Matt sat hunched over something. My breaths stalled when I saw what he read.

He looked up, his eyes clouded. They cleared after a moment and he nodded toward Kyle. "Kid's getting lazy. Been sleeping for two hours."

I smiled. "You're here early."

"I skipped out, wanted be with you guys on this day." He pointed to a small boxed cake, half eaten. "There's some left."

I put my purse down on one of the seats near Kyle's bed and pointed at Elizabeth's journal in Matt's hands. I'd brought my copy several days ago because Kyle had asked. "You've been reading it?"

"Yeah, when he sleeps or has an appointment, I've been

working at it." Matt wasn't a big reader. I thought it strange that he would read instead of flip on the television. "Kyle said it meant a lot to you."

"How far did you get?"

"Just finished it. Amazing. It's real?"

I nodded. A real person, just like us, who struggled with decisions of the heart. "You want to see the rock?"

He didn't hesitate. He put the journal on the table, scribbled Kyle a note, and we left the center, this time together, Matt driving.

We pulled into the parking lot of the library, and I led Matt through the same woods Elizabeth walked more than three hundred years ago. Early autumn light filtered through the changing leaves. In a few weeks' time they'd fall, burying the ground in crunchy, beautiful decay. I breathed in the scent of pine and earth.

"It's nice here," Matt said. "I should have come before now."

I walked in silence, resisting the urge to move closer to him. I was scared that the images of his unfaithfulness would again fill my mind, scared we'd get caught up in one another before we'd healed enough.

I broke away and continued on the large path up a slight hill. "You ready to talk about your father yet?"

He rubbed the back of his neck, stepped over a large root. His work boots landed on the other side. "Truth is, I don't remember much about my dad, other than he left us to chase gold when I was young. 'A regular old forty-niner,' my mother always said." He laughed with disgust. "Every week he had a new way of getting rich. If he only settled down and stuck with a job, he could have provided for us. We didn't always live in the trailer park—we moved there after he skipped out. Strange thing is I didn't blame him as much as I blamed my mom."

"How come?"

"It hurt less to have someone else to aim my anger at. I

didn't want to think I was the reason my dad left; I wanted to think it was all her. When she started bringing boyfriends around, when they drank too much and beat the crap out of me, well, it made it all the more easy."

"I'm sorry, Matt."

He shrugged. "It was really never about my father. I mean, yeah, he started the whole thing, but I don't remember him ever being in the picture. I knew it wasn't right though, just me, my mom, and her boyfriends. It made sense to put the fault with her."

"You still do."

"Yeah, I guess so."

"Lorna loves you."

"I know. And it was crazy of me to expect perfection out of her. This summer has shown me that. I mean, she was a single mother working full-time. She made bad choices, but that's something I know all about. I went to talk with her a few days ago."

I tried to hide my surprise. Matt went to see Lorna. Huge. Another hurdle in a long line of changes he seemed determined to make.

"How'd it go?"

"We talked a long time. We both apologized. We both forgave. It was . . . good."

"Good."

I pointed through the changing leaves where Abram's Rock loomed ahead of us. "There it is."

Matt walked ahead of me, his hands in his pockets. "No kidding. Just how she described it. Crazy."

We poked around in the cave portion and when my foot slipped on a pile of old leaves, he caught me. We stared at one another, and a burst of something new filled my heart.

Grief and sorrow clung to this rock, but so did hope. I knew Elizabeth's story. She hadn't given in to despair. She'd moved forward, chose to love. To believe. To have faith.

I wanted the same.

"Want to climb it?"

I led Matt up the large hill to the right of the rock and we scaled the rocky steps until we reached the top. He held my hand as we looked down. A breeze swirled around us, sweeping up a burnt orange oak leaf and settling it on a long journey to the ground.

"Poor Abram," Matt said. "Think he met his God that day?"

"I do. Through all this I think I have too."

Matt looked at me. I couldn't find words. Words to tell him how I had come to know a God as solid as this rock we stood upon. Unchanging, even after years of rain or snow or storm. Never swayed by even my own wavering heart. How He'd filled up a hole within me—a great need I hadn't even known existed until all I valued had been stripped bare.

Matt looked out into the woods, thinning in vibrant colors. "I . . . I wish I'd been more like Caleb. I wish I had shown extraordinary love. I wish I had—" His voice cracked, a thousand unspoken words in the broken sound.

I tucked my hand in his, assuring him that I understood. I'd also fallen short of showing the type of love Caleb showed Elizabeth, the type of love God showed me.

He squeezed my hand. "I was thinking it might be nice if we started going to church together."

I couldn't help the doubtful expression that crept on my face. "You do?"

"Yeah, I do. Who cares what denomination . . . if the God Elizabeth believed in is there, then I want to be there."

My spirit leapt at his words, and I felt we embarked on a grand adventure. Together.

He put an arm around me and drew me close. I lay my head in the crook of his neck, enjoying the woodsy scent of his deodorant, the soft smell of Ivory soap that still clung to his skin from his morning shower.

"I love you." He buried his face in my hair, and I returned the words.

"I've been thinking a lot about how our marriage started," he said.

"You mean my father forcing you to marry me? Yeah, me too."

"It was the wrong way to start things, but I want you to know I don't regret it. You know how Elizabeth talks about beauty coming from ashes? Well, I think that's like our marriage. It was a crazy, rocky start, but good came out of it. Good still comes from it. This summer too. It was a nightmare, but I think I'm trusting something beautiful to come forth."

He turned to face me and ran a thumb along my cheek. "Love is an emotion, but I'm learning it's also a choice. I can't promise I'll never hurt you again, but I can promise I'll never leave you again, never be unfaithful to you again, never stop believing in our marriage. Sarah, I want to share my life with you."

He lowered his lips to mine, and I melted into his kiss. As it deepened, I couldn't think of the past or the wrongs done, or doubt whether or not trusting Matt again was a good choice for my heart.

Right now, in his arms, it was the only choice. I didn't want to live without him. I was excited about our relationship, about the newness and beauty that could come from pain and hurt.

As he ended the kiss, I realized I hadn't been haunted by dreaded images of his unfaithfulness. Certainly it wouldn't always be this way, but right now it stood as a firm promise in the waning sunlight.

"I want to move forward too. To forgive. With you."

He kissed me again and a fresh breeze swept over us, almost as if Caleb and Elizabeth and maybe even Abram were blessing the new chapter we were writing for ourselves.

"Let's go home," I said, standing.

"You mean . . ."

"If you're ready."

He nodded, vigorously, reminding me of Kyle when he was four, and I asked him if he wanted a piece of candy. A no-brainer.

"I am."

We descended the rock and I marveled at how tomorrow our family would be back together under one roof. A new beginning. I spoke of my plan for the proceeds of Barb's estate.

He slung an arm around me. "Yeah, and if you ever want to downsize—you know, when Kyle's in college or something—maybe we can look for something smaller, something you like."

I shrugged. Right now, there was no place I'd rather be than with him and Kyle in my boxy home.

We reached the foot of the rock. Matt stooped to pick something up from the ground. But he didn't straighten. He continued digging with his fingers.

"What are you doing?"

"I want a piece of this rock—a pebble even, to help me remember this. Us."

He swept aside a few fresh leaves and some wet, old ones. "Hey."

Something shiny caught a glimmer of sunlight skipping through the trees. Matt picked it up and held it in the palm of his hand. "This isn't your—"

"Yes! Yes, it is. This is where I dropped them!" My engagement ring lay cradled in his palm, dirt crusted to the sides of the diamond rock.

He knelt down and swept the area clean. I knelt beside him, the knees of my jeans soaking in wet dirt.

"Here. I found it." He shimmied over to me on his knees, both my wedding rings now in his hand. I slipped off Lorna's ring.

"If you'd rather wear my mom's, I understand," he said.

I shook my head vehemently and pocketed Lorna's ring.

Matt caught up my left hand and held the rings at the edge

of my finger, gazed at me with sincere purpose. "Sarah Rodrigues, with these rings I promise to love you until the day I die, to always be faithful, to cherish you with every—" he swallowed down a crack in his words—"every last breath God gives me."

He slid them on. They felt light and secure on my hand. Somehow stronger despite—maybe even because—of the brokenness we'd been through.

Matt kissed me beneath the majesty of the boulder above us. The sunlight cast our shadows—now one—on the solid face of Abram's Rock.

AUTHOR'S NOTE

This is a story that caught me up and refused to let go until it was written. It was my first attempt at writing a time-slip novel, and it would be nearly five years before it would see the light of publication.

These characters and their struggles are dear to my heart. Growing up, I watched my parents go through a lot of marital strife. The details aren't important, but the very real struggle I witnessed was. Yet, do you want to know what else I witnessed? Perseverance. Work. Love. This summer, my precious parents will celebrate their thirty-ninth wedding anniversary. I saw how hard it was for them to get to this point. But I also saw them fight for one another, work for the vows they promised all those years ago. If you see anything of authenticity in this story, it is likely because of them, and what they taught me by living out their love, even when it wasn't the easy path.

At the same time that I am grateful for my parents' happy ending, I remain cognizant of the fact that not everyone gets such an ending as theirs, or an ending such as Matt and Sarah's. Sadly, marriages end, and hearts hurt. Dear reader, if this is where you're sitting today, please know my heart aches with you. Please know I am praying for the God of comfort to minister to you in a special way. Thank you for walking with me in this story despite a raw or vulnerable heart.

An obstacle I ran into in the writing of this story was creating the genuine point-of-view of a colonial woman. To obtain this, I looked to the writings of Mary Rowlandson, who wrote an account of her kidnapping by Native Americans during King Philip's War. While the account proved tremendously insightful, in many ways, it left me with a bigger problem.

I longed to be true to history, and yet I did not want to offend readers with that history—namely with the many prejudices held against the native settlers at that time. It is a fine rope to walk, and I hope that I have conveyed it with authenticity, yet in a manner worthy of God, who has declared that "there is neither Jew nor Greek, there is neither slave nor free, there is no male and female, for you are all one in Christ Jesus."

Now, about that rock... I first discovered Abram's Rock as I prepared for a local hike for my son's Tiger Cub den. When I learned of the legend of Abram's Rock, I knew a story had to be told. While the story of Abram is only a legend, the story of King Philip's War is all too real. As I read of this tragic war, my heart ached for both sides. While Elizabeth would no doubt have hard feelings toward the Wampanoag tribe, Native Americans were far from the only ones at fault. Many of the narratives I read were from a colonist's point of view. There are few accounts from the Wampanoag viewpoint, but ample evidence shows the colonists could be just as cruel and fierce in their fight for land as they perceived the Native Americans to be.

As with any war or argument, and as Elizabeth and Sarah learned, the blame often lies with both sides. I pray that in history as well as in our own lives we can move forward beneath grace, casting all blame not on one another, but on the Rock who took all the blame upon himself some two thousand years ago.

Dear Reader,

I hope you enjoyed this story! If so, I would be extremely grateful if you would consider leaving a review wherever you purchased this book, or on Goodreads. And if you love to talk about books on social media, I'd be tremendously appreciative for a shout out! Please feel free to tag me so I can engage in the fun.

Writing stories is nothing without you, dear reader. Please know I count it a privilege to be a part of your story time, and I'd love to keep in touch. To be the first to know about book releases, new covers, or special sales and announcements, please sign up for my newsletter (and receive a free short story!) at heidichiavaroli.com

ALSO BY HEIDI CHIAVAROLI

Freedom's Ring

The Hidden Side

ACKNOWLEDGMENTS

This book has had quite a journey, and as always, the final product is not mine alone. I am so very grateful to the many who have helped form and shape this novel.

Thank you to Susan Brower for being one of the first in the industry to believe in this book. I can still hear your words of encouragement, which buoyed my spirit and made me think, "Hey, maybe I *can* write after all!"

Thank you to Jan Stob for your early feedback which served to strengthen this novel immensely. Thank you to my agent, Natasha Kern, for your constant support and encouragement. Thank you to Nicole Miller for designing such a beautiful and perfect cover.

Caleb Sjogren, it is an honor to work with you. I can't help but be drawn to some sticky topics and having your careful insight is invaluable along the way. I appreciate the time and thought you put into helping me improve not only my words, but my characters. Thank you.

Thank you to my critique partner and sanity-keeper, Sandra Ardoin. Thank you to Melissa Jagears for her support and willingness to answer my never-ending questions. Thank you to Susan Meissner for looking at the first few chapters of this book at its beginning stages. Thank you to my sister, Krystal Leffort, for answering some of the medical questions that came up in the writing of this book.

Thank you to Rebecca Griffith, Associate Curator at Pilgrim Hall Museum for answering my questions regarding the museum and the handling of 17th century materials.

Thank you to my parents, Scott and Donna Anuszczyk, for not only supporting me but showing me that love—and marriage—is hard work, but worth it. I love you both so much.

To my boys, James and Noah, it's beyond fun to release this book after so many walks in the woods and conversations over the local legend that began the seed of this idea so many years ago. Thank you for your excitement and support.

Thank you to my husband, Daniel, for not only supporting my writing when no contract had yet been made, but for showing me true, unconditional love that serves each and every day. I love you, honey.

Thank you to my readers for eagerly awaiting another book. Your emails and social media notes warm my heart and remind me why I do what I do.

Lastly, thank you to my God, the God of Hope. May all glory go to you.

LEGEND OF ABRAM'S ROCK

excerpt from *The Swansea Stage Coach—A Local History*
Chapter written by Marjorie E. Walkden

A large boulder north of Swansea Village is known as Abram's
Rock. The tall oak trees at its base whisper of the Indians who
once trod the ground beneath them or rested in their shade.
King Philip himself might have rested here when hard pressed
by his enemies. Farther than the eye can reach were the lands of
Massasoit.

The most familiar legend handed on to us about Abram's
Rock is that he was a poor Indian who had deserted his tribe,
coming to this settlement where he made his living in peace. But
King Philip of the Wamponoag decided to take Abram back,
fearing his friendship for the white man. Abram found this
towering rock as a hiding place. On the west side is a room
formed by boulders. It is still called 'Abram's Bedroom'—after
300 years. He is said to have lived there for several months, til
tracked down and captured. He was given a chance for his life.
The sentence was death or three leaps from the top of the rock
to the ground below. Abram took the chance, and tradition says

that his first and second leaps from the towering rock were safely
made, but the third jump killed him.

DISCUSSION QUESTIONS

1. Sarah's parents forced Matt and Sarah into a marriage because of her pregnancy. What do you think of this sort of reasoning?

2. Matt and Sarah share a troubled marriage. Is one more at fault than the other? What do you think of Matt's decision to "take a break" from one another as a solution? How is Sarah at fault?

3. Elizabeth is confused over her feelings for Abram and Caleb. How do you interpret her feelings for each?

4. Elizabeth's feelings for her Native American neighbors are complicated. At different times in the story, she feels different emotions. How do you perceive her feelings? Are they due to culture or circumstances?

5. Matt does not like to talk about his troubled childhood. Why does he hide his pain? How can we heal from past wounds?

6. Elizabeth writes, "were it not for Abram, I would not have

loved Caleb with the intensity I did. Even as love is an object of but two people, it is shaped and formed by others, by the circumstances that surround it. It can grow, or it can shrivel. Had Caleb and I not suffered the times of adversity, we would not have grown together, into the man and wife we are today." Do you agree with her assessment? If so, how has this played out in your life? If not, why do you disagree?

7. Sarah acknowledges that marriage requires more than those first heady feelings of love. She says it also seeks out faithfulness, perseverance, and belief in the vow originally taken. What do you think of this?

8. In the hospital, Sarah clings to 2 Corinthians 12:9. "My grace is sufficient for you, for my power is made perfect in weakness." There is a lot to unpack in this verse. What does it mean? Have you ever known this grace when going through a difficult time?

9. What is the significance of the grandfather clock in this story? What small things do you depend on?

10. What do you think the author meant when she wrote, "Belief didn't walk well alone"?

11. If you had to choose a theme for this book, how would you word it?

12. Both Elizabeth and Sarah feel a connection to God through nature. Where do you see God in your daily life?

CPSIA information can be obtained
at www.ICGtesting.com
Printed in the USA
LVHW031347100721
692144LV00003B/17